D1609895

CONTENTS

ILLUSTRATIONS

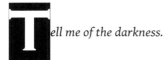 *ell me of the darkness.*

The words echoed down the tunnel, through the moist gloom and into the traveler's mind. This was it: the threshold.

If the traveler turned back and exited now, the madness and destruction outside would continue. It would go on and on until someone else made the sacrifice and offered themselves to the sleepless fiend, Yvo-Ket. The Empty One. Thoughtless Demon.

The legends told of the enigma, pranced around the birth cycle of the ageless curse. It was spoken of somberly in the decades before, but with growing intensity in recent years. There was no denying the world was in turmoil, and Those Who Remember had agreed to send forth a surveyor. The traveler. One final attempt at the legend's instruction to end the chaos.

Yvo-Ket required verbal stimulation to keep its idle mind distracted from breaking the threads of existence, told the legends. Without a constant string of tales to keep its not-imagination entertained, it would continue manifesting violence onto the world. In its boredom, Yvo-Ket would make the physical and mental planes its phantasmal playground; a prison of misery for every living thing.

Why did it desire such madness? Why was it obsessed with hurt and anger and depravity? With—

Darkness.

"Tell me of the darkness . . ."

The traveler was finally succumbing to the strains of the long journey. Fatigue gnawed at every nerve and ligament. Still, there was no choice but to go forward.

The traveler stumbled into the great room. The puppet-doll version of Yvo-Ket, the one it revealed itself as most commonly to humans, sat propped against a large stone altar. The symbol in its blank face glowed with the intensity of magma. Behind, in the shadows, slithered and coiled the restless true form of the demon; an agitated mosaic of angst, crawling around its throne and the walls like smoke and dancing from one shape into another.

Sitting before the puppet, the traveler was consumed by grief. The voyage to here had been physically and mentally draining; fleeing from and battling the behemoths in the wilderness had exhausted what little energy the traveler had left. To come so far and be so weakened . . . there was no telling now if completing the task was even possible.

Yvo-Ket regarded the traveler with its doughy moon-eyes. A subtle nod of its head and the smoky vileness behind it gyrated. The traveler watched as the air above the tapestry on the floor shimmered. Shapes began to blossom there—

And smells.

The traveler's tongue exploded with saliva as ornate plates of meat, cheeses, breads, and fruits materialized from the ether. Steam wafted through the air and mixed with the foamy fizz that bubbled from a goblet full of woody wine.

It was too much to bear. The traveler sampled some of everything before the thought surfaced above primal desire: this was a pact in the making. This was how the curse worked. The traveler knew that Yvo-Ket would continue to provide sustenance and drink (and possibly conjure *more*) as long as the tales continued to flow from the traveler's lips. The traveler was sure that the tastes of the delicacies would instantly turn to ash on the tongue . . . but they didn't. They remained delicious. Nourishment could be felt coursing through every vein and vessel.

"Tell me of the darkness."

Was this a fair trade? A life spent in the spectral gloom with a fiend, forever telling tale after tale to satiate its hunger for mayhem and misery? It was hardly a difficult decision to make. With a full stomach—and the inexplicable knowledge that the destruction outside had ceased since Yvo-Ket had sensed the traveler's presence—there was really no arguing the agreement.

The quest had not been a failure after all. In the traveler's mind there was a vision: chains wrapping around wrists and ankles, binding their owner to a life of entertaining a demon's lusts—but there was another vision as well. The traveler could sense those chains that had for so long strangled the world outside crumbling and being retrieved back into the void.

Buttery grease and apple tang were licked from a corner of the mouth; a soft smile formed thereafter. It was a pleasantly defeated one; sincere, but not without a bitter purse.

"Tell me of—"

"Alright. Okay. I will." The traveler raised the goblet, shook it lightly to watch the wine's perfect legs cling to the inner walls. The doll nodded. The few drops at the bottom swelled upwards until the liquid nearly overflowed the cup. Lips pressed into a smile, more confident this time. The traveler relaxed and leaned backwards. A comfortable assemblage of pillows had formed behind an aching back.

A sigh; a thought.

And then . . . the words began.

LONGBOAT

BECKY REGALADO

Two glittering specks hover over the bow like moonlight reflected in dark glass. I tell myself they are dim stars, or lamplight from the sinking brigantine some fifty yards ahead. I can almost believe it. Until they blink.

Those flecks are not stars. They are not candlelight reflected on the water. They are the wet and watchful eyes of whatever monster brought us to this lightless world.

I am the only one left alive.

Yesterday I awoke heaving my guts into the ocean. I looked through watering eyes at the slimy green threads of bile connecting my mouth to the water. The retching held me captive for several minutes, my gut clenched so tight I could not draw a breath. When my stomach released me, I collapsed against the hull and shut my eyes, then sucked in great lungfuls of the clean salt air. The freezing Atlantic wind cooled my flushed cheeks and eyelids, relieving my nausea for a time but doing little to ease the terrific pounding in my head or remove the sour taste of vomit and absinthe from my tongue.

I did not have to open my eyes to know I was no longer aboard the *Raven*. I was in the longboat . . . again. I had only the dimmest recollection of breaking into the shipment with the third mate and punching the quartermaster in the mouth when he tried to take it from us.

Damn.

I pried opened one gummy eyelid to see the brigantine just where I expected her: fifty yards ahead, towing my sorry drunken ass behind her. I groped for the waterskin in the floorboards and sucked down half its contents. I splashed a little on my face to wash away the sticky remnants of bile and excess before I dared lift my head again.

I considered signaling for my mates to reel me back aboard, but thought better of it. I was in no rush to feel the kiss of the bosun's lash peeling ribbons from my back again. Mary. He named the cursed whip "Mary".

I took a few more pulls at the waterskin and lay back to sleep off the aftereffects of my idiocy.

I awoke again at midday to gray skies and a vague sense of unease. They ought to have pulled me back aboard by now. Forgetting the promise of Mary's embrace, I sat up in the longboat and looked around. Naught but the gray Atlantic in all directions, aside from the *Raven* herself. I stood and whispered a swift thanks to whatever gods were listening that my head no longer pounded like a drum.

I waved at the masthead, but no one signaled back. I stuck two fingers in my mouth and whistled. Someone stuck his head up from the deck, and I gestured for him to reel me in. He watched me for a moment, then gave me his back and walked away. I frowned as the minutes passed and the line connecting the *Raven* to my longboat remained motionless. No one else came astern, neither to taunt nor to comfort me. After a half hour of shouting myself hoarse and fruitlessly gesticulating at the crow's nest, I gave up and plopped myself down on the thwart. Only then did I look around the floorboards. My heart sank.

It seemed I was not destined to feel Mary's gentle kiss this time. A week's rations lay at my feet. So that would be my punishment: a week in the longboat. Alone. The sun baking my skin until it bubbled and blistered and left scars no less painful than Mary's. Damn. The bosun was more clever than I thought.

After a month at sea, four drunken brawls and thirty lashes had done little to curb my taste for absinthe or the blessed numbness it brought. I needed the drink or the work to distract me from the pervasive ache in my leg. The pain was always worse with nothing else to focus on. Every sailor aboard knew I would rather swab for a month than take a single lonely watch in the mizzentop.

The brig was too kind for me, I suppose. Too near my mates, who might take pity on me for an hour or sneak me a bottle of lovely green oblivion. No; I was to be granted neither fellowship nor torture, outside of my own unpleasant company. If I knew the bosun's stubborn heart, he would not allow me back aboard early unless we ran afoul of a hurricane.

I knocked weevils from some hardtack and unleashed my frustration upon them. I squashed them beneath my bootheels, grinding their crunchy little bodies into the floorboards until they stained the wood. I tore off a hunk of salt pork with my teeth and tried to focus on reducing the hard, chewy mess into something I could swallow.

After my violent and unsatisfying meal, I glared at the *Raven* and cursed myself anew. The least they could have done was leave me a few bottles of absinthe, or anything else that might dull the nagging, ceaseless spasm in my leg.

The pain had hounded me like a shrewish wife for the last three years, ever since a musket ball shot clean through my thigh. I had terrible fever dreams while recovering from the infection. Nightmares of pain and fire and darkness. Others told me later that I called out my father's name. The ship's barber declared me dead at one point, only to hear me sputter back to life as he turned his back.

But I lived, and after a few months I could walk and scuttle about the deck with only a small limp. But the pain . . . gods, the pain was never truly gone. Even with laudanum or absinthe—sometimes both—there were times I came perilously close to weeping. Distraction had ever been my only remedy.

Now I faced a week adrift without conversation to divert me. Without the ceaseless tasks of working a ship to drive me to exhaustion. Without palliatives of any kind to numb my torment.

I might go mad.

Already I found myself massaging the ugly pit in my leg with one hand. By the end of the week I might toss myself into the sea and thank the spirited waters to suck me down.

I gazed across the thunderous waves, already considering when I might throw myself into it. Then I noticed the surface of the waters all around me were not tumultuous as I imagined. All around me, the sea lay as still as a bath. It so perfectly mirrored the leaden skies that for a moment I thought we were not sailing, but floating. The Atlantic is never so calm. Never.

I considered for a moment that we were caught in the eye of some vast, unseen storm. I dismissed that thought almost immediately; unless I'd killed a man, they would never leave me out here to die. Probably not even then. No ship has too many hands during a tempest.

The calmest harbor and the tiniest inland pond suffers wavelets and ripples, but not here. Not a single flicker of light or shadow played off the brine. The wind blew, not enough to fill the *Raven's* sails, but enough to crease the waters. Yet the sea was as still and smooth as glass.

I leaned over the side, purposely rocking the boat, but saw nothing but my own ugly face staring back at me. Not even a ghost of a ripple moved out from the hull. As though the boat rested in pudding rather than seawater. The hair on my neck and arms stood on end.

The sailors still aboard the *Raven* knew something was amiss. They held themselves stiff and watchful, jumping at every common noise or creak. They gestured sharply at one another and pointed at the sea with accusing fingers. More than one man staggered drunkenly about the deck, yet no bosun called them to task.

An unwelcome wind, lightly scented with carrion and long illness, whispered a dark prophesy to me:

You are all going to die.

So certain was I that some demon hissed the words into my ear that I whirled around and made myself dizzy looking for it. No one was there. No monster whispered cruelties to me, other than my own superstitious mind. Still my heart thudded like a cannon in my chest.

The skies cleared as evening fell, and my sense of unease grew as the light shrank. Unless my watch was broken and my own sense of time corrupted beyond redemption, the sun did not set at three in the afternoon.

I nibbled at a biscuit and watched the setting sun turn the waters pink and gold. Stars peeked through the swiftly-vanishing veils high above. Those cold divine fires, at least, gave me some measure of peace. The familiar shape of the Bear and the comforting twinkle of the Pole Star gave me bearings. Home still lay to the northeast. I began to relax. Surely this was all some strange weather phenomenon, some irregularity that learned men would laugh at a common sailor for trembling at.

But the sun lingered at the horizon as though stuck between worlds, hovering half-set for almost an hour, and my fragile peace deserted me. I knew a fleeting moment of relief when it finally resumed its natural motion, and then a panic so fierce I nearly went blind from it.

What would happen when darkness fell?

I glanced up at the cloudless sky. There would be no moon tonight, but at least the clouds were gone. I could still see the stars. I looked back at the sinking red disc of the sun, my heart pounding a little louder and a little faster as the darkness spread. I un-clenched a bit when they lit the lanterns aboard the *Raven*. How I wished I were on her deck. Night is never so dark with other voices to anchor you.

I glanced down into the bath-still waters and startled when I saw how clear they were without the constant motion of waves to distort them. I could see the bottom of the ocean. Fascinated, I leaned over and squinted into the gloom to get a better look. The sand and rock looked almost close enough to touch. I could not help myself; I reached down to touch the water . . . and came back screaming.

My flesh hissed like a lobster in the pot as my fingertips bubbled and smoked before my eyes. Agony crippled me, and I shook from the pain and shock. I wiped my smoldering fingers on my shirt and screamed louder when my flesh sloughed off like burnt chicken skin. White bone glared at me in accusation from my two ruined fingers. My next scream was not from pain, but horror.

Suddenly the pain in my leg flared to a level I had not believed possible outside of death, the muscles clenching and quivering in uncontrollable spasms. The old injury had not tortured me so since I first received it. I doubled over and bit down on my uninjured fist

until my knuckles bled. The pain in my leg subsided after what felt like half of my life, yet could not have been more than a few moments, for the sun still clung to the horizon.

I heaved and vomited over the side of the longboat, keeping well away from the surface of those poisonous waters. My half-melted fingers thrummed and tingled, but no longer pained me, oddly enough. I watched in horrified fascination as the half-digested hardtack and salt pork steamed and dissolved away, leaving the view as flawless and crystalline as before. In the last light of that dark day, I saw what truly lay at the bottom of this waterless ocean.

Bones. Countless bones, from all manner of creatures, painted crimson by the fading light of the sun. A triangular skull longer than the *Raven* glared up at me, connected to a spine I could not see the end of. The skeleton of a three-headed horse lay beside that of a bird with wings like the mainsail of a Chinese junk and a hollow tube instead of a beak. But most of the bones appeared—to my unlearned eye—human. Countless skulls and ribcages, pelvises and finger-bones. All seemed no farther away than I could reach, and stretched out farther than the eye could see. An entire seafloor, an entire *world,* built of bones.

This biting sea was not brine, but hunger. Why it did not consume the boat, I could not fathom. Perhaps the acid had no taste for wood. Even as I thought this, I glimpsed shipwrecks scattered along the bottom. Masts and hulls, keels and sails, the outlines of sailing vessels and skiffs all lay in pieces beneath me, unmolested since their sinking. This ocean revealed new horrors every time I looked.

Then came the monsters.

The sea boiled to life not with howling winds or whitecaps, but with odd bulges moving at speed toward the *Raven.* Hundreds of them. Thousands. They made no noise, no waves. They skimmed below the surface without breaking it, like rats scurrying beneath a blanket. All sped toward the *Raven* like moths to light.

I leapt to my feet to cry a warning, but it caught in my throat as the first of the monsters breached the surface. The grotesque silhouettes stood out in stark relief against the last light of the dying sun, each one powerful enough to tear down the main mast with a gesture. The hunchbacked fiends had too many limbs and tails like paddles, their backs covered in spines, those unthinkable jaws filled with too many teeth that stuck out at odd angles and dripped with fluids. They threw their heads back and howled to the sky, a noise like shattering glass and crumbling stone and the tortured pleading of the damned.

Wood shattered and splinters flew in all directions as the beasts dug their claws into the *Raven's* hull. Some tore pieces from the ship and fell back into the bitter sea without a splash or a sound. Other slithery bodies fell onto the deck with wet, heavy flops.

They swarmed the ship within seconds. Those aboard had no time to launch an attack or even sound a warning. Less than a minute after the first leviathan scaled the hull, the *Raven* was no longer recognizable as a sailing vessel. Only a writhing hulk of flapping tails and thrashing limbs remained, outlined sharply against the last violent, blood-red light of sunset.

My mates' death screams I heard only too well. I clamped my hands over my ears and stifled my own cries by biting down on my vest. I could not help them. God save me; what could I do against monsters like that? My ears resounded with the cries of brave men being eaten alive. I huddled down in the floorboards, shuddering with each cry for help or mercy that went unanswered. Hot tears rolled down my cheeks and stung my wounds.

I looked up at the sky, longing for the scant and hollow comfort of friendly stars, and could not keep myself from moaning in despair. The stars winked out as I watched, one by one. Not masked by clouds or drowned out by moonlight, but snuffed out as one snuffs out a candle flame. Gone. I was left in utter darkness.

I cowered in the dubious shelter of the longboat long after the screams of the dying faded away, lest any noise or movement on my part alert the demons to my presence. I remained curled in the floorboards until the longboat rose and fell as one of the monsters passed directly beneath me. They were gone. I waited a few more minutes before I dared lift my head.

The only light in the world came from the swaying lanterns aboard the brigantine. I could no longer see her silhouette, but I had heard her masts fall. I had seen pieces of her hull ripped away by claws I did not want to imagine. She would sink soon, and if I did not untie the rope that bound my longboat to the *Raven,* she would pull me down with her.

Perhaps I should have sat there and waited to be taken under. A few moments of suffering, and then all that would remain would be my naked bones. They would tumble down and become yet another addition to the macabre collection at the bottom of this alien sea.

But when I felt the first tug of the line pulling me toward the wrecked *Raven,* I leapt forward, knife in hand, and sawed at the rope until it fell away.

I sat back down, my heart pounding. The knife slipped from my shaking fingers, and I startled when it clattered to the deck.

My heart sank into that murderous ocean along with the lanterns aboard the *Raven.* One by one they hissed and winked out, leaving me in darkness and silence.

Something shook the bow and startled me awake. I did not remember falling asleep, and I was not certain I was awake even then, for the blackness that surrounded me was darker than the void behind my eyelids. But something had made the boat move. Something heavy. Something that was still there, for the longboat listed forward.

Then I saw them: two tiny specks, bright only in this inky darkness, hovering at eye-level above the bow. At first my heart leapt, thinking they were stars or perhaps even the lights of an approaching rescue vessel, until I heard the breathing. Wet and whispery; jagged breaths like those from a sick old man. My mouth went dry and I trembled all over as the lights winked out and came back in tandem. I tried to control my shuddering breath and the pounding of my blood in my ears. In a world so devoid of sound, such whispers were deafening.

The creature blinked again. I could not tell what light was reflected in those black eyes. Perhaps some inner fire lit them; I did not know.

I dare not move. I dare not breathe. For hours the creature has sat there, watching me, blinking and breathing its wet and whispery respirations. I fight down the urge to scream at it, to leap across the boat and attack it until it either leaves or devours me. I do not know if I can bear this stalemate much longer.

The pain in my leg flares again, white-hot and virulent, and I cannot quite suppress a whimper. The monster before me growls and snaps its jaws at the sound. A hundred tiny lights flash as its teeth spark against one another, and for an instant I see the monster's face.

It was the face of death itself. Of burnt and gangrenous flesh, crawling with slithery, corpse-white insects. Its eyes are so black and so fathomless they could devour the world and still hunger. Its teeth are rusted metal and splintered stone. Its tongue is the bloated, purpling mass of a dead animal left to rot and float in stagnant waters. Steaming white saliva drips from amorphous jaws. Shivering, shapeless growths stick out from its head, jiggling bonelessly and oozing poison.

How had I not noticed the smell before? Of carrion and infection, of cesspools and vomit and shit? If there had been anything left in my gut, I would have emptied it into the acid sea once more.

The sound of my retching sets the creature to snarling again. The boat moves as the beast quits its perch and crawls down inside it. Unseen claws carve gouges into the wood and something wet plops and slithers across the floorboards.

I push myself back, back away from the monster until I have nowhere left to run. The stern digs into my back and I lean out over the water behind me. I brace myself against the bench and my bad leg spasms and crumples. I wail and fall down into the floorboards, clutching my thigh. The creature echoes my howling and falls back; whether in surprise or something else, I cannot say.

When the pain eases, I find myself huddled into a ball in the bottom of the boat, shaking and drenched in sweat. The monster sits back at the bow, watching me in silence. Perhaps it does not savor the taste of pain not inflicted by itself. I do not care. It has retreated, and my tiny world is safe for a few moments longer.

I wish for the sound of wavelets splashing against the hull. I long for the swell and bob of the rolling ocean beneath me. Even the crack and liquid fire of Mary's scolding tongue. Anything. Any sound but the diseased breathing of the monster. Any sight but those shimmering black lights at the bow, waiting for me to give in and die.

When will the sun rise?

Once more, the carrion-scented wind whispers an unwelcome answer in my ear:

Never.

The monster before me makes a garbled sound that I pray is not laughter.

As the hours pass, I know that I shall never see the sun again. My life is over. The only choice left to me now is how to end it. Slowly, so as not to alarm the creature, I pull myself up and sit on the gunwale. For a few moments, I balance myself there between one choice and another, and then I fall backward into the ocean.

The monster screams and flies at me when it senses my intent, but it is too late. I plunge into the liquid. My whole body spasms and shrieks in agony as the acid begins its work, liquefying me one layer at a time. It burns and freezes and stings and shreds. Pain beyond imagining. I open my mouth to scream and the scorching liquid pours into my mouth and down my throat, setting my insides afire. My memories flicker and desert me as the acid trickles into my ears and devours my brain. Still I burn.

It does not stop. Oh, merciful God in Heaven, why will it not stop? How long, how long? When will I die? I burn, I burn!

I burn for days. Forever. It will not end. The acid is not death, but torment.

Then, through the agony, I feel myself begin to change. The monster above lurks in the longboat still, watching me twist and scream but doing nothing as my arms soften and split into four, five, seven limbs. My fingers are reduced to jelly before they harden into bony talons. The liquefying skin of my face, chest, and legs thicken into quivering, fleshy growths. My teeth splinter into daggers that project from my too-large mouth at weird angles. My eyes blister and clump into hard black orbs. Tiny maggot-like fishes swarm over my face and peck at what remains of my old flesh. My bones melt and reform as scaly armor that lessens the burning, but does not end it. Nothing will end it.

Others fly around me as my agony dulls to a nagging ache. This cannot be water, for I can breathe. We do not swim; we fly. The air-ocean above is a tasteless void we cannot move through, and as the hours pass, it fills with the hateful light of a fiery demon-god I once called the sun. All day my brothers shield me from the light. They show me how to hide from it in the skeletons of the monsters who once lived in the air-ocean. All day I change, growing more familiar with my new body, even as my hunger grows.

As the demon-god slowly retreats, the others grow excited. I follow them and join the hunt.

Dark shapes loom above us. The others chitter and swirl around one another in excitement. They say the dark shapes carry meat. My brothers swarm toward the larger shape before the demon-god is gone, but I linger behind, uncertain. I let the others feed and rend the unnatural shape asunder until it collapses and joins the bones below us.

I watch the smaller shape instead. There is meat here, but the others are long gone, fat with the bounty of the larger shape. I have no competition for this one.

I wait for the light to fade completely, for my eyes are new and more sensitive to the light of the demon-god than the others'. I breach the surface and realize I can breathe a little, though I am not comfortable. The meat does not move as I crawl into its container. It appears blind and deaf in this air-ocean. I watch it for some time. Something about it seems familiar. But that makes no sense, for there was nothing before the burning.

The meat clutches its leg and makes a noise. The noise reminds me of things I cannot remember, and it vexes me. I grind my teeth until sparks fly all around my face. The meat makes more sounds, which irritate me further. I move toward it, hungry and angry. My body is clumsy in this void, and the meat hears my approach and it retreats to the back of its container. I open my mouth to bite its head off when it clutches its leg and howls.

Memories flash through my skull at his cry of pain—memories of Men and ships and the world before this one. His pain is mine. I remember the pit in his thigh. No; in *my* thigh. It is gone now, replaced with armor and bulbous growths, but I remember.

I try to speak to the man, but he cannot understand me. He huddles down in the bottom of the boat—I know its name again— and lies still.

I am distracted when I smell tiny deaths in the floorboards. Weevils. Tiny, soulless things. I crushed them for stealing my not-meat.

I watch the man for some time. I try to comfort him, to assure him I am no longer hungry, but he seems more horrified than ever when I attempt to speak. So I retreat to the bow and watch him in silence. It is easier to breathe now. I could stay here a long time.

He finally rises and sits on the edge of the boat. He stares at me, then smiles and falls backward into the ocean. I know his intent, for it was mine—ours—once, and try to call out a warning. But my mouth is no longer shaped for human language, and he cannot understand me.

I watch from above as he fizzles and boils, his mouth open in a scream I cannot hear, until he changes. Again. Eventually, I slither home and let the liquid sky wash the memories away once more.

Tonight I will feast with the others.

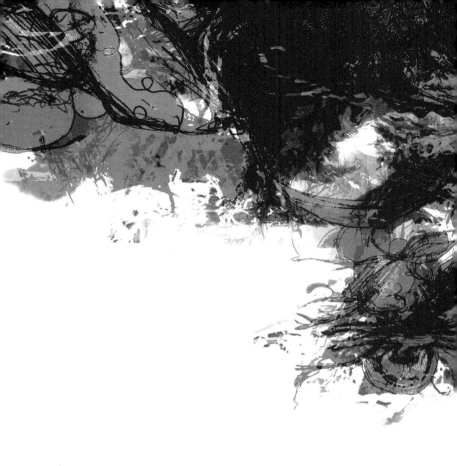

IN THE WALLS

ADAM MILLARD

They were in the walls; he saw them, on occasion, when they were bored and decided to reveal themselves to him. He would be sitting in his chair, reclined and relaxed with a good book or a crossword puzzle, a cup of tea or coffee—depending on his mood—in hand, when all of a sudden one of them would poke their spindly fingers through a plug-socket, wiggle them as if to taunt him, and then snatch them back in, quick as a flash. He would notice, from the corner of his eye, something glistening, only to turn and find an eye staring up at him from between the unlit faux coals of his gas-fire. Most of the time he would tip his drink down before clambering to his feet and chasing the things away; though they were always gone long before he managed to climb from his chair.

They were simply playing games with him. He didn't know how many of them there were, but he had it at around six, perhaps seven. *What* they were was also unclear. He knew that they had two eyes, like humans, but their hands seemed to be limited to three fingers each, and the central one—the *digitus medius,* he supposed—was much longer than the others, almost twice as long, which was why it always shocked him to find it probing from electrical sockets and the like. There were no fingernails attached to the elongated appendages, and he doubted the presence of fingerprints simply because he had, on two occasions, managed to grab onto the hand, hoping to frighten the thing, or at least make it realize that enough was enough. To touch, it was one of the smoothest things he had ever come into contact with; a strange, undeviating skin that felt as if it had been grown that very morning. That was the first time he had heard one of them make a noise; perhaps him latching onto its hand had frightened it, forcing that terrifyingly shrill sound out of its mouth. The noise had caused him to release the hand, and the thing had snatched all three fingers back into the wall.

The second time he'd made contact had been pure chance. He had been drilling a hole to affix a newel post to the staircase when his hand slipped. The drill shot straight through, his fist plunging with it. The pain had been almost unbearable, but nothing compared to the strange texture beneath his mangled fist. Unable to move—momentarily—he'd slid his hand across, trying to fathom what he was stroking; and then he knew, for it shifted quickly away, also aware of the impending danger. He'd pulled his hand back through to his side of the staircase, and stared into the darkness; but it was too late.

It had gone.

And tonight, during his silent supper, two of them had pushed him to his wits' end. He had been enjoying cheese and crackers, as was his wont, when he heard them beneath the kitchen sink. There was a hole back there—something to do with the plumbing, he guessed, though he wasn't entirely certain—and they could clearly be heard scratching about just behind the plasterboard. He'd listened discontentedly as they had skittered around, no doubt mischievously searching for something to break or cause him alarm. How stupid did they believe him to be? The initial fear he had once felt at the sight of them had abated; all that remained now was anger and disgust at having to share his house—his dead *mother's* house—with hominid vermin.

He had finished his cheese and crackers, chewing slowly so that he could maintain a clear idea as to where the things were in the walls. He'd walked his empty plate across to the sink, lowered it into the soapy water, and stood breathing softly, hoping they were still there, within reach . . . for he had a plan. He'd taken enough of their jesting; they didn't belong in his house, and they were no longer welcome—not that they ever *had* been. He had stood, waiting patiently, listening for the shuffling that betrayed their position.

He didn't have to wait long. Just in front of him, slightly above the lemon-yellow tiling at the back of the sink, came a rattle that could only have been caused by one of the things. Without pause, he'd snatched the largest knife out of its block and rammed it straight through the plasterboard, straight through the wall. There had come an almighty squeal, followed by a thick, viscous gargling sound that was both satisfying and terrifying in equal measure. He had hit his target; the knife was rocking from side to side as the thing flailed in agony behind the wall. He couldn't grasp the handle; such was the creature's spasmodic reaction to having a knife penetrating its oh-so-soft flesh.

He had laughed, knowing that he'd finally managed to inflict pain upon one of them. Served them right for the many times they had caused him sleepless nights; the times they had startled him during what should have been periods of repose. How dare they, in his own house, cause him to sit up restlessly in the early hours, afraid they were conspiring against him, concocting tricks and ruses to terrify him so the very next day?

He'd watched as a thick, viscous fluid poured out through the plaster; the creature was still screeching in its unbearable manner, even as the knife clattered from side to side and the dark green ooze that seeped from its open flesh slowly dripped down the tiles and onto the draining-board.

He had wondered in that moment—and as he had often pondered during the course of his residence—if the things in the walls had always been there. If so, his mother had never made mention of them. Surely she would have brought it up in conversation, especially knowing her son was to inherit the house after her passing, and subsequently the unwanted guests between the framework.

Suddenly, the creature had fallen silent, the knife came to an anticlimactic halt. He had watched, momentarily mesmerized, as the Phthalo green lifeblood continued to paint a trail across his work-surfaces, knowing that he would have to clean the mess up sooner rather than later.

A noise behind the wall—no, two separate walls and *three* distinguishing voices—startled him from his rumination. He had stepped away from the wall, the motionless knife, the dead thing hidden in the wall, and came to a stop in the center of the kitchen.

The sounds emanating from the walls weren't angry; at least not yet.

The creatures were mourning, and it was a sound that turned his blood to mercury.

Later that night he sat in semi-darkness, book in hand. The tiny lamp sitting on his side table was enough for him to read by, and he much preferred it to the glaring beam of the main bulb. The book he was reading was a parody of the bible; he found himself enjoying it a little too much. His faith wasn't entirely gone, not just yet, and reading such a book made him feel ever-so-slightly guilty.

Though, he assured himself, it was a work of fiction and should be judged as such, for nobody would believe that God created the earth by accidentally passing wind after a particularly strong curry; nobody could seriously agree that Adam and Eve were in fact executive bankers from the year 2029. His faith was not being called into question at all with such literature, and he suddenly felt a lot better by simply reminding himself of that.

He was almost at the end of Genesis when the things in the wall began their cruel trickery. At first, he believed that the voice he was hearing did actually belong to his dead mother; that she had somehow returned from the afterlife to palaver with him. He dropped the open book into his lap and scrambled to his feet, scanning the room for the glowing figure of his deceased mother. After a few seconds, and once he gathered his bearings, he realized that it was, indeed, not his mother's voice that beckoned him.

It was the creatures—for they knew better than anyone the pitch, the drawl, the occasional upturn of a certain word—that belonged to the previous owner. The question, left unanswered from that very same afternoon, had been answered. His mother had had to tolerate the creatures, just as he had to now. Though her secrecy was still beyond his comprehension.

"You must leave this place, son," her voice said once again. "They'll *kill* you if you stay."

If it was the creatures, and it *had* to be, then it was the first time he had ever heard them speak with words. Sure they growled, grunted, screeched, whined, whispered and cawed, but with nothing remotely close to the English language.

He spun on the spot, almost tripping as his feet tangled beneath him. The voice seemed to come from everywhere and nowhere. The entire room shook as the vibrations of the faux-mother voice played along the skirting, the walls, the coving, and shelves.

He screamed out, hoping that the mere sound of his voice would be enough to perturb them. The voice that replied was still that of his mother, and once again he found himself searching the room for signs of ectoplasm or glowing orbs.

"You killed one of them," the voice said, "and they will not rest until you are dead. You must leave now, sell the house . . . just go away and never return."

How could they sound so like her? For primitive creatures—which is what he had always regarded them as—they were remarkably talented at impressions. They must have been listening to every word his mother had said to be able to mimic her so thoroughly. It was, he thought, quite disturbing to think that they were always there, and then he thought back to all the times he had spoken on the telephone, to the times where he had invited guests over to share a dinner, to all the times when he had simply conversed with himself for no other reason than sheer boredom. The hackles rose on the nape of his neck, and it was all he could do not to pass out.

There came a scratching, and then a steady hissing as one of the creatures moved within the wall. From his periphery, he saw an elongated finger jut out of the electrical socket, and then it was gone, moving along the innards of the house—*his* house . . . his dead mother's house.

"I won't be moved!" he called out. "I didn't mean to kill it. You forced my hand. A man can only endure so much!" He didn't know why he was trying to justify his actions to the creatures. They were vermin; horrible, disgusting, squatting, mother-mimicking vermin.

And then, the sounds came from everywhere. He didn't know which way to turn; such was the scope of their shuffling and scratching. One minute they were all behind him, behind the chair in which he had previously been sitting, minding his own business and enjoying the company of a good book; the next minute they

were over by the window, beneath the sill. A three-fingered hand shot out through the wallpaper, and he almost cursed in anger at their selfish vandalism. There was a hole back there, behind the paper, of which he had not been aware. His mother, God rest her soul, was not much for home-improvement, nor maintenance, and the hole that the creature's hand now poked out of would have been near the bottom of the list of things to get done. Perhaps she had never intended to fill the godforsaken thing; her death had not been a surprise. Maybe she had left it purposefully, something for him to do when he got bored.

Though he *never* got bored, not with all the chasing around after "things in the wall" he did. There was never a moment of rest, never a peaceful day; it was all stress and no release, and he was glad he had managed to kill one of their kind that afternoon. It was in Hell now, where it belonged.

He watched the fingers twirl spasmodically, certain that the thing's only motive was to annoy him. From the kitchen there came an almighty clatter; he felt his heart jump up into his throat. He rushed through, forgetting all about the protruding fingers in the lounge, to discover an arm had managed to break through the north wall. A skinny, pallid thing that looked less like an appendage and more like something you might see in an aquarium.

Thrashing wildly, the arm retracted back into the masonry, leaving a twelve-inch hole behind. He reached for the nearest weapon, which happened to be the knife he had used to kill the thing above the sink, and paced across to the unsightly aperture. "You think you'll get rid of me like this?" he bellowed. "I won't be moved by your reprehensible pranks." He lashed at the hole with the blade, knowing that it was pointless, that the thing had already moved on.

Breathlessly, he staggered back to the lounge. The scratching and shuffling was becoming intolerable; he needed to lie down, to forget the things were there, to gather his strength for a battle of wits and determination.

He clambered up the stairs, pushing earphones into his ears in an attempt to drown them out with loud music and late-night talk shows.

He would not be beaten by the things within the walls.

"I can't play bridge today," the voice of his mother said. "I've got that useless sonofabitch son of mine coming over to visit."

He pushed himself up from the bed, not knowing how long he had been sleeping. The earphones had fallen out at some point, which is how he heard his mother's voice say such a wretched thing. He knew it was the things, the ungodly creatures in the walls, using the voice of his deceased mother to once again provoke him. He could hear them shuffling along the skirting, searching for the best place from whence to attack.

He swung his legs off the bed and rubbed the sleep from his eyes. He was so tired, so exhausted from the day's malarkey—though he knew that he would sleep no more tonight—not with the things continuing their torment.

Just to the right of him, where his wardrobe housed several suits and shirts that he had not worn for several years and not much more, the voice of his mother said, "Pathetic he is. I will be glad when I'm dead so that I don't have to suffer his stupidity any longer."

These words cut him to the bone, for he had never heard his mother speak with such venom. Her tongue could be cruel, but against others—not against him. As he sat there, listening to the barrage of abuse creeping out through the walls, he started to believe the words had indeed fallen from the lips of his dead mother. The things were intelligent, certainly; but how could they know about his afflictions, his depression, his inability to find love in any form? His mother had spoken ill of him on the telephone to friends; the things in the wall were simply re-enacting scenes they had witnessed.

No.

Mother, no . . .

"You should have *seen* him, Bettie," one cruel voice said from over by the suede ottoman. "He looked like he was going to cry, or piss himself, or *both.*" It laughed in his mother's voice, and he knew of the instance she had been speaking of.

He had confided in her, told her about a romantic encounter that had gone terribly wrong; and she had comforted him, told him that everything would be alright. She had even slipped in the old adage about fish in the sea, and how there were plenty more where that particular girl came from.

And all the while she had been laughing; secretly reveling in his misery, probably waiting for him to leave the house so that she could ring *Bettie* and tell her how pathetic her son was. It crippled him to think about it, and he toppled back onto the mattress, screaming at the voices to stop, to leave him alone for God's sake and his.

"His father would have *beaten* him, Bettie. Good job he died a long time ago, for he would have been just as disappointed as I am."

No please, make it stop. Make them go away! I'm losing my senses; I'm going insane . . .

He sobbed that night, watching as the creatures occasionally popped out from the wall somewhere. The voices soon subsided, and he was able to ponder in silence the enormity of the callousness he had heard spill from behind the walls. There was no way he could live with the knowledge of his mother's—God rest her evil, obdurate soul—disappointment, her indifference to his many plights, her downright hatred of him. He had to move, or risk insanity. There was always suicide, though his faith was not quite lost yet and he was to still hold true the laws regarding eternal damnation.

They had won, *after* all. The creatures; the things that lived in the walls.

Love Grudge

Dot Wickliff

I hope her lips were worth it.

Sleep well, my frail prince,
my Knight of Death,
and pay your fare to dreamland.
While she's beside you in our bed,
my charred soul runs nightmare's errand.

Clock's faces can't breathe and a slut's eyes
don't really see; you've been buried beneath
talus of flesh toys avalanche. And still
my stringy love, tactful beige, like a glue
Two at once? I laughed, I'd rather be dead
. . . but for you, I probably would have.
Even now it's still funny. That star there?
I'll take each piece down for you—

As I choke on jagged stars wrought from cold heaven,
frail prince, in your bloodsleep hear my words:
This act shall not easily be undone.

You'd better bury me in the desert;
you'd better bury my head separate.
Slaughter the white lamb the first dead moon
in August, and sleep fitfully with all three eyes open
. . . bed full of plastic crosses.

Instead may I suggest you invest in silver,
acreage of boneset, barrels of myrrh,
Talismans of Saturn carved into your chest
and tattooed ideograms of fresh juniper ash.
The musky tang of Corvus sweat and feathers,
edges burnt and sharply folded under,
    sharp just like jagged stars feel
permeates the woodshed, parches your heart—
the head turns, looks your way from under coals;
those blistered black eyes know your secrets.

Love, you'd better bury me *deep* in the desert,
and I suggest you bury my head separate.
In an expensive box of imported ivory
with inlaid symbols of gold; prettiest trinket—
and still, I can't promise those hinges will hold.
    Sleep with all three eyes open
Frail prince,
because I might just be coming back.
For you, my brave Knight of Death,

    I'll be clawing my way back.

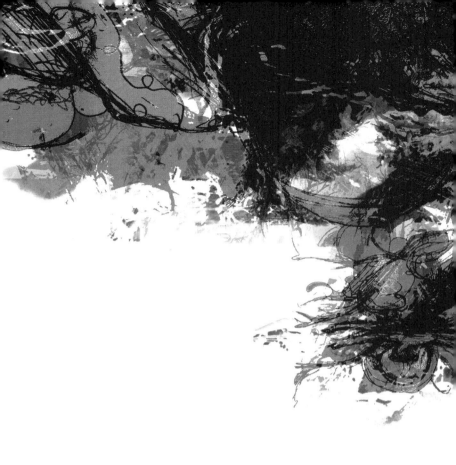

EARTH, RISEN

PETE CLARK

The last few words on the page burned his eyes like fever. The sculptor read them again and again until they blurred into insensibility. He let the book fall to the floor and left it where it fell, the soft flapping of closing pages like a balm to his mind, the sudden loss of stimulus like a cold compress over his hot eyes. He rubbed them until he saw stars and spoke those last few words out loud. In doing so, he not only confirmed to himself that it *could* be done; he knew instantly the way to do it.

It would not be enough to build the thing of clay alone. He knew that. He had read the lore, of course—had in fact taken much of it with a pinch of salt—but much had touched something in him, something that bypassed his blinding grief. It had to do with hope and belief. It had to do with the fact that so much truth was hidden within the myth . . . so much that *had* to be true. It was this he clung to, a raft hopelessly battered upon a sea of nonsense. And then he had found the book. Simply called *Earth, Risen,* it was written anonymously in flowing script onto dark parchment-like paper in a mixture of Hebrew and English. It was this book that had finally convinced him that it could be done.

Are you sure you want to know? the bookseller had asked him. *There are some things a man should not be party to, and I believe with all my heart that this is one of them.*

But the bookseller was as driven by money as anyone else, and he had accepted the payment graciously, holding the sculptor's gaze for perhaps longer than necessary. And so the book had been bought and devoured in the way important books so often are. The book had such simplicity to it that he knew at once it was genuine. So much of the lore he had studied had been hyperbole, covering up lies and misrepresented fact with drama and shocking revelation. Not so with this book. It was, in essence, an instruction manual—a description of the how and why of it. He bent now to retrieve the slim volume and turned immediately to the last page.

"...and so with truth, and with their own vitality, or substantial part of it, they will live. And when truth dies, as it eventually must, it will be the end of them, and they cannot revive..."

And then that last line, as with the bookseller, holding his gaze just a little bit longer than he would have liked.

"...be aware of what you do. Wrath, like love, has to be earned. Be determined which one you truly seek. Because all is possible, and all is truth..."

The sculptor stood, and the candles set all about him danced as he moved. A soft wind blew about his feet, sending dust motes into frenzied choreography. He poured a large glass of wine, took half of it in one swallow, and set the glass down on a long low bench that flanked one side of the room. In the center of the room lay a table, high and sturdy. Next to this was a box—an old tea chest, rough-hewn planks making up its walls, a hinged lid open to the floor. He reached into the chest, grabbed the neck of the sack within, and hefted the load onto the table. A muted clunk broke the silence, and pale dust sifted through the open weave of the sacking. He opened the sack, and lifted out the contents one by one, arranging them roughly, discarding the sack when he was done.

The assortment of bones on the table sent a cold shiver through him. They were small and dull and off-white. Dried sinew and tiny shreds of black flesh clung to some of the larger ones; the femur and skull, a shoulder blade. He had bagged hand and foot bones so as to keep them together, and released them now in a clattering pile like druids' rune stones, beginning to arrange the tableau as if it were nothing more than a jigsaw puzzle. He had once studied anatomy and bone structure and human physiology for his sculptures. It was this knowledge he used now to reassemble the skeleton. Some bones were missing—a rib here, vertebra there, lower jaw hopelessly crushed when his shovel had broken through the rotted coffin lid—but it was only a matter of hours before he had something on his table that he recognized.

It was an almost complete child's skeleton.

He took a battery-powered drill and fitted the smallest bit he could find. It looked no thicker than a toothpick. With whining monotony, he set about drilling holes into the ends of each and every bone, sending tiny puffs of foul smelling blue smoke into the air. He was fastidious, clamping each in steady fingers, blowing gently to send the smoke spiraling away from his eyes. A faint burning smell began to surround him, and he worked on. The bones in the feet were drilled now, and he moved onto the hand, and vertebrae. He used a slightly larger bit to drill the leg and arm bones, and the complex machinery of shoulder blade and ribs and collar bone. The rib cage was almost completely intact, apart from the missing rib, and he set this down on the floor as he worked. As each hour passed, tiny drifts of browning bone dust appeared at the ends of each cluster of bones.

His excitement grew as each bone was holed, and he began to relish the sweet burning aroma as drill met bone. The sound became the soundtrack to his work, and when he had finished, the last vertebra drilled and placed back with its brothers, he stood back from the table, unaware that the drill was whining redundantly in his hand. He stayed that way, eyes scanning the skeleton over and over to spot any missed bones, until the battery died and the drill fell silent. He dropped it and kicked it absently away from him.

From under the bench, in between sips of steadying wine, he sorted through a jumble of boxes and settled on two. The first contained wire—yards and yards of hair-thin silver wire, wrapped fastidiously with strands of spider silk so that they shimmered like dull moonlight. It had taken months of painstaking and ultimately painful work to collect the silk from his battery of captive spiders. It had to be spider silk. This was one piece of lore that he truly believed, and the book was specific about it.

The second contained a lump of wet clay about the size of a football. It was this he brought to the table now, along with a book detailing human anatomy. His skilled fingers worked quickly to separate a piece of clay and draw it into a rough cylinder, about an inch thick and eight long. With it, in between long consultations with the diagrams in his anatomy book, he fashioned a rough flattened semi-circle. He drew each end into a paddle about twice the width of the rest. He moulded the piece into a rounded V, and set it next to the skull for sizing. With further modifications and trimming of excess clay, he fitted the piece exactly to the skull.

He had made a jawbone.

He removed more clay from its box and set about creating a rib, the missing vertebra. He was soon satisfied, for he was an accomplished sculptor. He removed the clay pieces carefully and walked with them over to his kiln in the far corner. His hands were stained with the clay, calloused and sore from hours of painstaking drilling. He placed the pieces into the kiln, watching for a moment as the haze of fire shimmered around them. The smell of hot clay surrounded him. He washed his hands and changed clothes, throwing the clay-streaked shirt and jeans into an uncomfortable heap next to the kiln. He allowed himself a short sleep.

Hours later, the pieces fired and cooled, he sanded their jagged edges and drilled their ends. They fitted into place perfectly, as he knew they would, and a short frisson of excitement ran through him.

The skeleton was complete.

He began to thread the silk-wrapped silver wire through each and every holed bone. He snipped each piece to size and loosely twisted their ends together. The purpose of the wire was not for strength. It was not to hold the skeleton together, although he hoped the silk wrapped wire could bear the skeleton's weight for a short time. Rather it was a symbol of completion, a tying together of spirit and bone; locking the loose pieces so that they might know they belong together, and behave accordingly. As sweat ran through the mask of dried clay on his face, his tears joined it; tiny tributaries swelling like a river in a cracked river bed. He wiped the moisture away, smearing the clay like claw marks under his eyes and across his cheeks, red ochre where his fingertips had cracked and added their own moisture. He noticed neither the pain nor the tears as he worked. He merely fitted bone to bone, knit them gently together as they had once been. He thought of those times, and the tears came harder.

When the final wires between skull and clay jawbone were secured, he moved a second table into place alongside the first. On this he slapped down great chunks of wet clay, relishing the earthy smell, the living quality of the mineral. Fresh spatters of brown water coated him. He fashioned a rough silhouette of a human body, arms and legs and torso about three times their natural width. He pressed a large disc into place where the head should be. He offered up a silent prayer and slipped his hands under the skeleton, one at the knees and the other under the fragile puzzle of vertebrae below the skull. He hefted the wired bones off the table, and had a moment's panic when the head lolled backwards comically and the legs clattered towards the floor. The wires held, however; and, its feet kicking in the air, he transferred the skeleton to the second table, laying it lovingly onto the clay silhouette, as a father might lay a sleeping child into bed.

Next he filled a large bucket with water and set it next to the skeleton. Immersing his hands in the blessedly cool water, he let them sit there for a while, absently rubbing fingertip against fingertip, scrubbing the blood and grime away.

Okay, he said softly, and the words echoed around the dusty room.

He removed his hands from the bucket and, still dripping, set them about their work bringing the soft clay silhouette up and around the collection of bones. He filled the hollows in the rib cage and between leg and arm bones with rough blocks of clay. Hours he spent kneading and molding and knitting edges, filling gaps, adding here, taking away there. He gently turned the body over and began to work on the back, cleverly shaping the muscles in the back and neck, rounding the clay at the back of the skull, remembering the tiny flat spot just above the nape that he loved. Turning again, he set the body down, heavy now, its heft just right; the still wet clay falling as it should, legs turning slightly out, hands resting palm up. He worked on them now, separating fingers, molding knuckles and joints, carving delicate lines and creases. Toe and fingernails were shaped, the minute curls of excess clay from his knife falling around his feet. He roughed the body into shape, content to have the idea of it just right; but the detail he forewent in favor of the tiny outfit of clothes hanging from the door. These he would dress the body in once dry.

At last he could do no more, and sat back heavily, the table and its body lying at face height. He gasped at its likeness, despite the blank face. He ran a hand across its chest, cupped the narrow chin, and, with a fingernail, described a rough mouth and the position of the eyes. He teased a rough pyramid of clay from the middle of the face and shaped absently into its nose. He could do no more and fell back, exhausted. From his jeans pocket he drew a picture. Its edges were torn and crumpled, but the face staring from it was crisp and clear.

His boy.

He slept where he had fallen, the clay on his hands drying to pale ochre dust, the body above him hardening slightly in the dry air. He dreamt no dreams save for the face of the boy, and the sound of screaming.

It seemed when he woke that he had been gripped by fever anew. He rose and almost instantly started his work, as early morning arrived without acknowledgment. With an array of shaping and cutting tools, he set about the body's face. With memory alone he teased and shaped and moulded. The nose that he had roughed out the night before became exact, the small bump on its bridge so lifelike he bent to kiss it as he had so many years before. He worked tirelessly, cupping the shape of cheeks with his moistened palms, creating tiny flaps of clay that he pressed into place over eyes that stared into his with uncanny reason. He went as far as to scratch tiny lines at the corner of the eyes, extracting signs of life almost absently. The tiny, full mouth; pointed chin with its smooth dimple; high, full forehead. All these features became reality in his hands. With strands of clay rolled into straw thicknesses, he began layering the dome of skull with hair, each layer subjected to a barber's scrutiny to ensure that the strands lay just right. He created the flick of fringe that half-covered one eye, and turning the body carefully, let the longer strands at the back just reach to the body's shoulders. He looked at the face, and with a calculated flick, opened the mouth like a wound; remoulded the lips and added the impression of teeth within. Stepping back from the visage, he let out a coughing cry, hands covering the lower half of his own face, muting his shock. He reached suddenly to remould the ear lobes, but let the knife fall, content.

It was perfect.

His son lay on the table before him, androgynous from the neck down, but utterly right and beautiful above. The sculptor spoke his name over and over, and his sobbing words grew slowly quieter, and night fell once more.

As the sun burned away a ground mist, a sweet smelling breeze blew in through the recently opened door. He dressed the figure quickly, allowing the soft folds of cloth to mask any imperfections in the moulding of the body. He had slept well, and changed into clean jeans and a shirt. He rescued the book from the floor and smoothed the pages.

Almost subliminal in their placing, the symbols he had searched for were in the middle of the book, scratched with faded ink into one margin; one truth, one death. To mark his son with the first would bring life. The second would end it. He had practiced their curling form over and over, until he could draw them in his sleep.

He swallowed the dregs of his third coffee that morning and held his shaking hands up to his face. With a huge effort, he willed them to calm, and they did. The father became the sculptor then, all thoughts erased except for that of rendering the symbols perfectly. He turned once more to his clay son, smoothed the hair as if it were living, feeling, and hearing the soft rasp of dry clay under his fingertips. It wasn't until he saw the first drop of moisture on the face, sinking like rain on a cracked river bed, that he realized he was crying.

He selected a knife from his tools, and laid an elbow next to the face, cupping the hand holding the knife with his other. He breathed deeply and held it. When all sound had ceased, when all he could sense was the slight pressure and throb of blood in his ears, he lowered the knife to the forehead and watched, as if he were a mere observer, as the tip scratched into the clay.

תמא

Truth.

The symbols came easily. Indeed, they seemed to form themselves, the knife cutting into the clay like it was fresh and soft. Tiny parings muddied the edges, and he blew on these absently. It was done. The last thing was to feed them. His blood was the only choice, obviously; and so he used the same knife, heedless to the clay-soiled tip, to part his skin on the tip of his thumb. Seconds passed until blood welled into the cut, spilling silently. His mind still blank other than thought of his task, he pressed the wound onto the symbol on his son's forehead. He felt pain then—almost a sucking sensation—as the dry clay eagerly sought his fluids.

It happened very quickly. A slight hum filled his ears—the sound of electricity, perhaps—and he felt a thrumming under his hand, still pressed to his son. He lifted his hand quickly and stepped back from the body, rigidly upright, eyes wide with shock. He'd known it would work, prayed for it; and yet now he was chilled to the bone with fear. A finger curled. The fabric of the figure's garments shifted and settled. The sculptor moved nearer, clutching the knife tightly, breath rasping faster and faster, nostrils flared. An eye opened, the sound like one stone scratching across another. Another eye. The perfectly rendered eyes, complete except for color *(why hadn't he thought to add color?),* turned and moved and rolled in their sockets. They found him suddenly, fixed on him, blinked slowly, and stared.

The sculptor let out a cry, fell to his knees, and moaned his son's name. The body sat up on the table, dried clay falling from it like leaves, as if they had been playing in an autumn garden. The mouth opened noiselessly. A heartbeat later, impossibly, almost silent but *not* silent, it breathed. It reached to him, flexing its fingers, working them like it was trying on new gloves. It smacked its lips silently, discovering the configurations of its face, learning movement and sound and form even as it shifted its bulk to the edge of the table. A further icicle of fear pierced the sculptor's spine as the boy raised one hand and made a fist. Slowly, exerting utmost control, it extended one finger and pointed to him.

daddy?

came a scratching question. The body shifted nearer the edge of the table until gravity took hold. With no knowledge of balance or of the mechanisms needed to stand, the body pitched helplessly onto the floor and lay silent. A soft mewling sound broke the stillness.

The sculptor moved quickly to its side, all fear gone. He moaned the boy's name over and over, convinced he would find the body hopelessly broken. But whatever magic had brought tragic life to his sculpture, it seemed also to have brought a physical sturdiness; for even as he reached the body, it was pushing itself into a sitting position, limbs and face and body intact.

daddy

it said again, confident this time, its voice still no more than a scraping whisper. The sculptor reached his hands to cup the boy's cheeks, chilled anew at the pulsing warmth beneath the clay. He pushed the fear aside, closed his eyes, and bent to plant a kiss on the boy's forehead. If he had expected the kiss to land on soft, pliant skin, perfumed with fresh air and the exertion of play, then the reality could not have come as more of a shock. Gritty powder coated his lips, and he tasted the alkalinity of clay, the earthiness of the boy's flesh. He moaned again.

The boy moaned with him, a helpless

wa wa wa wa wa

and the sculptor ran his hands across the waving hair, so lifelike to touch, but smelling like the earth it was. He kissed him again, this time knowing the feeling and so relishing it. His son, born again.

As he drew closer, folded his arms about the boy, the sounds he was issuing suddenly became clearer.

wa wa w . . . w . . . wh . . . wh

why?

Ford

Ford

why?

why?

why?

why?

The sculptor sat back, unable to think as the boy repeated his desperate question again and again. In all his planning, years and years of searching, never had he thought that this would be the first question the boy would ask. Tears streamed down his face, and as he reached out, the boy backed off, shedding dust and clay particles as he went, backing up, backing up until he reached a wall. He continued to push with his legs, and in doing so, learned the mechanism of standing. The sculptor stood with him, and moved to stand in front of him, imploring the boy with eyes and gestures and words, to come to him, to let himself be held and to be a son again. The boy's eyes flickered around the room, landing on the sculptor's face, the table, the chairs, the window, the open door, the open door

the open door

the open door

Before the sculptor could gather his wits, before he had chance to move, the boy pushed roughly past him, knocking him aside, and crashed through the open door, morning sunlight highlighting the contours of his exquisite face. The sculptor let out a shout of fear and confusion, but ultimately he was too late. The boy had gone.

Time passed of which the sculptor had no recollection. The air seemed muted and grey, sounds muffled. Indeed, solace could only be found in darkness and in such a state of drunkenness that he felt nothing but the burn of cheap wine. Even the hollow pain in his chest seemed diminished. For a time after his creation had fled he had raged, hurling tools and lumps of sodden clay about the room, erasing any sign of his work, erasing any sign of the loss he had faced twice now. His son. His poor son. Panic fluttered constantly at the edge of his mind, his hands shook, and sounds issued from his ragged throat that bore no resemblance to human noises.

What have I done? he cried to the room. *My son!*

He began to piece together anything that might help him find the boy. He read and re-read *Earth, Risen,* hoping, searching desperately for some nugget he had missed. Where might he have gone? Who may have found him? And all this was affording the sculpture sentient thought. What if it was mindless, nothing more than animated clay? What if there was none of his son left? But the first word from its mouth had been *daddy.* Surely it must be his son. It *must* be. He took a drink of wine then, and another followed, and another after that. Bottle after bottle was consumed, and the sculptor began to dream that none of it had happened. Darkness turned darker, sound failed him, and he lost his fight with sleep. But even sleep could not protect him from images of moving clay, great lumpen faces with stretched maws, grasping hands, tearing, pulling. And always the questions.

why why why why why why why why?

He woke screaming.

" . . . be aware of what you do. Wrath, like love, has to be earned. Be determined which one you truly seek. Because all is possible, and all is truth . . ."

Was it love he wanted, truly? Or was he really seeking the boy's wrath? He closed his eyes and saw the boy's face, heard screaming, heard the breaking of glass and shrieking of tires. He lived the moment that his son died, over and over.

Died because of him.

Because he took the boy from his mother in a drunken rage, drove in a drunken rage, killed his son in a drunken rage.

He read the words again. In a second he knew. Knew everything. He knew somewhere in the back of his mind that he could never have lived with the sculpture like he would have his own son. And so love was not his aim here. That left only wrath, and as soon as he thought it, he felt a great weight lift. At last he felt the burden of his son's death lift from his shoulders, and he knew where to find him.

The door stood open still, flecks of clay marring the surface. It was a short walk to the bridge. The place where he had driven from the road, plunged the car into the icy river. To this day, he could not have said it was truly an accident or truly deliberate. But it happened, and as the black water flooded the car, and he struggled with his own seatbelt, he heard his son screaming and screaming until water smothered them both. He lived. His son did not. And now as he approached the small bridge, the replacement railing his car had destroyed still a shade lighter than the original all these years on, he saw the figure sitting on the wooden boards. It had lost its clothes, and he saw again how unfinished its body was. A mere suggestion of form, and yet hands as perfect as they had been in life covered a face he knew better than his own. It sobbed as it sat there, whispers of pain and sadness reaching the sculptor's ears. He bent to it and rested a hand on its shoulders. It reacted violently, snatching itself away, its mouth open in a silent scream, a suggestion of fear in its eyes. It locked gaze with him, and in a heart-lifting moment, its mouth curled in a smile. Faint and stiff, as the clay had dried . . . but it was there.

daddy

it said.

my son, he replied, holding his arms out wide. It came to him then, and wrapped its arms around him. He sobbed and sobbed, tears dappling the dome of its head, running along the cleft of its parted hair. He dropped to his knees, knowing what was to come, and yet feeling nothing but the joy of finding his boy. He smiled and kissed the face lightly. He picked the boy up, rested his weight on the railings above the roiling water. It was as black as he remembered. Reaching a hand up to the creature's forehead, he whispered two words into its tiny ear.

i'm sorry

Its grip on him tightened and its eyes widened slightly as it somehow realized what he was about to do. He rested a thumb on its forehead, and with a scratching stroke, scraped out the first symbol drawn there. He remembered the text from *Earth, Risen;* remembered the symbols perfectly. In scratching out that first, he effectively turned truth, תמא, into death, תמ.

The transformation happened quickly. Suddenly, the sculpture was just that. In its eyes, there was nothing. He looked down into its face and saw not life there, but only the numerous faint marks of the tools that he had used to render it. The body was a dead weight, and its arms a hardened clay sculpture around his middle. As it dropped and he had neither the strength nor the desire to stop its fall, it took him with it.

The water hit him with a slap of iciness, and he didn't hesitate to finish what he had started. His first breath was air and foamy water, and he coughed it out reflexively. His next, and the next, and the next, were not air. It was black freezing water he was filling his lungs with now, and he welcomed it. His son would have breathed the same water, would have felt the same panic; the same pain in his chest that was fading remarkably quickly now that he had resigned himself to it. As darkness came over him, he felt the clay sculpture begin to disintegrate in his hands. Faintly, he felt the scrape of its hands as it released him into the water, and he reached with the last of his strength and wit to catch hold of its face. Clay crumbled under his touch, and he brought his hand back and kissed the residues. The action of the water gave the face a lopsided grin—one he remembered so well—and his tears added infinitesimal volume to the raging river.

The pain was gone. His sight and hearing were gone. There was no feeling as the current tore him this way and that, scraped his trailing legs along the river bed, tore into his flesh with loose rock and branch. There was just the feeling of floating and the heart-bursting joy as a small hand took his and a whisper of love from a small voice echoed in his ear. He was content to lose his life for this; as if he had sculpted love from the very bones of despair and guilt.

To have that hand in his, and those whispers of love and forgiveness in his ear.

To have those, without life?

It was enough.

SMUDGE

JONATHAN TEMPLAR

The apartment was *perfect.*

It was everything Alan had been looking for and had begun to think he would never find; a central location, open plan, modern fittings, sleek white fixtures. It even had a floor to ceiling window that looked out over the city, but from a high enough vantage point that nobody was looking back—and even if they did, the exterior glass was tinted to avert their gaze. Living there would be like living inside an iPad. It smelled of pine and lavender when he was shown around, a smell that stayed with him for days afterwards— and he knew in one glance that every item of furniture he owned would fit in there snugly.

And on top of all that, it was a vacant possession.

"Guy who lived here just up and went," the realtor told him. He looked about twelve years old, wearing a slick suit too big across the shoulders, like it belonged to someone else and this kid was just playing make believe. "Happens all the time these days. Property becomes such a burden that folks just hand their keys in to the bank and run rather than stretch out another payment. This guy, he didn't even do that. Just left his stuff here and bailed."

"Anything decent?" Alan asked, sniffing for a bargain. After all, one man's misfortune was another's gain.

The realtor sniffed. "Just the kind of shit you'd see at a yard sale, if you pardon my French. Guy had a fucking eight-track and a Betamax in the closet." He leaned closer for a conspiratorial whisper. "Fantastic stash of porn though. Imported stuff. European. Real sick shit, you know?"

"I'll take it," Alan had said. And he hadn't meant the porn.

It was his within the week. A cash sale at a bargain price. Ten days after he'd first seen the apartment, he was unpacked and had his feet up on his sofa with a beer in hand, watching *Dexter* on his 50-inch plasma in his brand new home.

And that was when he noticed the smudge.

In was in the far corner of the apartment, on the ceiling to the right of the window. He could have lived there for months and never noticed it, but he'd placed an uplighter directly beneath it and it was the one spot in the room that would shine the brightest when he turned off the regular strip lighting. It wasn't much, the size and shape of a saucer. But as soon as Alan had seen the smudge, he couldn't see anything *but* the smudge.

At first he'd stood on a chair and reached up to the ceiling to examine it. It was yellowish-brown, but wasn't wet or cold to the touch. Water damage, perhaps? Some old piping between floors that had leaked and stained the paintwork? The damage didn't look new, but there hadn't been anything about it in the realtor's report. The fact that Alan didn't notice it before didn't mean that it hadn't been there.

"Son of a bitch." He squinted at the damage. That close to the ceiling, he could hear the sound of footsteps in the apartment above. It occurred to him as he listened to his vertical neighbor that this might be someone else's fault, that the liability for repair might not have to be clawed out of his own insurance broker. If the guy (or girl—he *really* hoped it would be a girl) in the apartment above had left their tap on for too long and flooded their bathroom, then let *them* foot the bill. He found this thought comforting.

Alan's apartment was on the seventh floor. He took the elevator up to the next level. The fucking thing cost him enough in maintenance charges . . . he was going to use it at every available opportunity. The ride took a couple of seconds, which he spent happily scrutinizing his own reflection in the mirrored walls. He liked what he saw.

It was a simple task to find the right door. The layout was identical to his floor: four doors leading to four different apartments, a stairwell at the very end of a straight corridor lined with tasteful carpeting. The same brand of fire extinguisher, the same safety notices. If it wasn't for the plaques on each door showing the apartment number, you'd never find your way home.

Alan knocked at number eighteen. He waited, and was toying with the idea of knocking again when the door opened inward and the occupant glared out. It was a guy, of course; younger than Alan and, by the look of him, just as successful. A media type. You could tell from his carefully cultivated beard and the small black spectacles that screamed affectation rather than requirement. The space behind him looked sparse but carefully considered, cold blue neon light spilling out like an open refrigerator in a dark room. The guy gave an irritating sigh that instantly flagged him as a prick of the highest order.

"The new guy in fifteen, right?" he asked.

"Right."

"Well, before you even start, I haven't got a dog and I've never had a dog. I'm never going to get a fucking dog. Let's make that perfectly clear."

Alan didn't know what the fuck he was talking about, and said as much.

Number Eighteen just took it in stride. "I had your predecessor up here once a week, regular as clockwork, moaning about my *dog*," and he used his index fingers to show the inverted commas, the universally accepted warning that the speaker was an asshole, "and how much noise my *dog* was making on his ceiling, and how my *dog* was against the rules of the building. I've never had a dog in my life. I fucking *hate* dogs."

"I'm not here about noise," Alan said.

"Okay then," Eighteen said, and suddenly looked a little apprehensive as to what it was Alan *did* want.

"There's a stain on my ceiling that looks like water damage. I wanted to know if you'd had any leaks or such, anything that might have run down through the walls."

"Oh," Eighteen said, and pushed his glasses up. "I'm not getting into any of that. You got a problem with your pad, take it up with the building super. I'm not saying any more in case it gets taken as an admission of liability."

And he shut the door on Alan without another word.

"Prick," Alan said, though it probably went without saying.

So he called the super, and the super called his guy.

The guy looked as if he'd been doing this job since the Eisenhower administration. He was seventy if he was a day, maybe five foot five in his workman's boots with a barrel chest and a thick white moustache that made him look like an aging Mario brother. He seemed to know what he was doing—Alan certainly hoped he did, as the old man had smashed a two foot hole in the ceiling before Alan had a chance to object.

"Thought so," the old man said, his voice carrying down from the hole his head was stuck in.

"Thought *what*?" Alan called up.

The old man pulled his head out and climbed down his step ladder, wiping his hands on his overalls. "There ain't no pipes up there, just supports. Any water leaked through, must have come through the structure from the outside, and I can't see any sign of that. No sir, best bet is you got a rodent stuck up there at some time, couldn't find its fool way out again, just died and just rotted through the boards."

"That doesn't exactly fill me with confidence regarding the general state of this building."

The old man shrugged. "Where there's a city, there's gonna be rats. Fact of nature. Just coz can't you can't see the little sons of bitches, doesn't mean they ain't there."

Alan tilted his head, indicating the cavernous hole that his uplighter would now shine into. "I take it you're planning to put that right."

"Why, naturally," the old man said with a well-practiced grin. And he did. Eventually.

For a week or so, everything was fine. And then one evening, Alan happened to look back at the spot on the ceiling, now masterfully re-plastered and repainted so that you'd never see the join, and there was the smudge again. It was smaller now, little more than a dime in size and circumference, but it was back all the same.

Alan pulled a chair over from his breakfast bar, hopped up and scrutinized the smudge. It had the same dirty brown center, the same yellowing edges. Whatever had caused the original damage had also caused it to return.

Alan cursed. He'd have to call out the not-so-super Mario brother again. The old man was going to get a fucking earful this time—whatever was tainting the apartment, it was no dead rat.

Then he heard footsteps upstairs. It was a scampering, scratching sound, not at all like the padded footfalls of a human occupant, but the scuttling, sharp clawed passage of an animal.

No fucking dog!

Suddenly, the smudge made perfect sense if that prick in Eighteen had a mutt pissing all over the place. No wonder he had tried to hide the fact. And more than that, the damage was going to be his fault as well.

"Admission of liability, my ass." Alan got down from the chair and headed up to Eighteen. "Let's see who's so fucking superior *this* time."

He called the lift. The indicator above the golden call button was flashing 3. Alan waited, and still it flashed the same apologetic number. He stabbed at the button, but nothing seemed to move.

"Four hundred bucks a month for this shit," he said, and kicked the steel door. He stomped down the corridor, pushed open the emergency door, and made his way up the stairwell. It was the first time he'd had to take the slow route since moving in, and he didn't like it. The stairwell was made of narrow, concrete steps and a metal railing painted white, with none of the finesse reserved for the more commonly used areas of the building. There were strip lights encased in clear plastic boxes that hummed as he passed them. It was cold on the stairwell; a chill breeze seemed to whistle past Alan as he climbed. Suddenly, four hundred bucks seemed a small price to avoid this pleasure on a daily basis.

There seemed to be an awful lot of steps. He looked over the railing and thought that the ground floor looked a lot more than eight flights down. But he swallowed that idea for now.

He pushed the door to the next floor open, and as soon as he stepped through, he knew something had gone seriously wrong. He'd only been up here once before, but once was enough for him to know that this time round, he was somewhere else entirely.

The layout was the same: a straight corridor, four doors at regular intervals, a window at the end that looked out onto the brick façade of the adjacent building. Not that you could see anything through this particular window. It was filthy, smeared with a black, greasy residue that you wouldn't have been able to see your own reflection in if you were standing two feet away. There was no plush carpet here; the floor leading up to the window was bare concrete—bare if you choose to ignore the layers of dirt that had accumulated and the scattered piles of strange garbage and debris that lined the walls. Two of the doors hung from their hinges; one of them was missing altogether. The rooms were sheathed in shadow, but they appeared to be barren and un-occupied.

Only the door to what should have been apartment Eighteen was still intact. Across its warped and swollen surface someone had written the words

Not here, Not there, Not anywhere!

The penmanship was clumsy; the letters dripped and smeared into one another. It might have been made by a finger dipped in something that Alan did not want to imagine. He put out a tentative hand to touch the words, but withdrew it as if he had been stung.

He stood there for a minute or two, confused but not completely disturbed by what he had come across. Alan had heard of things like this, of buildings where one of the floors had been sealed off and forgotten due to some colorful event in the past best left forgotten, or to avoid some tiresome building regulation. Landlords plastering over their sins and hoping they'd just go away. Shit, hadn't he read about a hotel somewhere in the city that had left the whole thirteenth floor empty?

But as he pondered, he began to appreciate that it made no sense. He'd seen the plans; a surveyor friend of his gave them the once-over before he'd signed the lease. And he'd stood outside the building the first time he'd looked over the apartment, and then a dozen times since, just taking in the smooth beauty of its glass exterior, the sheer windows that looked out but wouldn't let you look in. *I want to live in a building like that,* he'd said back then, and had there been the scar of a dirty level, a tainted watermark across the otherwise perfect canvas of his new home, he'd have known before now. He'd have seen it and he would have walked away.

So where the fuck was he?

He walked along the corridor, even though the voice in his head that normally kicked in at time like this, the voice he thought of as Sensible Alan, started to protest.

Are you out of your fucking mind? it said. *Whatever this place is, it's gone bad. It's sour. There is nothing good here, get out, go home, close the door and forget you ever stepped foot here.*

But If Alan spent his life listening to his sensible voice, he'd never have gotten anywhere. Sensible Alan had warned him not to ask Debbie Selznik to the senior prom in case she said no, and if he had listened he wouldn't have discovered to his delight that Debbie never said no to *anything.* He'd warned Alan not to blow a whole summer's wages from working at the burger joint on a snazzy suit just so he could impress during interviews in the fall—and impress Alan most certainly did. If he'd listened to Mr. Sensible he would never have risked half the investments that made such a name for himself and brought him enough wealth that he could take a "career break" at the age of thirty-five that would likely stretch until he was eighty. If Sensible Alan had his way, he'd probably still be at the burger joint flipping patties like half his graduating class. There was a little box inside his head where he locked Sensible Alan at times like these, so he shut the lid down and threw back the bolt.

Alan opened the door that should have been Number Eighteen. Something was messing up his ceiling, after all. If it was coming from in here and he could find it, then maybe he could have his perfect home back.

The room was a dark echo of his own apartment; the dimensions were the same, but somehow it felt larger, and certainly colder. He had a moment of disorientation; the space was *so* similar, like this really was his home—like he had fallen asleep and woken up a hundred years in the future after the apocalypse had come and gone. The walls were gray and sometimes green; the plaster was bloated and bubbled in a dozen places. All the surfaces were covered in a white film of greasy sludge; what mold became when it grew up. The floor was bare and felt sticky beneath Alan's sneakers. And the smell . . . it was like being under the blankets with a gorilla who farted. It made his eyes water and bile rise in his throat.

Alan peered through the gloom into the far corner, the spot where the uplighter stood in his own apartment. Where there was a full length window downstairs, here there was just a boarded up void through which rancid air was whistling. There was indeed something there, filling the corner. It was a pile of . . . *something.* From this distance it looked like rags; a heap of old discarded clothing made into compost heap. So he wandered over, ignoring the entreaties of Sensible Alan as he rattled at the bolts of his cell.

Upon closer inspection, he could see that it wasn't simply rags. It was a sac of some kind, almost like a clumsy wasp's nest. Alan had seen plenty of them growing up; his father would remove them carefully from the rafters after the occupants had been gassed into oblivion, then let Alan poke around with the newly emptied home. That nest had felt like paper; brittle and hard. He poked a finger at this specimen, and the surface yielded—it was moist and spongy. Sticky. The surface was as gray as the walls, but the stickiness came from a yellowing ichor that coated the skin of the sac, and was now smeared on Alan's finger. It stung—burned almost—and he rubbed the finger down his slacks, hoping it wouldn't leave a stain.

Alan got to his knees and looked at the base of the sac. Yup, the ichor or whatever the fuck it was had pooled around the base, was seeping into the exposed floorboards, and was no doubt dripping slowly but surely through the wood and onto Alan's otherwise perfect ceiling.

"So much for Grandpa Mario and his fucking rats," Alan said louder than he had intended.

The sac started to thrash. Alan let out an involuntary yelp and fell backwards onto his ass.

There was something inside it, pushing at the skin. It pulsed, the surface rippling. From within came a muted groan. Whatever had made that sound was no fucking wasp.

Alan crept back closer, making sure he wasn't too close. "Hey, anyone in there?" he whispered, and felt like a tool for doing so.

But there came an answer. Nothing discernible, just another sighing moan.

Sensible Alan was having a fit inside his box, but his keeper ignored every instinct that screamed at him to run and keep running until this room was nothing but an unreliable memory. He reached in his pocket, pulled out the key to his apartment and used it as a makeshift knife, pushing it into the skin of the sac. The sac was thicker than it looked; the texture and strength of a cotton sheet rather than the paper Alan had expected. But he pressed the key in, straining with the effort, using it to saw the surface until it tore. Then he pulled the key out and ripped open the sac with his fingers, forgetting the stinging effect of the ichor until it began to kick in and his hands started to burn. But by then, his attention was so captured but what he had uncovered that he barely even noticed.

There was someone inside the sac. At least, they had *been* someone once. What was left was only human in the same way that a hamburger was still a cow. The shape was still vaguely that of a man, but the thing was twisted; parts of the body ran into each other as though it had been made of wax and left on a radiator. Bone protruded though skin, and it was impossible to tell which bone was which as they were all in the wrong places, surely. But what was left was a face—even though it was longer than a face would normally be, the features spread out as though their maker's hand had squeezed the clay of their construction into new and hideous shapes. The mouth hung down, past the point at which you would expect the chest to be, drooping open. Above it were only hollows where the eyes should have been, voids that even in their emptiness still managed to express the agony of this tortured creature.

Alan said something, but it was unintelligible. He knew that this was the guy who had lived in his apartment before him. The guy with an eight track in the closet and a penchant for a peculiar shade of porn. He didn't know *how* he knew that, but he was certain he was right. This was who had written those words on the door. He'd come up looking for a dog, just like Alan had. But there was no dog to be found, not up here. And he had gotten very, very lost.

"Hey, pal! How the fuck did you get in there?" Alan asked.

The previous occupant of Apartment Fifteen twitched, and a reddish-black fluid ran out of his mouth and down the elongated chin. There were no teeth in there, nothing that could still be a tongue. This poor guy looked like he'd been liquidized from the inside out.

"Don't worry," Alan said pointlessly. "Just hang tough, I'll get you some help." And then for no sane reason he added, "You made a real mess of my ceiling, you know?"

The ruined man started to thrash, and the sounds he made as he moved should never have come from a human mouth. Alan gave him the kind of sympathetic smile he reserved for situations when he didn't have the first fucking clue what you could possibly say and got back to his feet. He noticed that his hands were itching, and when he looked at them he saw that the ichor had burned into the skin and his fingertips were a livid red.

"Better get some antiseptic on these babies," he said to his predecessor, and started to back away.

The resident of this twisted apartment had lowered itself down from the ceiling while Alan's attention had been focused on its larder. It had learned to be furtive on the rare occasions when prey ventured into its territory. When Alan turned back to the doorway, he finally saw it—and his already challenged mind struggled to process what he saw.

"You're not a dog," he said, but he didn't even realize that he had spoken.

It landed on the floor and scuttled toward him, eight segmented legs clattering across the boards, a sound that nobody could mistake for a pet, not now, not when the thing that made that sound was facing you. It had a lot of eyes: they were all black and they all reflected Alan's face back at him, showed him his terror eightfold. The thing's maw opened outwards, a drooling hole in an arachnid face that parted to allow its tongue, sharp-tipped and lined with razor hairs, to slither out with a hungry hiss.

Alan's bowels voided. His sanity fled to the box at the back of his mind intent on hiding away, but Sensible Alan wouldn't let it in. *This is all your fault,* he reminded him, and kept the lid firmly closed.

The resident spat a thick glob of something vile at Alan. It hit him in the chest, and began to spread, encasing his upper body, arms, and shoulders. *A web.* Not a sac after all . . . it was a bloated spider's web. Within moments it had stiffened into a vice-like grip. The resident loomed up above Alan with four of its legs pulled back. Then it pounced, wrapping those sharp legs around him. Alan was lost in its embrace, and it plunged its teeth into him, acidic drool passing through Alan's skin and beginning a slow mission to melt his insides so that he could be drunk at the spider's leisure.

And as he gradually melted, in the prolonged and inconceivable agony of his death, Alan felt himself dripping away through the floorboards, running through the frame of the building and becoming a smudge on the ceiling that used to be his.

He often wondered if there was anyone looking up at him, at the smudge he now was.

But no one ever came.

THE
HIGH PRIEST

C. DESKIN RINK

Beneath black cathedrals of forest, the wattle-and-daub grotto of the Oblivion Shrine writhed amid an umber gloaming cast by hexagrammic arrangements of weeping candelabras. Their guttering flames served only to push the night back far enough to create a suffocating hemisphere of shadow, entombing the open-air shrine in a layer of intangible, onyx masonry. Unto the crooked altar, fretted with all thirteen runes of the other-god Xethogga, Bethany Eves reverently laid the rotting body of an infant boy, his puffy arms, legs and face still coated in the grime of afterbirth. From the other side of the altar, Caleb St. Draco, Patriarch of the Death Clan, stared down at the tiny figure. Candlelight illuminated his goat-head from below, casting it in a ruddy pallor and further enhancing the already disturbing quality of his yellow eyes and rectangular pupils.

Bethany took a step back, then spoke. "On the eve of the Autumnal Equinox, Lady Gretel of House Jericho declared my coven heretics. We are protected by Imperial Edict, but this far from the capitol the Emperor's words carry little weight. Her soldiers slaughtered each one of my Sisters and burned our sacred groves to ashes. I alone managed to escape."

Caleb thumped the butt of his baroque long-rifle against the ground and shook his head so that the array of finger bones and vertebrae hanging from his horns clacked together. He touched the infant's brow with the ungues of his thick fingers, muttering a prayer.

Bethany continued. "I had been with child for twenty-six weeks when Lady Gretel's forces butchered my coven. After my initial escape, I hid in the jagged maw of a ravine; there, amidst the damp stone and moss, the strain of my flight brought birth upon me early. My son emerged into this world, but he never drew breath. Lady Gretel murdered him as surely as if she had wrung his neck herself."

Echoing from all directions, Bethany could hear the brays and howls of the rest of the Death Clan as they chanted praises to Xethogga, the hermaphroditic, sightless, mindless deity of the outer spheres—a deity which the Death Clan grotesquely considered mother of all creation.

Uuah! Uuah-Xethogga! As if in response to the chanting, a whippoorwill called mournfully from somewhere far away.

Bethany continued. "Long ago, the Death Clan swore blood oaths to the founding sisters of my coven. As sole remaining representative, I am here to beseech you to honor our ancient pacts. Aid me in hunting down and killing Lady Gretel."

The whippoorwill cried out again. A third figure loped out of the shadows encompassing the altar. Tall and muscular, it possessed of the bestial features and grey-on-gold pelt of a wolf. In the saffron glare of the candelabras, his fangs blazed like molten daggers—and his frost-colored irises, bisected by vertical pupils, shone like mirrors in the manner of cats.

"Bethany Eves," he said. "It's good to see you again."

She noticed fresh scars cutting like knotted furrows through the fur on his left shoulder, and the rows of gleaming studs newly pierced into the left side of his muzzle. The ritualistic body modification meant he'd defeated Darius St. El Nath, his rival, and been promoted to Spirit-Caller since Bethany saw him last.

"Ardan St. Cygnus. I knew you would defeat Darius."

He smiled, displaying far more teeth than cheer. Around his digitigrade legs, a long brush of a tail curled and uncurled slowly. He regarded her, the massive thews of his arms folded over his broad chest.

He flicked an ear, then said, "I accept and honor the ancient blood pact. Nothing would please me more than visiting death upon Lady Gretel and her entire House."

Despite his wedge-shaped, canine jaws, Ardan spoke perfect English without a hint of slur or accent. His voice was gravelly, deep, and almost deceptively soothing. To Bethany he sounded exactly the way she imagined a wolf would sound if it could talk.

Ardan's agreement made Bethany's breath come a little more easily. But she scarce had time to feel relief when Caleb struck a cloven hoof against the ground; at Ardan, he snorted a clear dissension and lowered his horns as though preparing a charge. In response, Ardan flicked his wrist to reveal a wicked set of retractable claws. Across the altar, across the pale body of Bethany's son, they eyed each other. The array of fetishes dangling from Caleb's horns rattled osseous music; Ardan's claws gleamed like brass razorblades. They argued in a thick, guttural language until, eventually, Caleb raised his head and Ardan's claws slid silently back into their sheaths.

"Caleb may be Patriarch," Ardan said, "but in this matter, he cannot overrule me. The Death Clan will join you against House Jericho."

Without another word, Caleb pushed his way past Bethany and clomped down the long flight of wooden stairs leading up to the shrine. Ardan padded over to her, then knelt down on his haunches so that they were eye level.

"Thank you for siding with me," she forced herself to say.

"You lied to Caleb, Bethany," he said. "Lady Gretel has always respected your coven's religious practices. She is too pragmatic to have attacked for solely ideological reasons." Softly, with his breath misting in the cold night, air Ardan asked, "How did she find out what we did to her sister?"

Bethany's jaw tightened. A year ago, a torrent of nightmares had invaded her every restful hour. The nightmares brought with them images of a cyclopean black castle or fortress, flung up against blacker mountains and glimpsed always beneath a boiling, glacial sky. The castle's jagged tiers piled atop one another: terrace upon terrace, battlement upon battlement, until its highest spires and minarets clutched at the very heavens themselves. In a manner possible only through the logic of dreams, she knew somewhere within the abyssal vaults and oubliettes of that horrid edifice, ensconced upon a titan throne of obsidian and jet, there sat the unlimited loathsomeness of Siosotep, High Priest of Xethogga.

The dreams persisted until one night, during the veritable peak of their horror, Bethany was awakened by the gummy, grasping hands of a cadre of pale, rubbery abominations. They were the servants of the High Priest, and they stared at her from her bedside with wide, rheumy eyes set in faces that were not faces but pulsating masses of gristle and jagged bone. In screaming, shrieking voices, they told her the High Priest knew of the life-long barrenness afflicting her womb and the unbearable anguish she'd suffered as a result. Because it pleased Him to do so, the High Priest offered her a trade. In order to complete his monstrous harem, He required a further three females. The first—Bethany was told in no uncertain terms—had to be Lady Fiona, sister to Lady Gretel of House Jericho. If Bethany delivered Lady Fiona to the High Priest's servants, He would remove her barrenness long enough for her to conceive and give birth to a child.

Bethany swiftly tracked down Lady Fiona: she was kept jealously by her husband in a fortified manor, defended by a legion of soldiers. Realizing she would need help, Bethany used her coven's close ties to the Death Clan to secure the aid of Ardan St. Cygnus. Together, beneath a bloated, fungoid moon, they abducted Lady Fiona from her tower and traded her to the servants of the High Priest.

For his role in procuring Lady Fiona, the High Priest's servants bequeathed Ardan a large, coffin-shaped box, heavy with ominous contents. To Bethany, they bequeathed nothing, but assured her that a child was forthcoming.

Yet afterward, Bethany felt no different. She thought at first the High Priest had deceived her, and after several desperate trysts with rustic paramours, she grew increasingly certain her womb remained as unviable as ever.

Then one somber afternoon whilst traveling, Bethany met a bearded, filthy man at a crossroads. He shook her by the shoulders, and screamed and screamed with the shrill wail of the mad. Through cracked lips he described terrible dreams wherein a voice boomed amidst the halls of a cyclopean, black castle—a voice that told him to wait for a woman at a certain crossroads—a voice that told him he should lay with that woman. Bethany let him take her, as repugnant as he was, and over the following weeks grew overjoyed when she found herself with child.

But now that joy was long gone. Her son had been cruelly taken away and she found herself once more before Ardan, once more in need of his help. In the distance, the whippoorwill called out for a third time. Bethany touched the altar and glanced hesitantly at Ardan.

"At first, I thought you somehow told Lady Gretel that we were responsible for kidnapping her sister," she said.

Ardan flattened his ears against his head and pulled his jowls back to reveal a sliver of fang. "I know you didn't tell her," Bethany whispered. "You swore an oath of secrecy, and I know you'd never break an oath you made to me." Ardan's ears relaxed to their normal orientation.

"It was the High Priest," Bethany continued. "I know it. A few days before Lady Gretel butchered my coven, the dreams returned: a black castle flung up against blacker mountains. I don't know why He told Lady Gretel. But I know it had to have been Him."

Atop the altar, flies gathered upon the body of Bethany's son. He'd started to rot days ago, but she'd been unable to bring herself to perform the funeral rites and burn him.

"The High Priest," Ardan said. "To Him, we are just insects, just puppets, just toys."

Over and over, Bethany pushed her hands through her long black hair until it splayed out, wild, above her head. From behind a veil of stringy locks, she gritted her teeth and stared into Ardan's eyes. Something flickered across his face, but his canine features made the emotion hard to read—pity? No, something else— sympathy? Or maybe just concern? He looked for a moment as though he were about to speak, but instead he lifted the body of her son, almost tenderly, from the altar. Then, taking her by the hand, he led her down the stairs.

At the bottom, amongst the open spaces betwixt mighty pillars of sequoia, countless bonfires raged. About each, the Death Clan gathered while howling praise to Xethogga, Hastur, Nothoth-Yamon, and Dionysus, their foul gods. Leaping and cavorting in circular bacchanals with skins of dark wine held high, they matched horns and fangs in ferocious orgiastic combat. Caleb galloped back and forth amongst his warriors, shaking his rifle and extorting them with earth-shaking bellows. In return, they brayed, roared, and shrieked, beating their hooves, claws, and rifle butts against the ground.

The bodies of the Death Clan displayed almost limitless per-mutations of animalistic grotesquerie: some corpulent and ele-phantine in stature, others lithely muscular and graceful of limb; some with naked pink flesh, others with lupine pelts or corvid plumage. The heads of wolves, ravens, goats, rams and bulls intermixed freely between them; sometimes attached to bodies of comparable species, other times attached to utterly incongruent forms. Amongst the larger organisms, the Death Clan's slave caste furtively crept: stunted ovine creatures possessed of only rudi-mentary intelligence. When one of them tugged curiously at Bethany's robes, Ardan struck it with a backhanded blow that sent it tumbling head over heels.

In a nearby clearing, Ardan directed a group of slaves in the construction of a pyre. When it was complete, he placed Bethany's son upon the apex. Thereafter, a pillar of flame climbed upward into the sky to push back the constellations until they clustered reverently just above the treetops. Bethany watched her son's body shrivel into a black husk, the oily smoke blotting out the stars. She did not cry.

That night, the dreams returned. In untold distances, Bethany beheld once more the cyclopean, black castle flung up against blacker mountains. A cadre of formless abominations evanesced beside her. They guided her inside the castle's walls; they led her into a high-vaulted chamber of such scale that no sane school of architecture could have possibly envisioned it. A throne of obsidian and jet, engraved with sigils of a monstrous, six-lobed eye, up-reared into the chamber's highest reaches to vanish amidst illimitable darkness. At the base of the throne, a troupe of muti-lated figures danced awkwardly to a chorus of haunting, shivering bells. At one time, they may have been women, may have been human—but such unspeakable tortures and gruesome surgeries had been visited upon them that they now resembled ghoulish, cartilaginous marionettes. From the way they danced, Bethany could tell that their hellish formation required yet two more members to be complete.

Then a hemorrhage of shadows spilt over the throne; the shadows waxed in depth until slowly, surely, they took on a *positive* quality. The bells went silent . . . the figures abased themselves upon their bellies . . . the shadows congealed. There, sprawling upon throne, a titan of carrion flesh, a colossus of rotten planets, a gargoyle of the death of stars—Siosotep, the High Priest.

And lo, the figures cried out in terror. *Uuah! Uuah-Xethogga!*

Bethany awoke with a surge of adrenaline. A shadow fell over her, and she clutched reflexively for the repeater rifle by her bedroll. It took her a few tense moments to realize that it was merely Ardan who had stooped into her tent. The watery light of morning streamed in behind him, and her dream evaporated with its touch.

He set something down in front of her: a sinister contrivance of dark steel plates and intestinal brass tubing which resembled, in exaggerated fashion, a massive rifle of arquebus. Bethany slowly traced her fingertips along its barrel, up to the swell of its muzzle brake, and grasped it firmly. The circumference was so great that she could not touch her fingertips together.

"What is it?" she asked.

Ardan knelt down. "We have sixteen of them," he said. "The High Priest gifted them to the Death Clan in gratitude for my part in bringing Him Lady Fiona. They are fully mechanized firearms based upon schematics recovered from the fallen Golden Civilization."

"I dreamed of Him," Bethany said. Ardan stopped. He concealed his emotions well, but she spotted the slight constriction of his pupils.

"The dream," she continued, "was similar to the one I had a year ago. He wants something *more* from me. What right does He have to ask anything of me? He betrayed me! He betrayed me to Lady Gretel. Is he not equally deserving of my hate? Of my vengeance?"

Ardan lightly brushed the back of her cheek with his fingertips. "To the High Priest, we are but insects. Should He choose to destroy us, it would be so. We exist always in His shadow, but in the darkness, we can take that which we are strong enough to possess. No one can deny you vengeance except you."

Bethany clutched his hand with both of hers. She squeezed it as tightly as she could. She had known he was right before he had even spoken the words.

The High Priest could destroy kingdoms with His passing, checking his inexorable progress only to laugh at the carnage left in his wake. If He had betrayed her, then it was because it was in His nature to do so. He was a storm—a thing to be suffered, to be endured—not a thing to be fought and defeated. A thing deserving of no more scorn or adoration than the uncaring sun, moon, and stars. Upon Him, her hate was wasted. It was not the High Priest, who had murdered her son, but Lady Gretel.

"Our spies and informants have reported Lady Gretel is aboard a Tailwind-Seven locomotive northbound for the city of Benediction," Ardan said. "This very night, her train will be traveling through a mountain range nearby."

From a pouch at his side, Ardan dug out a metallic object and passed it to Bethany. When she took it, her hand sank with its weight. It proved to be a firearm cartridge longer than her palm and thicker than her thumb.

"That is a fifty caliber round designed specifically for the weapons the High Priest gave us," Ardan continued. "At five hundred and fifty yards, it can completely perforate three-quarter inch of face-hardened armor steel plate. Under optimal conditions, our weapons can fire around six hundred of these rounds per minute." Bethany handed the cartridge back to him.

Arden went on. "When at cruising speed, the pressure within the boiler of a Tailwind-Seven locomotive engine is about fifty psi and the internal temperature is about three hundred degrees. Sufficient perforation will result in catastrophic boiler failure and instant depressurization: each gallon of water will vaporize into thirty thousand cubic feet of super-heated steam."

Despite his monstrous appearance which might seem to imply otherwise, Bethany knew Ardan actually possessed more than a passing understanding of physics and engineering. He claimed to have received private tutoring from no less a personage than Dr. Heinrich von Eichmann, esteemed laureate professor of Benediction University. Yet Ardan rarely flaunted his knowledge and his sudden digression into technical nomenclature confused her.

"Why are you telling me this?" Bethany asked.

"Steam explosions are not discriminatory," he answered. "And even if there are survivors, Death Clan tradition dictates that no quarter be given: every single person on that locomotive will die. Men, women, children—and not just those from House Jericho."

"So what?" she snapped.

"Lady Gretel's husband and three-year-old daughter are on the train with her," he said. "They made a special trip to surprise her at the station. If we kill them, House Jericho will demand retribution. It will mean war."

"Have you all become cowards then?" Bethany asked, "Do your kindred no longer welcome combat?"

"For too long, the Death Clan has been without the touch of Dionysus—the ecstasy that comes with battle," Ardan said. "*We* want war with House Jericho."

Bethany sat back. His point had become clear: war between House Jericho and the Death Clan would likely result in a Death Clan victory, but the Death Clan was not known for mercy, nor for the taking of prisoners. Hundreds, perhaps thousands of people who were mostly innocents would be butchered.

Bethany remained quiet for a long time, then whispered softly, "Can I show you something?"

She placed a sack in front of him and reached within to produce a handful of gritty, black gum. "I mixed this before I went to sleep last night," she said. "I know that your caste traditionally spikes the fur on the back of your necks into ridges before battle, and that an adhesive made from blood or wax is often used."

She paused to stare directly into his eyes.

"I would like to ask you if you would be willing to use this instead: it is a pigment made from my son's ashes."

His tail twitched and his claws flicked in and out of their sheaths as the magnitude of her request sank in. "Yes," he whispered. "I accept."

She knelt behind him and kneaded the black gum into the longer fur running from behind his ears, down his neck, and over his trapezius muscles. Reverently, she formed spikes in two descending ridges, like twin rows of flensing knives. Black plumage, like the flight feathers of a raven, grew in places along the back of Ardan's neck and she bound these with leather thongs strung with her son's charred finger bones. When she was done, she drew her face near and inhaled the scent of the ashes: dry and bitter.

"You are my wrath," she whispered. "If the world must burn to avenge my son, then I want you to set it ablaze."

Without thinking, she ran her hands around the side of his neck and over his chest. She could feel the heavy, steady rhythm of his heart and, quite suddenly, became aware of the warmth of his body. "I will never bear another child," she said. "The High Priest gave me only one chance."

She laughed sadly, as if noticing for the first time the growing gauntness of her cheeks and the deepening lines at the corners of her eyes. "I am too old for children now anyway," she said. "Grey has begun to streak hair that was once black."

"You are only thirty-eight," Ardan said. "That's not considered old for a human, is it?"

She laughed a little. "I am more than twice your age," she said. "You do not consider that old?"

"You're still beautiful," he said, and drew her into his arms. "Why do you want a child so badly?"

Her lips trembled, but she remained silent. "My father died from a tumor when I was very young," he said, "My mother raised my five siblings and me by herself. I loved her more than anything—but she always hated me. I knew she thought me a cruel and distant child . . . and maybe I was. But when I abandoned my tribe and forsook my familial name to join the Death Clan, she didn't shed a tear—didn't say a single word."

The softness of his touch, the strength of his arms, the caress of his fur and the scent of her son's ashes proved too much for Bethany. Her eyes glistened wetly and tears rolled down her cheeks as she reached up to trace her fingers down his muzzle and across the silken fur along the sides of his face.

"You're not the only one looking for family," he said, "I . . . I should have told you how I felt a year ago. I should have asked you to stay with me."

"I would have said no," she said.

"And now?"

Bethany answered by pressing her lips to him. The kiss they shared was savage, inhuman. And though Ardan's fangs left scratches on her cheeks, it was the best kiss of Bethany's life.

She took him then—climbed into his lap and consumed him utterly. He responded with a passion so fierce that Bethany suddenly grew concerned that he might accidentally injure her. But his initial fury quickly subsided into a surpassing gentleness and, within the grey fortress of his embrace, she felt safe. Within his embrace, she almost felt her loneliness subside . . . almost.

When it was over, they held each other, the silence disturbed only by the sound of their breathing and the distant screech of a hawk.

Already, the sun peeked from behind the treetops, and soon Ardan was forced to whisper, "We have to go."

They broke camp and traveled through the grim forest in the company of eight other Death Clan warriors. After a few miles, the trees gave way to a sepia expanse of raw earth that undulated with lumpy, tawny-hued mountains. A particularly sheer escarpment, covered in rocky detritus, leaned from the side of one of the mountains. They climbed up it to conceal themselves amongst scattered piles of rubble and heaps of nodular stone. Below, train tracks threaded their way between various mountain passes only to vanish abruptly in the horizon's vermilion haze.

Hours fell away as they silently awaited their prey. Clouds spilled over the horizon in tumbling waves. The sun sailed slowly across the ecliptic until it finally plunged to extinguish itself betwixt the horns of two great peaks. In its dying light, the land-scape ignited into gemstone bands of color.

Just as Bethany grew convinced the train would not come, she noticed Ardan's left ear swivel northward. The steady chug of a locomotive became increasingly apparent. Puffs of chalky white smoke rose into the burnt ochre of gathering dusk, and presently there came into a view a gleaming, silver engine tugging a long line of cars.

The train approached so close that Bethany could make out the blurry faces of people talking behind little curtained windows—she even made out the palms of a young boy, pressed inquisitively against the glass. She knew there was no way the boy could see her, but she could not shake the sensation that he somehow stared directly at her. She wondered, for a moment, if her son would have looked anything like him had he lived.

Bethany began trembling and set a hand against Ardan's bicep to steady herself. Her eyes burned, but she denied the power the emotion had over her. She remembered the pine flavor of the stick she'd bitten down on as she pushed her son into the world. She remembered the way his hands clenched into tiny, blackened fists within the flames of his pyre.

"Kill them," she whispered.

Ardan waited a moment longer for the train to achieve optimal range before howling: *Uuah! Uuah-Xethogga!*

Ardan and his warriors opened fire as one. Despite her understanding of the weapons' specifications, Bethany was utterly unprepared for their raw, unchained fury. Each discharge produced a concussive blast that pounded her ribcage like a drum; shrubbery flattened as though subjected to gale-force winds; spent brass cartridges spilt to the ground in metallic rain; and an endless roar shook the mountain range from end to end. With precision that spoke of experience, the Death Clan coordinated their fire until nine distinct streams, marked by phosphorous tracer rounds, converged into one single hurricane of molten lead.

The locomotive's engine shuddered beneath the impossible punishment. Its steel hide burst apart into thousands of bleeding rents. Unstoppable, the storm of bullets raked back across the passenger cars and blew them apart, section by section, into fiery matchsticks. Bethany watched as pressure distended the side of the train engine. Rivets popped, and a jet of steam lanced out—followed immediately by a thunderclap as the boiler ruptured. A solid ring of steam and shrapnel tore through the passenger cars and tender with such violence that they lifted from the rails and slammed against the hillside.

Without waiting for the train to slew to a halt, Ardan and four of his cohorts dropped prepared rappelling lines over the cliff face and made their descent. Bethany followed as swiftly as she was able, unslinging her repeater rifle as soon as her feet touched ground.

With remarkable bravery, a few battered House Jericho soldiers had already pulled themselves from the rubble to return fire. Bethany dropped one with a pair of shots from her repeater rifle, its staccato pop remarkably feeble next to the whirring gears and howling blasts of the Death Clan's mechanized weapons.

She reached the smoldering wreck of the first car and clambered up alongside Ardan just in time to see him direct an avalanche of bullets into an open compartment. A House Jericho soldier caught most of the onslaught in the chest, and it tore him apart in a crimson supernova of limbs and entrails. His companion, more fortunate perhaps, was merely sheered in half. Ardan did not waste the ammunition to finish him off, and Bethany felt dizzy when she caught a glimpse of the man feebly trying to gather a slimy pile of his guts back up into himself.

"Cover me!" Ardan said, ending her distraction.

He knelt and pulled back the bolt of his weapon, releasing the meager remains of its ammo belt. As he fed in a fresh one, a window nearby slid open. Bethany caught the glint of a rifle from behind the curtains, but a quick pull of her weapon's trigger blew out the back of the man's skull before he could draw a bead on Ardan.

Ardan thanked her as he chambered the first round of a new belt.

Weapon reloaded, he leapt from car to car until he reached one which was yet relatively intact. Without pausing, he heaved the main door open. A group of dazed House Jericho soldiers, along with more than a few civilian passengers, greeted him with hands raised in surrender.

Bethany leveled her repeater rifle at them. "Where is Lady Gretel?" she demanded.

No one responded. Ardan fired off a few rounds and echoed her demand.

"Where is she?"

A woman in a torn petticoat, her sunhat still somehow perched upon her head, pointed with a trembling hand toward the front of the train. Ardan thanked her, then held down the trigger until the compartment was drenched with gore.

Bethany followed close behind Ardan as he clambered along the length of the train. Gunfire thundered from the ridgeline as the Death Clan warriors who had remained there cut down anyone trying to stumble away from the crash; Bethany winced when she heard a woman scream as a bullet punched through her abdomen. But she gritted her teeth, remembered her son, and kept running.

Ardan paused at each relatively intact compartment he came across. He opened each in turn and whenever he found one occupied, he discharged his weapon until the screaming stopped. Upon reaching the front of the train, he leapt atop the coal car. Bethany saw his ears shoot up.

"There!" he pointed.

Bethany could just make out a group of House Jericho soldiers helping a white-armored figure, who ran unevenly as though carrying a burden, flee up a nearby slope. She recognized Lady Gretel instantly. Ardan had planted his feet, pulled back the bolt on his weapon and lined up the group in his crosshairs. Bethany realized what he was doing and shouted, "No!"

He growled in irritation, but upon seeing the look on her face, he nodded, slung his weapon across his shoulders, and charged up the hillside. The House Jericho soldiers tried to intercept him with a fusillade from their repeater rifles, but Ardan utilized all four of his limbs for locomotion and fell upon them with such swiftness that not a single bullet found its mark.

Bethany caught up with him just as he'd finished ripping the last soldier's throat out with his claws. Ardan caught the man by the tunic before he fell, holding him up and looking into his eyes. Arterial blood gushed over Ardan's forearm in thick rills and he bared his fangs, laughing with ecstasy as the man gurgled and sobbed. Bethany caught sight of a ring on one of the man's fingers; she realized he was Lady Gretel's husband just as Ardan let him slip to the ground like a broken doll.

Lady Gretel stumbled backward up the slope, her white armor spattered with blood and soot. She tugged at the holster upon her hip, trying desperately to free her revolver.

Bethany leveled her rifle. "Don't," she said.

Bethany could see now what had so hindered her: in her arms she bore the kicking, crying, screaming form of her three year old daughter.

"Let go of her," Bethany ordered. Lady Gretel pleaded for mercy, but Bethany only drew back the hammer of her weapon. "Put her down!"

Once set on the ground, the little girl clutched hysterically at her mother's leg. Tears streamed down her face and snot dribbled from her nose. She wore a little frocked dress, the satin still shiny and new where the explosion and escape had not damaged it. It must have been a gift given to her specifically for this trip. Bethany could imagine her twirling and curtseying in front of her mother at the train station, showing off her pretty new clothes.

Bethany's heart hammered in her chest. Sweat beaded on her brow. Behind her, the other Death Clans warriors gathered. Above, a conspiracy of ravens wheeled slowly against an increasingly black sky. From all around came the tortured moans of the dying. In shaky hands, the barrel of her repeater rifle dipped ever so slightly.

"Kill them."

Ardan unslung his weapon, but did not aim it. "No," he said. "This part has to be yours."

A cold wind swept up the hillside, carrying with it the stench of blood and charred flesh. Lady Gretel petted her daughter's head, trying to calm her whilst trying equally hard to remain resolute. In her rifle's iron sights, Bethany lined up Lady Gretel's throat.

"Just spare my daughter," Lady Gretel begged.

Bethany's eyes burned and her hands trembled. She *wanted* her vengeance. But the girl's little hands looked so much like those of her son—and the mask of horror Lady Gretel wore looked so much like the one Bethany wore when she realized her son would be stillborn. Her finger tightened around the trigger, but she just couldn't pull it.

The sun plunged below the horizon, cutting the mountains into silhouettes. Against the gathering nightfall, their peaks and escarpments took on the resemblance of titanic spires and battlements—like the architecture of a cyclopean, black castle.

Bethany suddenly felt a pang in her abdomen. She lowered her rifle. "Bind them," she told Ardan.

"What?" he snarled. "Kill them and be done with it!"

"I'm not going to kill them," Bethany said.

She looked at Ardan, looked at the fur and feathers running down the back of his neck—looked at the twin ridges formed with the aid of her son's ashes. A beatific smile fell softly upon her face.

"I'm going to give them to the High Priest."

She laid a palm on her stomach, just below her navel. Humans and Ardan's kind were not supposed to be able to produce offspring, but she could already feel the life growing within her. The High Priest had planned this all along. She realized that now. Lady Gretel and her daughter would be the final two individuals He needed to complete His harem—and she was going to, at last, give birth to a child.

STEALING DARKNESS

GEOFFREY H. GOODWIN

The skinny boy tapped seven digits into his cell. He listened distractedly while the other end of the connection rang.

"Hello?"

"No names, okay? Someone might be listening. Beauty or life?"

"Wow! I know what you chose. Did you really do it?" Jaclyn's voice jittered with almost as much pleasure as William felt.

"Somebody had to," he said, rejoicing. Balancing the phone against his jawbone, William kissed his fingertips and stroked them along the whorls of the antique wooden frame.

The front of the beach house was almost all windows and flooded with sunlight, so he'd uncovered the felt wrappings and hung the painting in the darkened sitting room. Its effects were far greater than the rumors Jaclyn had heard. William would've sworn the painting made every wall move farther away. The painting made the entire world move farther away.

"I'm impressed that you'd do it for me."

"You fucking should be. It's more impressive in person. Don't come over."

"I don't know where you are."

William poked his tongue through his teeth, felt his lips curl to a smile. "Perfect."

Of course she was worthy of seeing it, but not yet. She was the one who repeated the tales of the enchanted oils, that the painting could reveal splendor beyond dreams. It was unbelievable that the artwork hadn't been on display. Instead, it had been wrapped up in a musty corner in a rich estate's basement. He hung up on Jaclyn, stared at the canvas, and masturbated carefully.

Later, William walked in a small circle, focusing on the barren off-white walls and feeling the breeze blow in through a cracked kitchen window. He lifted his gaze and fixed his attention back on the masterpiece. It devastated anything he'd ever gleaned from brushstrokes. His hands quivered, and he laughed for a moment before going to the kitchen. The refrigerator contained nothing but a soft plum, which he grabbed. Then he unplugged the machine, whispering goodnight to that goddamn hum. But it was too late . . . the hum was already gone.

Yards away from the painting, he bit through the fruit's skin and felt its juice dribble from his chin to his hands, then down his bare chest. He shivered, dropped the plum, and collapsed to the floor.

William dreamt of a blood-red ladder that jutted into the sky. Climbing upward, he realized that the rungs and rails were made of gristle and flesh. His eyelids flipped open with a start, but he was still asleep, dreaming of the painting as it floated just above the white wisps of clouds.

It was dark. William tasted salt in the air, heard the night surf, and enjoyed the growling hunger in his stomach. He didn't want to go anywhere.

Blades of morning rays reached in through the kitchen, but the shades in the sitting room were still pulled tight. William sat up, feeling stiff. He rubbed grit from his eyes and looked at the painting. The artwork was exquisite.

A partially eaten plum was resting by the fireplace, coated with ash. William spat on it, trying to clean it off. He was hungry but didn't want to eat.

He found his phone near the front door, but had forgotten being there with it. He called Jaclyn and got her voicemail.

"The rush of the new . . . the joy of self-possession . . . every inch is entirely ecstatic . . . I sense pulsations, a varying magnitude . . . none of it makes sense . . . that's its . . ." William wasn't sure if his message cut off or if he forgot he was talking and just set the phone down.

A brown vial of cocaine was in the back of the freezer. The refrigerator was unplugged, but it didn't matter—there wasn't any food in it. William wasn't much of an eater, even before, but felt the skinny boy inside him should try. He found a cube of beef bouillon in a drawer, chewed it for a moment, then spat it out onto the linoleum. The lump of brown muck looked as salty and grainy as it had tasted.

Coming to, William's tongue felt thick with nasal drip and soot. Probing an incisor with his tongue, the coarse tang made him cough. It was night again. William wanted to wake up.

Turning on every light in the beach house didn't help. He went to the bathroom and splashed bleach all over his body, rubbing the corrosive liquid in with a stained towel. He barely felt it. Frustrated, William yanked a fluorescent light bulb from its fixture and smashed it on the porcelain sink. He took the jagged edge of one end and thrust it into his left arm like a claw. In the bathroom mirror, William smiled as he watched the skinny boy's nerve endings scream.

Feeling himself being attacked, he shuddered and became alert.

"How are you here?" he stammered, as Jaclyn's stiletto heel jabbed into him a third time.

"You called me. Have you killed yourself?"

"No." William looked at the angry red swirls in his arm, the pocks in the skin of Jaclyn's face, her wilted eyes. He gagged as he realized how flawed it all was.

He tasted blood drooling from his mouth, and turned his head, surprised to see a thread of thick, violet saliva dangling from his bottom lip. William noticed that the pit of a plum was resting amidst flakes of frosted glass, splashes of blood, and white powder.

"You're naked. So skinny. *Emaciated.*" Jaclyn grimaced as she took in how much damage he'd done to himself.

"I had to be thin to sneak in through the window and get it. Come. Have you seen it?" A burning string of pain knitted along his left side. His breathing hitched. Barely able to lift himself up off the bathroom tile, William felt his penis growing erect again.

Jaclyn tried to shrug. She was also injured, bleeding from a slash that ran down her back. William decided she'd already seen the painting.

She pointed to the powder scattered on the bathroom counter and floor. "Is that blow?"

Standing up increased the blood coming from William's arm—but he was vaguely comforted by the idea that his breathing was improving.

"Maybe from inside the bulb tube. There was some. Somewhere. Once. How did you know where to find it?"

"When you steal, you hear things."

William wobbled into the sitting room and crouched against the back wall, far from the artwork. His dick started pulsing in rhythm with the throb of his wounds. Jaclyn was already there, her pants half off. She looked like she was in pain, yet somehow comfortable. The blood smeared along the wall next to him was probably his, but might have been hers . . . he wondered if they took turns. William watched her nostrils flare outward and back. Her mouth released a loud whimper as she pulled at her genitals. She was quiet for a moment.

"Fresh flowers . . . in a glazed vase . . . dying from a poison touch. The touch matters, even when no one believes." Her voice had acquired a husky quality that William thought of as a tireless bitterness. The entire spectacle was the crescendo for their private ceremony. *Maybe a* timeless *bitterness instead.* Everything was exhausted. Not knowing what to expect, he hadn't dreamed anything could be as divine as this moment.

"Better than you said. That's what we wanted . . . its magnificence."

William watched Jaclyn's eyes change from ice blue to woolly gray. He climbed atop her body and began to ram himself into her. She didn't make a sound.

Waking again, despite his bleach burns and gashes, William jerked off. He stared at the painting until the borders of his vision dripped. A crimson pool was spreading along the planks of the wooden floor. His eyes began to dry out and feel wrinkled. Too drained to move, William wished he could crawl to the canvas to touch or lick its oils. Peering deeply into the century-old browns and greens of the vase and dying flowers, he finally saw a hint of motion. A kind and smiling face emerged in chartreuse, vermilion, and cadmium blue. A hand reached out and offered funereal flowers. William knew he'd never move again, and hoped it would be weeks before he bled to death or starved.

The
WESTHOFF VERSION

PATRICK O'NEILL

Dad, what's foie gras?"

It had been a long night, lost in blurring hours of darkened motorway and streaming white lines. We had driven out of Cherbourg and headed south through the night towards Nantes, then further still past Bordeaux, only stopping to refuel or take toilet breaks. We were destined for Masseube, or rather a remote farmhouse with Masseube as its nearest point of significant civilization. We had planned to share the driving but sometime after midnight Kelly had fallen asleep and not come around again.

Until now, Joseph had slept most of the way too.

Near our destination, the roads narrowed and dipped in and out of valleys. On the edge of the horizon, the snow-capped peaks of the Pyrenees were silhouetted against the first hesitant shades of dawn. But even in the early hours, the air was warm here; and as rolling landscapes carpeted with endless rows of dying sunflowers steadily emerged from darkness, I began to realize just how secluded our holiday location would be. Every now and then the headlights picked out battered wooden signs with the words *foie gras* scrawled across them in painted letters.

There was no way I would have found this place without satellite navigation.

"Dad?"

I had been hoping Joseph would fall back to sleep, but there was no chance of that now. He was eleven and eager to begin our summer holiday. He had seen the pictures: the swimming pool, the snooker table, the ping pong set. And now, as morning light grew in strength, there was no way he would sleep again.

"You're sure you want to know?" I asked. "It's pretty horrible."

This ignited interest, as I knew it would, and he craned his neck between the seats to hear the explanation.

"Foie gras means, *fat liver*—and you eat it. It's actually made of duck's liver."

"Urgh."

"Disgusting, hey? But it gets worse than that, you know why? Because of how they make it. You want to know how they make it?"

Joseph smiled at me from between the seats and nodded slowly.

"Well, first they get the duck and they put it in a metal cage. But it's not a normal cage. It's a really small cage with a big hole at the top so the duck can stick its head out. But the cage isn't just *small*—it's so small that the duck can't even move. In fact, the only thing it can do is move its head."

"Why do they do that?"

"Well, if the duck can move it means it can exercise, like a duck is supposed to, right? But they don't want that. They want the duck to stay exactly in the same position and get fat. And so they feed it and feed it and feed it every day through a tube down its neck, and in the end that makes its liver all fat and swollen up. And when it's fat and swollen up enough, they kill the duck and make its liver into a nice pâté so they can eat it."

"Who are *they*?"

"Tom, that's enough." Kelly was suddenly awake next to me. "That's a horrible thing to tell a child. Absolutely horrible. What is wrong with you?"

"Look. I'm just telling him how it is. He's old enough to hear these things now."

"Yeah, Mum. I am old enough, you know."

A long silence followed. I had inadvertently managed to do it again: pit the boys against the girls. But therein, as always, lay the problem—there was two of us, and only one of her.

"You're right," I said. "I'm sorry."

"Mum, have you ever eaten foie gras?"

"No, I have not."

"Dad, have—"

"Wait. This is it."

The sunflowers had given way to bare, unfarmed land, and the road narrowed to a small junction where a crumbling memorial rose from the dried earth like a Norse god silently watching over the landscape. Beyond this, the ruined chapel of Le Carde stood derelict amongst crooked headstones and rusting crucifixes. I recognized it all from the photographs. Our destination was less than a hundred meters from this place.

Isolated from the road by a gravel driveway, the farmhouse was exactly as I had imagined. Set on one level, it looked over the chapel of Le Carde and across the hills beyond, its pale structure lined with dark veins of stained oak. I found the keys amongst the bright flowers in the ornamental cartwheel that lay beside the pond, just as we had agreed with the owners. My legs ached from driving and I felt like hell. We had arrived, and I was done.

"I have to sleep."

Hours later, I woke to the comforting sound of Joseph splashing in the pool, warm French sunlight beaming on my face from the skylight above the bed. I knew we had nothing in the house and that I would need to get the local village of Masseube to pick up essentials, so I got up straight away. Joseph got dry and dressed quickly, unable to contain his curiosity to explore the locality. Within minutes we were on the road again, crossing the eight kilometers towards the small settlement and leaving Kelly to sunbathe beside the pool. We were halfway there when I realized the satellite navigation had stopped working.

Nevertheless, we had no trouble in finding the supermarket outside Masseube, which was well marked and larger than I had expected. Simply stepping out of the sunshine and into its air-conditioned coolness made me feel exhilarated for the first time since arriving. Alongside the wine, cheeses, and fresh bread, we crammed the trolley with unnecessary treats and I made the mistake of telling Joseph that he could have whatever he wanted.

When he returned, he was grinning and holding a jar of foie gras. I made him put it back on the grounds that it was too expensive, but part of me wanted to buy it because I knew exactly what he would have done with it. He would have taken it back to England, carefully wrapped in clothes, where it would have taken pride-of-place on the *special shelf;* that most hallowed of all sanctuaries, reserved only for the most bizarre and exotic trophies from across Europe and beyond: the clear vodka lollipop, complete with scorpion inside; the shiny remains of a long-dead stag beetle; a dried, baby crocodile, and finally, the foie gras—in all its glory—potted in glass with roughly-woven sacking fastened about its neck by a ribbon. But it was not to be.

While checking out, I asked in staggered French for directions to Le Carde because I knew I would struggle to find the farmhouse again without satellite navigation. The girl behind the register drew a map and gave it to Joseph with a kind smile.

When we got back in the car, I noticed a little old French woman who I immediately recognized from the supermarket queue hobbling towards us, carrying shopping in one hand and waving frantically with the other.

"What does she want, Dad?"

I opened the window as she approached. Her hands were gnarled with arthritis but her misty blue eyes caught me with an unnerving intensity. When she spoke, she did not blink.

"Monsieur, faire attention. Il ya des serpents sur les collines dans Le Carde. Il n'est pas sur. Il est très dangereux," she pointed to Joseph in the backseat with a twisted finger, ". . . pour l'enfant."

I thanked her hastily and drove away in the direction of Le Carde. In the rear view mirror I could see the old woman standing alone in the supermarket car park, pale faced and hunched, staring on at us intently.

"Dad, she was creepy. What did she say?"

"She said there are snakes on the hills in Le Carde. And that we need to be careful, because it's dangerous."

We drove in silence for a time. In the back seat, Joseph had rolled down the window and was staring at the dried foliage on the verge as we passed the sunflower fields. He was looking for snakes. Less than a kilometer from the farmhouse, he called out.

"Dad, behind us!"

I barely had time to check the mirror before the Daimler was right up against us.

Up ahead, the road meandered to a blind corner, but I instinctively knew what was about to happen. The Daimler silently accelerated and came alongside us, passing in a blur of tinted glass and black metallic paint. I caught a fleeting glimpse of the driver: a silver-haired man with sharp nose and high cheekbones. But almost in the same instant, the car was gone, into the blind corner and out of sight.

Later that evening, after we had eaten and Joseph was taking a final swim with Kelly, I wandered to the end of the driveway and leaned against the wall to light a cigarette. From here, and at this time in the evening before sunset, the countryside was absolutely still. At the very edge of a wooded area across the dry landscape, a motionless deer stood in a parched field. Far above it, a solitary bird of prey circled the area. A warm breeze stole across the fields for a moment, carrying the scent of dry earth and sweet wild flowers.

And then I saw it for the first time: the other farmhouse, across the fields, half-hidden by tall fir trees. I could see that it was accessible from a track that snaked past the chapel ruins and down into the valley to the other side. The black nose of the Daimler poked out from the side of the house and though the fir trees offered only a limited view, I could see the thin silhouette of a man standing on the main lawn, staring back at me. In the stillness, he raised a hand and waved once.

I did the same, and we stood motionless for some seconds before I turned and walked back to the house. It was a strange moment. It stays with me, even now.

Later, when Kelly and Joseph were sleeping, I strolled down to the wall again, where a faux Victorian lamp post cast a pool of amber light over the entrance to the driveway. Bats flickered in and out of its humming brightness, undisturbed by my presence. Across the fields, the lights from the other farmhouse shone out like a skeletal face leering across the blackness of the valley.

I began to relax properly over the next few days. In the period leading up to the holiday, I'd barely had a moment for Joseph. A sudden dip in the markets had caused a flood of investors to buy at what they considered to be a "low point", and we had struggled to make all the trades before the inevitable upturn began. But now, far away from anywhere, in the warm sunlight, I could forget all about the mundane and repetitive world of finances and con-

centrate instead on the important things: ping pong, swimming, and snake-hunting with Joseph.

Kelly and I hadn't taken a week's holiday in over three years and we were loving every second. The accommodations were basic—the furniture a mismatch of different styles and ages, the kitchenware a senseless combination of random sets—but it was all perfect for us. All we needed was the sunshine, and each other. It was bliss.

I always knew that the French were keen on recycling, so it was no surprise to find the collection of communal wheelie-bins parked behind the ruined chapel: green for bottles, red for cans and plastic, black for household waste.

The clouds had thickened that morning and hung like the belly of a huge grey beast over the fields. The humidity was high and had brought with it an unpleasant stillness that seemed to make the flies more active, especially in the dusty clearing around the bins. I brushed them from my face as I clanked empty wine bottles into the quietness. From where I stood I could see the crumbling head-stones and jagged iron crosses in the shadow of the ruins. There was a terrible smell about the place; not just the smell of rubbish, but something else beneath that—a sweet and nauseating stench, like the smell of rotten meat. I was about to close the bin lid when I heard the voice behind me.

"Good morning."

I turned to see the black Daimler parked in the road. The driver's window was open and inside a dark-haired woman smiled from behind large, bug-like sunglasses. I took her to be around sixty-five, although it was hard to tell given the amount of pale makeup covering her face.

"Judith Westhoff." She reached out her hand. "From the farm-house across the fields. How are you settling in?"

"Pretty well, thanks. I'm Tom." I shook her hand, which felt oddly wet and boneless beneath my grip and made me want to pull away immediately. She removed her sunglasses and peered with concern across the cemetery.

"The rain's coming. It's always like this before the rain. I *so* hope it does. It's been twenty-three days now."

I could see her more clearly now: grey roots against black hair-dye, eyes a fresh marine color that belonged to someone far younger.

"Yes, it certainly needs—"

"Morris and I were wondering if the three of you would like to come around to the house tonight," she interrupted suddenly. "For drinks. We could tell you all about the area. We're easy to find—just walk around the track to other side of the valley and we're there on the left." She pointed through the tinted glass of the Daimler to the fields beyond.

"Okay. I mean, yes that would be lovely. Thank you."

"Excellent. Let's say seven, then?"

Soon afterwards the Daimler purred away, leaving me standing in a cloud of swirling dust. I thought for a moment as the sky darkened that rain would come, but it did not.

Back at the poolside, I told Kelly about the invitation.

"I cannot believe you agreed to that without talking to me first. Did it even cross your mind that, just maybe, I would not want to spend the second last evening of our holiday doing *that*?"

"Oh, come one. It's just for an hour. Where's your sense of adventure?"

"Yeah, Mum," Joseph said, pulling himself out of the pool. "It might be fun."

Kelly stood up and wrapped a towel tightly around her waist. It was impossible to ignore the sarcasm in her voice.

"I tell you what then," she said as she walked away from us.

"Why don't we just take a vote? That would be the fairest way, wouldn't it?"

By six-thirty, all three of us were dressed and ready. Kelly was wearing a loose white top and jeans. I had forgotten how beautiful she was with a tan; the way it lifted her green eyes. Joseph had copied me to the letter in beige shorts and a navy blue t-shirt. He had even combed his dark hair back and used my gel to realize the most perfect imitation ever.

We locked up the house and walked slowly in the oppressive heat, past the war memorial and towards the ruined chapel of Le Carde. Joseph raced on ahead to get there before us and Kelly stopped and turned to me.

"I'm sorry," she said. "I was wrong to react like that before. It's just that I've loved it so much here, just the three of us. It's been perfect. I couldn't bear to think of anything spoiling what we've had. I am sorry. And I'm sure it will be fun too."

She reached out and touched my face. We kissed tenderly for a long moment, and then continued towards the chapel.

We took a break when we reached the dilapidated wall of the cemetery so that we could take a proper look. The structure of the chapel remained more or less intact, although the roof was collapsed and dried ivy tendrils crept from its shadowy interior and flowed over its thick, flint walls. The cemetery was a mess of brambles and reeds. Fragmented gravestones rose from the foliage and only glimpses of the fractured soil could be seen beneath. The scent of old death hung in the warm air.

"It must have been like this for decades," I said, wiping sweat from my forehead.

"I don't think so," Kelly replied quietly, as though worried she may disturb the quietness around us. "Look."

She was pointing to a clearing in the brambles where, beneath a crumbling headstone, the soil was darker and did not have the same line-cracked quality as the rest. There was no doubt the earth had been disturbed there.

"Dad, check it out."

I turned to see Joseph gazing into the distance where black clouds had gathered over the jagged outlines of the Pyrenees. Tiny veins of lighting flickered intermittently from the darkness and into the mountains. A flock of white geese flew overhead in formation, winging away from the storm. One cried out like a child in terrible pain.

"It's coming our way," I said. "Come on, let's get going."

The Westhoff residence was bigger than I had imagined. As we crunched along the gravel driveway beneath the fir trees, lawns rolled out before us, perfectly trimmed and impossibly green. The swimming pool looked brand new, too. Swallows glided down to skim its surface in turn before rising up again and disappearing into the heavy skies.

"Dad, what's that?" Joseph had stopped and was looking at a large wicker object at the edge of the lawn.

"It's a lobster cage," I said. "They use it to catch lobsters."

The house itself was constructed in a similar style to the one we had rented—red brick with oak-stained beams lining its breadth—Tudor in style, but on two levels. The windows were leaded in the traditional style but looked new. They had spent money here.

As we approached, Judith Westhoff appeared in the doorway to meet us. I introduced Kelly and Joseph before we were ushered into a wood-paneled hallway adorned with stuffed deer heads and antelope horns. I looked at Joseph, who was smiling in bewilderment at it all.

"This way," said Judith. "Just through here now."

I hadn't realized until now just how tall she was, and how thin. Her black evening dress hung loosely from her shoulders. She wore thin gold jewelry about her wrists and neck. Wafts of floral perfume lingered in the air as we followed her beneath an old stone archway and out onto the patio behind the house. I again saw the grey roots at the base of her hair as we stepped into the dim light, and it struck me that, in spite of the expensive surroundings, she probably didn't entertain very often.

From there, the view to the mountains on the horizon was breathtaking. Fields overlapped one another in pale shades of amber and green. Farmhouses and dilapidated outbuildings lay scattered around the valleys like broken bones beneath the heavy clouds. The storm was edging closer now. The first fragmented rumbles of thunder sounded across the landscape.

"It's beautiful," Kelly said. "Stunning."

At the far end of the patio, where the view was best, a white table bore wine glasses, canapés and clean plates, all sheltered beneath a pale blue parasol.

A man's voice sounded behind us.

"Yes, we are lucky here. Very fortunate indeed. You missed the sunflowers, though. A month ago the world was yellow."

Morris Westhoff was a small man with thick silver hair and high, feline cheekbones. His linen suit flapped about his thin frame as he approached us. He smiled to expose a perfect set of white teeth that spread impossibly across his tanned features.

Judith poured red wine and gave Joseph lemonade with ice. I left Kelly and wandered to the edge of the patio with Morris.

He explained that they had bought the house just over six years ago, after he had retired from his career as a Research Scientist at a cosmetics laboratory in Berkshire. I asked him if he missed England.

"God forbid! Look around. What could we possibly want for?"

I shared my views on current market trends and the world economy at large. Morris listened intently, taking in every word from behind small grey eyes. I got the feeling he enjoyed significant wealth and investment experience. His questions were detailed and company specific. In truth, I struggled to keep pace with them, as he must have known.

"The wine is fantastic," I said as he refilled my glass.

"It's the local drop. Very good, I agree. Try some cheese."

I thanked him and took a cracker with Roquefort.

"They certainly get it right with the cheeses and wines," he said, "but to my mind they fail abysmally on the cooking side."

Just then, Kelly and Joseph came over to join us. I put an arm around Joseph and smiled as Morris continued.

"For example, have you tasted the local duck foie gras?"

"No," I replied. "I can't say I have."

"Ah, well in that case, you must try some."

"That would be lovely."

I smiled over at Kelly who was staring hard at me with serious green eyes.

"When in France . . ." I said to her quietly.

"Judy, darling," Morris called out. "Bring out the foie gras, please."

I excused myself to find the toilet on the ground floor, which was situated off the main entrance hall.

Inside, the walls were clean and white. A solitary color photograph hung in a wooden frame above the sink—a portrait of Morris many years earlier, dressed in a clinical white lab coat, smiling his wide smile at the camera, all-white teeth showing. In the background, wire cages were stacked on either side of the corridor behind him. The face of a small monkey peered out from one of them, a forlorn expression stretched across his face. Until that moment, I hadn't really considered what being a Research Scientist for a cosmetics company actually meant.

"Now, here we are," Morris said as I joined the group again.

The table beneath the parasol had been cleared now except for two plates. A pale round slice of foie gras sat on each. Joseph craned his head to take a closer look, then moved away again as the rich scent caught his nostrils.

"Would you like some, dear?" Judith asked. "It's very tasty."

"No, thank you." Joseph recoiled in a clumsy backwards step. "I don't want any at all, thank you."

"Ah, now that is a shame. You look like you could do with some fattening up. How about you, Kelly?"

"I won't. Thank you, Judith, but I disagree with it entirely."

Morris cast a quizzical look in her direction. "What is it exactly that you disagree with, Kelly?"

"The way it's made is cruel and inhumane. I don't know how anyone could eat it."

"And yet we accept the idea of fattening turkeys for Christmas," Morris said, raising a silver eyebrow, "and all of the chickens that line our supermarket shelves."

"It's different," Kelly said evenly. "They're not force fed."

"Oh, is that so?" Morris nodded and smiled to himself. "That, I did not know."

A long silence followed and Kelly gave me her best *Can we leave now please?* look. I was surprised at how quickly Westhoff had rattled her. The thunder made itself known again, louder this time, like a train battering towards us from behind the dark clouds. Lightning blinked on the horizon and Morris clapped his hands together firmly.

"Right, then. To prove my point, try this one first. The local foie gras."

I took the plate and carved a small amount of the supple pâté onto my spoon. Joseph's eyes were fixated on me with a mixture of excitement and horror as I raised it to my mouth. The flavor was creamy and rich and smooth, with the faintest under-taste of liver. It dissolved away like butter on the palate, leaving a tingling sensation on edges of my tongue.

"I'm sorry, Morris," I said. "But I think that's actually very good."

He raised a small hand to quiet me before passing me the other plate.

"Now, try this one."

This pâté, a paler shade of pink than the first, was oval in shape, with a small, red trim of fat about its circumference. I knew from the moment my spoon cut effortlessly through its tender consistency that it would be even more delicate and buttery than its predecessor. As I put the spoon into my mouth, I saw that Morris was staring at me intently.

His grey eyes narrowed and a trembling, half-smile played around the edge of his thin lips. A small fly crept across his smooth brown skin before settling on the end of his nose, but he did not notice. Small beads of sweat had formed on his brow; one trickled down and landed in a dark stain on his perfect linen suit.

The taste was extraordinary: smooth and rich once again, but the under-taste of liver was a barely detectable dimension beneath the buttery, exquisite texture which melted away on my tongue in seconds. I had never tasted anything like it.

"That is possibly the most beautiful thing I have ever tasted."

Morris clapped his hands together in delight. The smile was back now, wider than ever, and I realized suddenly that the teeth were simply too white, too wide, and too flawless to be anything other than dentures.

"The first foie gras, as I have already explained, is the local attempt," he said. "The second however, is the Westhoff version, and, dare I say it, the *correct* version—created right here beneath our very feet."

"You made this?"

Morris nodded proudly, resting hands on his hips and pointing his beige brogues east and west.

"Foie gras is simply fat held together and flavored by what was once the liver. Essentially, it's all about this semi-solid fat—which, though neutral to the taste, is slightly meaty. If executed correctly, the solidi-fication point of the fat is such that it melts on the tongue, going from solid to liquid with the body's temperature, just as it's eaten—hence the *melt in the mouth* sensation. Now, the French do understand this, I have no doubt—but they have failed in the most fundamental way. Their basic ingredient is wrong."

Just then, Judith appeared on the patio.

"Morris, I'm sorry to interrupt, darling, but have you fed the kids yet this evening?"

Silence was again broken by the distant rumbling of thunder. Judith smiled on at us, and I noticed that her unnaturally blue eyes had changed somehow. Was it possible she was wearing colored contacts? Yes, I could see it now. The blue lens to her right eye had slipped to the side, revealing a dark iris beneath.

"You have children here?" Kelly asked in total bewilderment.

"Children? God forbid!" Morris laughed out loud for the first time. "My dear, we keep young goats in the stables under the house, that's all."

He tapped a brogue on the patio. "Right beneath us. They need a lot of feeding, though, I can tell you—especially in the last two weeks. That's the critical period. If you get that wrong, it ruins the taste completely."

I looked across the neatly mown lawn, where Joseph was crouching to inspect the lobster cage in the dying light. But I knew now, of course, that the cage was not designed for a lobster, but for a baby goat. I saw that it would be impossible for a small animal to move within in its tight wicker confines. At the top, the small gap would provide just enough space for the goat's head to stick out for feeding.

"So you're telling me," Kelly said quietly, "that you keep baby goats under this house, in cages, and that you force feed them to make pâté?"

"It isn't *just* pâté. And I can tell you now, my dear, most emphatically, that none of my subjects experience any pain whatsoever."

"How can you possibly know that?"

"Local anesthetic is administered to ensure that the subjects feel nothing during the fattening process and that the trachea remains numb throughout all feeding sessions. It is such a shame that you insist on being so narrow minded. What difference can it possibly make from an ethical perspective whether it's a duck or a goose or, indeed, a goat?"

I thought of the photograph in the toilet, of the monkey cages and Morris' clean white lab coat. I could still taste the faint iron-like tang of the foie gras. I simply could not speak. In the end, I didn't have to.

Kelly stepped forward and calmly rested her wine glass on the table.

"Mr. Westhoff, I am sorry, but I believe what you are doing here is immoral, despicable and, I suspect, illegal. I thank you for your hospitality but we are leaving now."

Morris only smiled and nodded. "As you wish."

The silence was broken again; not by thunder this time, but by a terrible and prolonged gargling sound that echoed up from beneath us, from deep within the bowels of the Westhoff house.

On the brisk walk back to our farmhouse, the rain finally began to fall. Darkness gathered with our every step. Joseph ran on ahead.

"I meant exactly what I said," Kelly whispered. "We're leaving. Now."

"But the Ferry isn't booked until Friday."

"Change it. Please."

"What will we tell Joseph?"

"Nothing. Put him to bed as usual. We'll put him in the car after he's asleep. When he wakes up, we'll be in Cherbourg."

She was trying to be strong, but I knew her better than that. I could hear the slight tremble in her voice that told me she was not angry, but frightened.

We walked in silence as the ruined cemetery came into view through the rain. It suddenly struck me then.

"Do you think they bury them in the—"

"Yes."

It didn't take long to pack up. I backed the car right up to the house; out of sight from the Westhoff residence, so that no one could know. I was surprised at how in agreement I was with Kelly about leaving tonight. I had felt it too. It wasn't just an argument about food, but something else beneath that. A sense that something was out of kilter here—something was not right with the Westhoffs—and it sent a chill through me. I no longer felt safe for any of us. The edge I had heard in Kelly's voice was all the more unsettling, because I seldom saw her shaken in this way.

Once the car was crammed full, I put my waterproof coat on and pulled the hood over my head. I made my way down the driveway for one last cigarette before the journey began. Darkness had fallen. The street lamp at the entrance shone light through the beating rain.

I stopped short of the entrance to the driveway when a rustling noise sounded through the rain from just behind the wall of the driveway. I peered through the rain drops, but saw nothing. Was it possible that someone was hidden behind the wall? It would have to be someone small—very small. Someone like Morris.

I stood frozen for a moment, feeling my heart thump wildly under my coat. I had definitely heard something there. I threw my cigarette down and ran back to the house.

I told Kelly we were ready to go and went to Joseph's room to lift him into the car. I walked in and turned on the lights to find his bed empty; the sheets a swirling mess about the floor. Panic took hold almost immediately. I searched each room of the downstairs, even the games room, which was a separate out-building from the main house. Nothing.

"Joseph! Joseph!"

I scraped my fingers down my face, as though it may bring rationality of thought. Kelly rushed at me with tears in her eyes.

"Where is he?"

Then it came to me. There was one place I hadn't looked: the bathroom off the main living area. We had barely used it because it was smaller and less clean than the other one between the bedrooms. I pushed the door open and saw the light was already on: a bare bulb dangling from the ceiling.

Joseph was standing absolutely still beside the toilet, a terrified expression stretched across his pale face. He looked at me desperately, and then moved his eyes towards the closed bath curtain beside him, and nodded slowly. I reached out my hand to him and he took it before running out of the bathroom to Kelly, screaming at the top of his lungs.

The bath curtain hung before me, straight and absolutely still.

I stood motionless for some time until my breathing had leveled to quietness. The panic had left me now, although my heart still thumped in my chest like a caged animal. Then I saw the thin white fabric twitch, just once, and realized that Joseph had been right. There was something behind there. I reached out and ripped the curtain back.

Inside the dry bath, a thick brown snake curled and writhed in anger, striking out powerfully at the curtain. I stumbled backwards and ran.

Within minutes, the house was locked with keys safely hidden amongst the flowers by the ornamental cart-wheel. The engine started and I locked the car from the inside before turning on the wipers and heading out into the rain. In the backseat, Joseph was whimpering. Kelly was silent next to me.

I reached the end of the driveway and turned right.

"This isn't the way we came."

"The sat nav's broken," I said. "But forget that. I've checked the map. This is quickest route to the motorway."

As the headlights beamed through the rain, the ruined chapel of Le Carde came into view. A small figure rose from the gravestones in the cemetery and stared back at us through the rain. Pale-faced and dressed in a trenchcoat, he held a spade in one hand.

"Jesus Christ, it's Morris."

"Just keep driving, Tom. For God's sake, keep driving."

And I did—and soon we were on open road, driving through remote French countryside. Every now and then I checked the rear view mirror to make sure we were not being followed. I remembered what Judith had said about the rain: *". . . I so hope it does. It's been twenty-three days now."*

"It's impossible to dig soil when it's that dry," I said aloud. "And twenty-three days is a long time to have to wait to bury something."

By why go to all the trouble? I thought as I squinted into the darkness. *Why bother burying goats? Why not burn them, or simply dump them?*

In the backseat, Joseph was snoring quietly and had wrapped a colorful duvet around himself. Kelly was quiet too, breathing regularly with her head rested against the window. We were still some distance from the motorway and would need to drive through at least three small villages before we reached the safety of the toll gates and the main highway beyond.

I slowed as the road narrowed and gave way to a collection of small houses. This was Saint-Médard, the first of the villages. Though the roads were empty, I was forced to stop at a traffic light with a small white flyer fastened to its post. It was the picture of a dark haired toddler. He was missing. This was a call for help. There was a police contact number at the bottom of the picture.

A few yards later, I stopped again at a deserted roundabout. Someone had fastened another flyer to a pillar beside the road. A different child this time; a girl of around four with pale features and curling blonde locks.

Dread crept through me in the coming miles, because as we left Saint-Médard and made our way through more country lanes to the village of L'Isle-de-Noé, it was the same story all over again: photographs of missing children in darkened shop windows, taped roughly to lamp posts and across stone bollards by the roadside.

"That's six now," Kelly said into the silence.

My heart sank then because I thought she was asleep, and had not wanted her to see what I had seen. But more than that, I could not face discussing the possibilities that now filled my thoughts.

I tried to speak, but no sound came. All I could think about was the lobster cage on the Westhoff's perfectly mown lawn; the photograph of Morris in the toilet, smiling proudly in his white lab coat; the terrible gargling noise that had risen up from beneath the patio; local anesthetic; and, worst of all, the faint iron-like taste that still lingered on the edges of my tongue.

THE
BURNING MAN

TONY FLYNN

The other night
I met a man;
a Burning Man
with eyes of coal.

The Burning Man
He smiled at me,
and singing songs,
He stole my Soul.

Where He is now
no one can know,
but if He sings,
you too must go.

So shut your eyes
oh so tight,
and pray to God
with all your might,

The Burning Man
won't sing tonight.

BLESS ME, FATHER

LISAMARIE LAMB

The priest stood, his knees creaking, his back cracking, his tired bones complaining. He blinked in the darkness and blew out a breath that stank of garlic and last night's broken sleep. With a moan of exhaustion he never meant to make—a pained noise tinged with the jagged slash of cancerous agony—he worried about the years he would not see. What would happen without him here? How would the world go on when he was finally gone? And what would he miss in death? In the minute after his soul left his body, in the hour afterwards, in the years and years and years that followed, when no one remembered him and his bones were dust and his headstone rubbed away by the wind and the rain, what would he not see?

And, saddest concern of all, what of his beloved church once he was gone?

This strange, ancient, lovely, mystical and lonely building—made of hand-hewn stone and heart-rendered glass—was set apart from the rest, high up on its hillside, and overlooked the new town. All beige buildings and concrete crowds; coffee shops and loan sharks, the only difference between this place and any other in the country—perhaps planet—was his beloved church.

Yes, the people below might scurry around like impoverished ants, not caring, not giving a damn about him and his building, the urban decay of the town settling on and crushing them, crashing about them like breaking waves of despair and neglect . . . but he knew he could have them. He knew he could entice them to climb the steep steps, to tug at the grass as they smashed their way towards him, answering the call he had put out to save them. To save him. To save the church that even now was being talked about in uncaring circles of ministers and governors and the ones who feared saying no to them.

Even the mayor was in on it. Even the mayor, the woman who appeared in the pews twice a year—Easter and Christmas—and pretended that she knew the place inside and out. Pretended that she knew the priest, come to that. Even the mayor was considering allowing the church and its land, its graves and its skeletons, to be sold to the developers for houses. Because of course, that was far more important than the church. God's house forsaken to let the unbelievers and the uneducated and the undeserving sprawl about on its ruined foundations, wallowing in their drink and drugs and cigarettes, their children running wild, running ragged, running the show.

The day finally breaking through the stained glass window above his head gladdened him. He had made it this far. He was left with red and orange smudges on his face, and the idea that this beauty would go on.

Tomorrow. He was dying, and tomorrow would be his last day on earth. And just because it happened to be his penultimate day, that didn't mean he could slack in his duties. He had so much to do before he met God at last, and the work would stop him from letting the terrible grief of it all go round in his head.

What would happen would happen. But, being a studier of human nature, knowing how mercenary and brutal brains worked, he could, if his plan went smoothly (and he prayed and prayed and prayed that it would), guarantee what would happen to the church.

It would become a monument to him and his mercy. A working museum dedicated to one priest and his incredible generosity.

That was for tomorrow. For now, the pain was back. Harder now, much harder—it was difficult to breathe sometimes and so trying just to survive. The priest had, over the past three months since his fatal diagnosis, asked time and again why he was being made to suffer. He asked the doctors, nurses, inpatients, out-patients, strangers in the street . . . he even asked his wilting congregation. He asked God. But no one would answer him. No one *could* answer him. All was silence or strange looks or uncom-fortable shuffles in the pews and sudden close examinations of the order of service. They pitied him, thinking of a good man's terminal illness and all this on top of the possible (although they were sure probable) compulsory purchase order looming.

Maybe, they thought, it was for the best. Because if the priest died, he would never have to lose his church.

There were no answers, then. Until one night last week, during a particularly painful and mournful hour. At that moment, a reason was given through sweat-soaked dreams of blood and thunder. And now the priest understood the pain and silence. He understood the meaning and the message. He was special. He was chosen. He was ready.

One more sermon. One last Lord's Prayer. One final Eucharist. And then he could close his burning eyes and sleep for eternity. Because this *would* be the last service, it should be something he would be remembered for—so that when his headstone was starting to fade, someone might think it worth tidying up. So that when his name began to be forgotten, someone might think it worth speaking again. Telling his story.

Reminding others.

And this is why he had plastered posters up around the town, deigning to walk in the cigarette butts and dog shit that were left as souvenirs of the area's best bits. The priest shuddered as he did it. He disliked venturing down to the town at the best of times; but now, with such an enormous task heaped upon his bony, fractured shoulders, he felt the judgement flowing from those who saw him. They distrusted him in his black, dress-like cassock and his dog collar, marking him out as something different.

Something special.

Unique.

Just like his church.

But despite their wariness, the townies were also curious. Most had never actually seen the man—he was just there—part and not part of the place, known and not known. And now he was in the midst of them, involving himself in their lives. Pasting up homemade, hand-drawn signs that told of promises and rewards. Of course, they wouldn't go. They would not attend church this Sunday just to find out what the wasted old man wanted. What he meant by his cryptic treasure hunt clues that all led to the same place in the end. What he could hardly wait to tell them.

The priest watched, safely back on his hill and surrounded by the peaceful dead, the grass so green as it fed on their moldering corpses. Plants grew well up here, and the yew trees were quite something to behold. Yews. Yes. He could no longer even look at his long-limbed companions, perfectly sculpted by nature, without recalling the developers and the name of the new estate. *Yew Tree Meadow.* It didn't even make sense. There was no meadow. And there wouldn't be any trees once the diggers came.

It didn't matter now anyway.

The priest watched as the little people far below scurried around the lamp posts and phone boxes, ignoring, as usual, the signs about littering; ignoring, for once, the doomed girls' calling

cards. He could see their interest, their curiosity. He could see he had them then, and that they would be there on Sunday. *I'll go if you go, it'll be a laugh, don't you get free wine or something? let's find out what the old git wants, let's go, let's go, let's go and then we'll forget.*

But they wouldn't forget.

No one would.

The priest finished his prayers and stood at his pulpit, reading through his well-prepared sermon, making sure. He couldn't allow for anything to go wrong. Engrossed in what he was doing, he didn't notice the church beginning to fill. It was only when the bells started ringing that he realized with a start and a jump of his heart that he had just ten minutes until he needed to begin—to inform and educate and entice, to embrace these new followers—because there would be so very many new ones, greedy and nosy, unable to stay away, unwilling to miss out. And he, of course, was just the same, exactly the same—so he understood and he would tell them so—and show them God. He would allow them in.

The priest trembled as his legs told him they had had enough. And he shook as his hands tried to grip the neatly printed paper with his beautiful words trip-trapping across it. And his mind swirled and curled around itself as he remembered that it hadn't been Sunday just now.

It had been Saturday, early afternoon, the day *before* now; the day before the end of it all.

The thought caused his heart to rattle and a spasm of pain to jolt through him. Time was passing quicker these days, in the final days, and he wondered what he had done in the interim; the time between his prayers and climbing into the pulpit. He hoped it was good. But he couldn't remember, and perhaps he had simply slept. His eyelids felt heavy and his tongue was full in his mouth, so that was certainly a possibility. It would explain his tired legs and numb arms if he had been asleep standing up like the mystics of India.

Ironic.

The faint smell of body odor may even have been his and not the hooded youths, dirty black boots stomping grit and turds and mud all over the priest's freshly polished floor. Along with everything else, his sense of smell was failing now, and it might have been that it wasn't there at all; that no one smelled, that everything was as light and fresh as if it were new born.

Except that it wasn't. If only. A new world, blinking in the sunlight, confused and mewling but free of all the brokenness that had been heaped upon it . . . now that would be something. That would be everything.

That would be the priest's world soon enough.

Not soon enough.

The bells were incessant, and the priest wanted to cry out, to tell them to please just stop—but he couldn't do it. They were a part of this as surely as he was, and everything had to be perfect. Who else had arrived amidst his reverie? There were some faces he recognized, or thought he recognized, and more that he had never seen before . . . unless *they* were the ones who taunted him in the town, who spat at him, who tried to trip him when he walked. Unless *they* were the ones who called him names and accused him of atrocities. Unless it was *them*. He saw them now, saw them differently; wanted to hold his arms out to them and thank them for coming, for allowing him this day.

But he did not.

The priest stood down from the pulpit and made his way out of the church and into the vestibule. The sexton was already there. Of course he was. And he was preparing the sacrament: stale wafers and vinegar wine bought bulk and wholesale from the local cash and carry. The men nodded at one another, silence needed for such an important task.

But the priest found he had to speak. "It's crowded in there," he murmured, nodding back towards the pews, which were filling and filling and filling with people; men, women, children; a couple of guide dogs. He didn't like the dogs shedding all over everything, but he accepted them for now, even though he hadn't invited them.

The sexton smiled, fiddling with a packet of wafers, trying to open them but unable to gain purchase. The priest snatched the bag from him, snapped it open, and handed it back with his teeth and gums showing.

"Full to bursting," agreed the sexton, carefully counting out wafers and then realizing what a pointless and thankless thing it was that he did. "I've never seen it like that, not even for the carol service."

Ah. Carols. The priest's favorite thing. And if he had thought about it, if God had given him more time to plan, he might have thrown a few into the mix, just because. He was sure no one would have minded, what with Christmas cards and decorations being in the shops now for a month or more. Too early, too soon, too much.

Another reason to be pleased to be out of here.

And yet . . . carols. It was too late now to ask the organist, limbering her fingers up with a bit of Pachelbel at this very moment, to change her playlist. It was too late now to expect everyone in the audience to know all the words without spelling them out, one by one, on a big screen above their heads. The priest missed proper hymn books, faded and tatty and loved. He missed the time when the congregation would be happy to sing, and wouldn't need any aid to get the words right.

Those were the days . . . but they were long gone now.

At least the screen kept the ones with short attention spans (and wasn't that everyone?) interested for as long as the music held up.

"Maybe this year we'll be able to recruit a choir."

The priest snorted as he brought his heavy head up to face the sexton again. "What? Sorry, what? I was a million miles away." Or further. What was the distance between heaven and earth anyway? A child at Sunday school—when there had been enough children to warrant a Sunday school—had once asked him that question, and he had laughed and patted that child on the head and not said anything. But perhaps there was an answer after all.

The sexton patted the priest in the same condescending way, the same way that told the priest he didn't entirely know what to say except to repeat himself. "I was just saying, maybe we'll get a choir this year. What do you think? It would be lovely to hear them raising the rafters again."

"It's been a good while," said the priest. He didn't elaborate, as he couldn't remember exactly how long it had been and he didn't want to embarrass himself by getting it wrong when he should know. He really ought to know; at least he knew *that.* That was a comfort in a time of such confusion and such soul shaking despair. "Too long," he added to seal the reminder. It probably had been. If he couldn't remember then it had to be an age.

It didn't matter.

Nothing mattered except what God had told him to do, what to say, how to die, how to live in these final few moments. The priest reached out one skeletal arm and gripped the sexton's. The other man flinched, surprised at the strength behind the decay. "Thomas," said the priest, looking at the sexton for the first time, looking properly, seeing a real human being there, a proper person, someone good, someone worth saving. "Get out."

The sexton recoiled, shaking his arm as though it were on fire. "Father, I—"

The priest shook his head and tried to soothe his almost friend. "You've done nothing wrong, Thomas, but I don't need you here. In this room, in this church. Go home, leave this place, leave me. Go back to your . . . mother, is it? Sister? Whoever it is you've told me about, the bedridden one. Go back to her, pray with her and for her, and don't be here."

Thomas gasped. Surely Father Fletcher was having a break-down; mental, physical, soulful. He tried again to press forward, to continue with the ordering of the sacrament, trying to do his job and forgive the priest as he was supposed to. But Father Fletcher was not going to allow it.

"It's your sister. I remember. Shannon. I can't quite . . . I don't recall what her illness is, but it's something . . . bad. Something unfair. But more unfair would be to ask you to be saved and not her. Do you see?"

Thomas did not see. He was scared. The priest's voice echoed around the small room in tune with the never-ending bells that rang above the world they had made theirs for the moment. "Saved?" Thomas squeaked. "How? Saved how?"

The priest smiled, soft and sad and sentimental, and he leaned in close and whispered to the sexton; "Saved by me. The ones who have come today, the ones who would never normally dare to step foot within such a sacred and beautiful building as this one, they will be saved. I will show them what they've been missing, and they will thank me."

The words tickled Thomas' ear and he sighed along with them, relief letting itself be known. So that was it. A sermon for the doubters, for the layabouts, for the scroungers and the wastrels. Thomas was none of these things. Thomas did not need saving today.

"All right. Okay," he said, placating his priest, thinking he understood beneath the weirdness of things. "I'll go." But he wouldn't. He would stay and bear witness, he knew that. How could he do otherwise, especially when Father Fletcher was so close to the end?

The sexton's words pleased the priest and he nodded. "Good man. Go on, now, I can finish off here. But do me one more favor—one last favor—would you, Thomas? Lock the doors. When everyone is in, lock the doors and then leave."

Thomas crossed himself, hoping he was doing the right thing. "Of course. Whatever you say." It was a peculiar request, an unsettling one, and Thomas wasn't sure what to do about it. "See you soon, Father."

"Not too soon, I think."

Strange words.

But Thomas put on a smile that meant nothing and disappeared out of the door that led to the car park strewn with empty crisp packets. He breathed in fresh air and felt the winter coming. Keys jangled in his pocket, and he used them, snapping the lock shut as he had been asked to do. Father Fletcher knew what he was doing. Of course he did. And it wasn't for Thomas to question him. Within seconds he was back in the church, using the main door this time; and he positioned himself at the back, hidden as best as he could be, surrounded by the monsters the priest was so keen to save.

Thomas doubted he would ever understand Father Fletcher. With that last thought of the man he had come to love, Thomas the sexton left the church, smiling at those strangers who passed him, those who were running in case they had already missed something, and locked the heavy, scarred oaken door behind him.

As though the mere thought of the priest could conjure him up, the bells stopped their maddening clanging and Father Fletcher took to his pulpit. He had never been one for too much ceremony. As much as the flinging of incense and chanting of Latin might inspire some, it deadened him. It had never been about that . . . it had never been for him. So instead he had no procession, and if the congregation hadn't been made aware of him from his hacking, violent cough, they may not have noticed him at all.

But there he was, resplendent, perfectly poised in the pulpit, ready to speak. There were certain words he needed to express, his own words. But he eased them in with what they were expecting—a short welcome followed by a hymn that everyone knew. Deliberately obtuse, Father Fletcher gave nothing away as he spoke. "In the name of the Father, the Son, and the Holy Spirit." Without Thomas there, Father Fletcher was the only one to make the sign of the cross. He ignored that fact. "The grace of our Lord Jesus Christ and the love of God and the fellowship of the Holy Spirit be with you all." There was no response. Now a little anger was beginning to build. It was written there, *right there,* in the order of service they were all so intently staring at. It wasn't hard.

He could not lose it now. He had to continue. Breathe, breathe . . . just breathe.

"Good morning, everyone, I'm so pleased you could attend. It's so wonderful to have a full church again, especially on such an occasion as this." He offered no elaboration, and no one called for it. Father Fletcher continued, noticing someone for the first time. "And look, we have a celebrity in our midst, our very own mayor. Welcome."

They two enemies smiled politely at one another, each baring their teeth, each territorial over this old building, crumbling and devastatingly perfect. The mayor considered whether now might be the right time to make her announcement, the letter with the details, every last one, was snug in her handbag and she couldn't remember the order of the service, couldn't quite think if there would be a better time later. But she left it. She'd have time, surely, to speak before the end.

"And now, we must sing a hymn that we all know from our school days, if there were any." His little dig at the idle and the indolent went unnoticed, of course. As always. *"Onward Christian Soldiers."*

They sang, if it could be called that, a caterwauling that went up to heaven and offended the sky as it passed.

And then it was time for the communion. Bread and wine and promises to be good that would be broken within seconds, within moments of the unfaithful falling back into their hard wooden seats. Would they come? Would they take the offering that he tried and failed to explain was the body and blood of Christ? There was no halfway here, no room for maneuver. It was real and it was true, even if he couldn't make them see it.

"For those of you unfamiliar with what happens now, for those who can't follow the order of service there, it's simple. I'll wait here for you, and all you need to do is to stand up, follow one another like sheep, come to me and let me save you. Eat the body, drink the blood. Be with God."

Father Fletcher held out his arms and blessed the chalice and the paten, blessed the wine and the wafer. Again. He could bless it as many times as he liked and still the result would be the same. The whole church was blessed—it was special and holy—and even if a church hadn't been built on the hill, it still would have been a sacred place to be. Surely they all knew that? They had to. Father Fletcher could feel it as he beckoned those closest to him, a gangly girl with blue hair and an older man, straggly and thin, to approach. He smiled so that they would not be afraid. And he felt the power surge through him, electric and light, static and thunder.

The girl reached him first. She was unsure, unhappy at the prospect; but the smell of the alcohol revived her and she took a bite of bread, staring at the chalice all the while. "The body of Christ," said the priest, watching her swallow. "The blood of Christ," he intoned, his voice cracking with fear and amusement as she took too big a sip of the wine and began to cough and splutter, spray flying from her and onto the altar. She held up a hand to tell everyone she was all right before anyone could rush to help—

although no one would—and fell back into her place, dropping her head to her lap not to pray but to catch her breath.

One down.

And when Father Fletcher looked away from the blue haired girl, he saw a miraculous thing. The entire congregation was standing before him, a long line of misfits snaking its way down the center aisle of the church and away, twirling around cold stone pillars and backing out towards the door to the car park.

"The body of Christ. The blood of Christ."

Over and over the priest said the same words, and each time he felt stronger, safer, more sure of himself than ever before.

There wasn't much left after everyone had had their fill, but there was enough. Father Fletcher downed the remainder of the wine and wiped the chalice with a white cloth, smoothing and soothing, enjoying the feel of the metal beneath covered fingers.

When it was finally over, the priest waved away the trappings of tradition. No one cared. No one was there for that. And as much as it pained him, he had to be quicker. He needed to grab their attention; and then, when the time was right, he needed to introduce them to his God.

The priest cleared his throat. He threw up a prayer for strength and another for solace and then he called for silence. His head was throbbing, and his stomach cramped and pulsated as though something were trying to escape from its cage of ribs. Sweat dropped in fat globules from his pale forehead. He didn't have long. No one did.

"You're wondering why you're here. It's no accident, and it's not what you might call free will. Just as I had no choice but to invite you into my church, to allow you to soil it with your brokenness, your filthy souls, your putrid excuses for lives, you had no choice but to come." A cough wracked the priest's entire body, shaking him down to his pointed shoes. Blood spattered his lips and he drew his starched sleeve across his mouth to wipe it away.

The ones at the front had noticed.

But they said nothing.

Everyone knew the priest was dying.

The ones at the very front had noticed something else, too. A pain in their stomachs, sharp and stabbing, gripping and grabbing at their insides, ripping and tearing, and it was getting worse, worse all the time.

The priest kept talking. "And once you were here, you had no choice but to do as I told you to. You ate and drank from me and not once did you question it."

They were questioning it now. Not just the ones at the front, but more, further back, a ripple effect as those who had taken communion first became more ill and those who had been last starting to feel the bite of the poison.

"My church—this beautiful building—was in jeopardy. It was. Once I was gone, they were going to take it from the town, tear it down, and build houses here instead. The graves . . . God knows what would happen to the graves."

He had to speak louder now, to drown out the dying cries of the congregation. Some, those with enough strength, those who had only taken the smallest sip of wine, managed to stumble to the doors; but they could not open them. The priest was pleased. Thomas was a good man; Thomas had done as he had told.

They had to die in here.

That was the point.

Father Fletcher gripped the lectern to deflect as much pain as he could. "I was told in a dream to make this place so special that no one would ever take it. To make it the final resting place of hundreds. Now, I believe my church is safe. And it is thanks to you." He waved an expansive arm across the pews.

The blue haired girl fell to the ground, convulsing, foaming at the mouth. The priest swallowed his own pain and held up his hand. "We entreat you, Lord, to look with favor on your servants who are weak and failing, and refresh the life you have created. Chastened by suffering, may they know that they have been saved by your healing; through Christ our Lord. Amen."

The Last Rites. His last job as a priest. His last act of mercy.

Father Fletcher didn't hear the screams of the saved as they scrabbled at the door, fingernails tearing, bodies folding in on themselves and each other, some crushed before the poison could have time to work.

It didn't matter.

He knelt on the altar and thanked God for allowing him this opportunity. And then he closed his eyes, dying on the stone steps, blood spewing from his mouth, his nose, his eyes, a smile on his red-stained lips.

It was Thomas who raised the alarm. The more he thought about Father Fletcher's words, the more he realized there was a problem. A huge problem. A problem that needed more aid than he could give. He called the police, the ambulance, even the fire brigade—anyone and everyone—and he rounded up the stragglers in the town, those who really *had* been saved.

And afterwards, when the bodies had been cleared away and the identities found, they had to make a decision. The mayor was gone, of course; and the letter in her handbag, the one that said they no longer wanted the church, that it was safe and sound and would not be razed for money, was shredded because it was no longer required to show anyone.

But still, what would now happen to the church?

They voted on it, those that were left, and it was unanimous.

The place of massacre would have to go; no one could bear to look at it anymore, and it was said that the dying cries of those trapped inside by the mad priest could still be heard. It was said that the silent bells still rung and that the priest's voice wailed through the windows; *The body of Christ. The blood of Christ.*

They would tear the church down.

They would plant flowers in its place.

Perhaps they would even grow.

A LIGHT
IN THE DARKNESS

LAWRENCE SALANI

The slick, rain-covered city streets were always deserted during the hours approaching midnight. Only an occasional warm light shone from the rows of blackened windows that glared onto the roadway from stern concrete towers. Silent and grim, a lone dark silhouette walked along the cold, deserted sidewalk.

Cameron had always hated the late shift, but money was difficult to come by these days. Darkness enfolded him as he hugged his warm woolen coat closer to his body and looked at the twisted silhouettes of trees that lined the distant roadway. The late shift, however, did have its advantages.

Rowland, one of his work mates, had introduced him to his wife Judy at a Christmas party some time ago. Cameron was surprised that she was much younger than Rowland, and remarkably beautiful. They had accidently met again in town while Rowland was at work not long after that, and she had been unusually friendly. At first, Cameron ignored her advances; but he was never one to knock back a good time. When they met a second time, a relationship developed. Rowland had never suspected their infidelity; even now, Rowland was blind to what was happening while he was at work. Cameron smiled to himself then looked around at the darkened street.

Tonight Cameron had decided on a different route, which, although unfamiliar, may have been a quicker way home. The towering buildings that surrounded him made him feel small and insignificant; their cold, hard surfaces seemed foreign and distant in the diffused lighting cast by the few streetlights that lined the roadway. Rubbing his hands together before putting them in his pockets, he quickened his pace in an effort to be home and out of the detestable cold night.

Nervous glances down the ominous openings of darkened alleys caused him much consternation. Imaginary things moved within the thick, black shadows; creatures ready to spring out of the cluster of rubbish bins and piles of waste eyed his solitary form.

Another alley yawned in the distance. Hastily, he walked past in an effort to avoid any danger; however, upon glancing into the murky darkness a soft light shone eerily halfway down the lane. The light was entrancing; it captivated him and held him fixed in awe with its warm iridescent glow. Hesitant at first, an intense need to see this strange phenomenon overwhelmed him until he unconsciously began walking down the darkened alley.

The light gently illuminated the surrounding area; its golden glow hovered in the darkness, beckoning. Approaching closer, Cameron could see that it came from an open door within a shadowed wall toward the far end of the desolate lane. When he finally stood before the strange glow, his mind became a soothing blank slate; all thoughts and troubles that had previously filled him suddenly disappeared. A premonition made him enter the doorway. But, after advancing cautiously along the long corridor that lay before him, the light began to dim. Still entranced by the surreal radiance, he continued following the dim light in an effort to find its source. There were strange doors on either side of the hallway, but the peculiar glow continued in a forward direction before turning left. It continued in this direction until the light disappeared into a room and could be seen emanating from an open door in the distance. Excitement gripped him; but the nearer the doorway, the dimmer the light became. Upon entering the door, only a thick, fetid darkness remained; the walls seemed to vanish, and only an empty, black abyss remained.

Darkness had never been frightening to him in the past, but the atmosphere in this tenebrous place was thick with death. A feeling of emptiness, as hollow as a tomb, filled the room. The silent, gentle caress of darkness sent a tingle of fear through him. Stress turned to panic; his mad scream was lost in the thick, black void.

Soft and featherlike, something scampered nearby. A sudden slither of fear made his legs feel weak. The sound repeated itself before it faded into the darkness leaving only a palpable silence. There was something inside the room.

An apparition, a face—faint but discernible, made its presence in the dark—then slowly faded into nothing. The repulsive, ancient shape radiated a feeling of intense evil that made him realize how vulnerable and defenseless he was. The weakness he had previously felt suddenly returned and he thought that he would collapse. A sudden surge of strength flowed through his body. He must go on.

The room smelled of dampness and decay. Death lingered in the shadows. Not just mortal death, but something that threatened his very essence. Again, that soft breeze-like presence caressed his body before slithering away. Then something emanated from within the blackness; a small glowing light. It did not illuminate the room, but hovered within the black void. He watched with awe as it drifted silently toward him and began to float before his face . . . then, without warning, it entered through his nose.

The feeling was ecstatic. Blinding colors flashed through his mind before he awoke to find himself standing in front of the empty alley. The strange light had disappeared, but a peculiar numbness filled his head. An illuminated clock on one of the distant towers tolled the hour. The sound was a thick, muffled note that drifted through the empty street before pounding softly deep within his head. He glanced at the white, glowing disk, then continued his journey home.

It was a cold and miserable night. The moon and stars had disappeared from the sky and left a silent, empty void above. Dreary, poorly lit streets unfolded a melancholy tale as he trudged wearily through the desolate gloom. He arrived home eager only for the warmth of his bed and the peaceful realm of slumber. The autumn rain persisted throughout the night and lulled him into a deep, tranquil sleep.

Although the peculiar numbness within Cameron's head had subsided the following morning, an inexplicable feeling still persisted within his skull. He thought the fresh air would clear his mind of visions from the previous evening, so he stepped outside his residence.

Brown leaves from the elm trees that lined the roadway thickly blanketed the footpath. A biting autumn chill hung in the air; the distant sun in the cold, blue sky provided little warmth as it drifted listlessly over the new morning. It had been raining constantly for the past few days, but the turbid sky had finally cleared and everything felt fresh and clean.

Tranquil pools of water by the roadside mirrored the cerulean sky. Vibrant colors of the morning allowed Cameron to forget the occurrences of the previous night. But when he walked past a large pool of rainwater, his reflection on the still surface attracted his attention. Time had etched marks onto his face, and when he stopped and gazed at his reflected image his thoughts drifted over the water and into the darkness within. A sad moan rose through the recesses of his mind—or was it his own thoughts?—as memories and hidden fears began to surface. Looking at the image on the surface of the water, he could see the blue sky framing his tired, worn face. Suddenly, a strange shadow crept over the cool blue before a deformed face appeared in the reflection behind him. Upon turning quickly, the distorted image disappeared. There was nothing there.

The vision broke his spell. Bewildered and confused, he rose from his crouching position beside the pool and looked around at the surrounding cluster of trees, but could see nothing untoward. *My imagination,* he thought.

Town proved to be a mistake. The crowds were irritating and strange. Talking to acquaintances had become laborious—their conversation seemed shallow and distant—so he decided to return home and seek rest.

It was then that the voice began.

At first, it was a distant hum in the depths of his mind during the dark oblivion of sleep. The sound was scarcely audible, but as he focused on the indistinguishable drone it gradually increased until the murmur began to resemble words. It whispered thoughts that were incomprehensible at first, but with time, its barbed, parasitic force entangled his consciousness and smothered him with vile suggestions that he previously would never have contemplated. At first the words were only a trickle, but the trickle became a cascade . . . until the voice within was screaming for release.

Malicious, twisted, and evil, it surfaced at odd times during the day until he began unwittingly talking to himself in a voice that was unlike anything he had ever heard.

The voice surfaced during periods of solitude, but as time progressed it became audible when people were present. Obscene suggestions that made them stare at him in disgust.

"What are you looking at, you maggot!" The virulence in his voice and the evil glint in his eyes were enough to make anyone nervous and quickly walk away.

The nights became restless, and sleep riddled with nightmares. Shadowed and barely discernible, the faint outline of the hideous, ancient face that had been glimpsed within the room he had stumbled upon a few weeks past appeared before him, its brown parchment like skin softly glowing in the blackness. Pernicious eyes glared through the shadows of his mind as it whispered:

Fear not the darkness; feel its velvety embrace as it entwines your heart. Feel its hard, black strength surging through your veins as the waves swell through your bosom and carry you into ecstatic worlds of nightmare. Silent and brooding, its soft caress permeates everything. Feel your longing as its power swells and fills you. Placid and timeless, before the first glimmer of light, in time immemorial, the eternal black void has always existed. What horror was spawned within its ancient depths? What lies hidden within the sempiternal blackness ready to devour those that walk within?

The ancient face lingered before him; the evil in its sinister smile was eclipsed only by the hatred that shone in the glare of its eyes.

As the face faded, dreams of madness filled his sleep. Nightmare worlds in other dimensions, other galaxies, overwhelmed him. Incredible, forbidden visions of landscapes, desolate and barren, filled with the very essence of death.

The strange vistas persisted well into the next day while he was at work. Rowland, his work mate, found him distant and slightly more quiet than usual. "You should take the rest of the day off," he told Cameron, who seemed unconcerned.

"It's only a passing problem," Cameron replied. "Perhaps a rest over the weekend will make me feel better."

But instead of alleviating the morose feelings, the days passed and the dreams persisted only to become more vivid while the landscapes became populated by strange beings. They wallowed in darkness as they crawled and moaned in their pain while pleading for release. Twisted, deformed shapes bred from the ancient night; alien beings that would tear the very fabric of existence in an effort to enter the wholesome world of sanity and light appeared before him. Within what resembled faces were globular, off-set eyes within which insanity lurked. Elongated mouths filled with teeth that resembled shards of broken glass were ready to devour not just flesh, but his very soul.

Such things could not possibly exist in a normal, sane world—they must surely be delusions created from dark dreams. The dreams began to fill his mind during his waking hours until the images became so vivid that reality and nightmare became indistinguishable.

It was then that the things began appearing amongst normal people during the day when the crowds were busy rushing to their respective destinations. *Why could they not see them?* Somehow, the creatures had escaped their dark, twisted world and had entered the normal sane world of man. There was one crawling amongst a group of school children. Another was sitting on a bench, apparently waiting for a bus; it dripped some sort of excrement onto the pavement below where it was seated. Its obnoxious form slithered and moved as it stared at him through protruding globular eyes set on its strangely shaped head. Ignorance proved the best solution. He mixed in with the surrounding people and continued walking along the footpath.

How had they escaped the darkness? Someone had let them into the world of light, and they would eventually overwhelm humanity. Looking around, he was relieved to find he could not see any more of the creatures within the crowds. But as he approached the curb and prepared to cross the road, a taxi pulled up at the intersection in front of him. He was overcome by a sudden shock when he looked up from his pensive reflections and into the darkened interior of the cab. One of the creatures was driving, and stared at him from the car. The driver waited for the road to clear before turning onto the main highway. Cameron watched the distorted head in the taxi cab drive away, and a spasm of fear flowed through him as the vehicle gradually disappeared into the flow of traffic.

No more creatures were present along the way home, but in the darkness of his room he could hear the sound within his head. Like a freight train, it began within the distant depths of his mind; a gentle throbbing that became gradually closer and louder until, within the darkness of his thoughts, the twisted, foul voice was instilling suggestions into his mind. The voice, a screaming bellowing horror, was intolerable. The intensity of his thoughts was so strong that he began repeating the suggestions loudly. Foul, twisted sounds came from his lips without him consciously willing them to be said.

Sleep would rid him of this horror, he thought. And, besides, he needed the rest. Tomorrow he would be back at work. But his sleep was a parade of nightmares. The aged, evil face again glowed in the darkness.

The filth must be destroyed. They must be eradicated and sent back from where they have come. Back to the darkness from where they were spawned.

The voice echoed within the chambers of Cameron's subconscious. Cameron needed to think. The shell-like hardness of their bodies made it impossible to destroy the beings, but the elongated necks would be easy to cut. Decapitation would certainly prove fatal to the creatures.

He selected a knife with a large, sharp blade—the biggest and the strongest from the block in the kitchen—and sharpened it to a fine edge before placing it in his work bag. The protection of the hard, cold steel felt comforting. There was no knowing when he may need it—the things looked ravenous and seemed to be watching him. They had selected him from the hordes of people who wandered the city. One was sitting on the bus across from him this morning. It just sat there doing nothing, making its obnoxious wheezing noises. He pretended not to see it until its presence, and the stench it emanated, became unbearable. When the bus arrived at the next stop he disembarked and walked the rest of the way.

Rowland had arrived at work earlier than usual and was waiting for Cameron. "The trains aren't running today, so we'll need to direct people to buses on the main street."

Cameron looked tired, for his night's sleep had been troubled. Nevertheless, he followed Rowland to the street above the underground station where buses were picking up people as a substitute for the trains. Crowds of stranded passengers were waiting buses arriving at regular intervals. Cameron followed Rowland to a makeshift tent and put his work bag in a safe place beneath a table before following Rowland back onto the street.

"You can direct these people onto the buses as they arrive. If you need any help I'll be just over there directing those passengers," he said as he handed Cameron a high visibility vest and indicated an area about fifty meters away. Cameron seemed preoccupied with something and seemed distant. Rowland noticed a serious look drift across his face when he spoke to him.

Rowland departed, and Cameron's demeanor became one of intense fear and loathing as he noticed one of the creatures in the crowd. The hellish being was sitting silently on a bench nearby; it seemed to be resting, and disregarded him completely. Passengers awaiting transport seemed oblivious of its presence; they walked or stood around it taking little or no notice of the thing.

The voice in his head was a screaming horror. *Destroy the abomination!* it cried. Cameron began whispering obscenities to himself before repeating the command in a strange voice.

The express bus had just arrived, and Cameron began to direct some of the passengers onto the bus. After the bus departed, more people arrived to await the next one, but Cameron's concentration was focused on the figure seated on the bench. The creature must be sleeping; its bulbous eyes seemed closed. This was the perfect opportunity. If he was careful, he could approach it without being detected. It seemed relaxed and unconcerned about what was occurring around it.

Cameron waited for a lull in the crowd before making his way to the tent where he had put his bag. A glint of light shone off the sharpened kitchen knife as he removed it. He could see his blazing eyes reflected upon the cold, smooth steel as he fondled the blade within his hands. Placing the knife beneath his jacket so as not to agitate the surrounding people, he left the tent.

The thing sat motionless. This was his chance. The voice within was a thundering, demonic rage of blasphemy. *Kill it,* it screamed. *Destroy the abomination!*

He slowly removed the knife from his jacket and approached the bench. The surrounding crowd of people looked aghast at Cameron and began to fan out in all directions. There were screams of horror and shouts of warning. People fled, panic-stricken at the sight of Cameron cutting the neck of the creature. The sharp knife slid through its tender neck easily until Cameron clutched the severed head tightly by the hair. He raised it in triumph, allowing the blood to soak him as it drained from the neck and onto the concrete path.

"The creatures must be destroyed!" The thin, twisted voice made the onlookers cringe in fear at the horror that lay before them.

Rowland could not see what was happening from his position due to the excited crowd that had formed. At first, he thought that an accident may have occurred and a passenger may need first aid. He was totally unprepared for the sight that would confront him as he made his way through the crowd of stunned people.

Cameron had severed the head from the body of a vagrant that had been sleeping on a bus stop bench. Rowland gazed upon the blood covered scene in disbelief; he had never expected anything like this. As the crowds swarmed about him, Cameron called out to the people, "They were spawned from within the darkness before light existed, and they will live even when the light fades. They are the darkness." He was holding the head aloft, displaying the abhorrent trophy to the horrified crowd.

When the police arrived, Cameron was standing next to the body of the man he had decapitated, holding the head in one hand and the bloodied knife in the other. Obscenities emanated from him in a voice that was unlike anything that they had heard before. His babbling about some sort of creature that had infested the earth had finally become more subdued.

But as he stood before the dismayed crowd, he repeated the words that the voice within his head whispered: "Silent, placid, and timeless, the eternal black void has always existed. Before the first glimmer of light, in time immemorial, what horror was spawned within its ancient depths? What lies hidden inside the sempiternal blackness ready to devour those that walk within?"

As the police were leading Cameron away, Rowland stood before him. A seditious smile lined his face as he glared at the blood splattered figure. The smile was replaced by a grim look; he realized that everything comes at a cost. Even before he had made the bargain, he had been aware of the consequences—and now, as he looked at Cameron, he felt that it had been worth the price. Suddenly, an entrancing soft light hovered in front of Rowland before it disappeared. An unusual numbness filled his head. Surrounded by the astonished crowd, Cameron looked distant and unreal. Black, deformed skeletal trees that lined the roadway moved oddly beneath the turbid canopy of dark, grey sky that had suddenly appeared overhead. Thoughts of his wife, Judy, began to drift through his mind. She had looked somewhat odd this morning when he had left home for work—somewhat alien. Rowland began to feel strangely lethargic before an overwhelming compulsion to sleep suddenly overcame him.

PILING UP

KALLIRROE AGELOPOULOU

He picked up the black chicken carcass by its foot, carefully avoiding the bloodied, cut-up neck. Giving it a good once-over, he decided that no one in the house was going to eat this foul, rotting corpse. Even the cat hadn't nipped at it, which proved that it must have been lying there for a while. This was a pointless murder, and while John felt that everyone was entitled to their own beliefs, he found he drew the line at the sacrificing of chickens.

The person to blame arrived just in time. With her hair tied up neatly and her broom in hand, she turned the corner and stopped mid-step to stare at him.

"Mrs. Martha? Um, it's not ok to cut up chickens in this house. Not for any reason other than eating them. Please don't do it again."

She looked at him, then at the bird, then at him again.

"Sí, señor."

"I'm glad we see eye to eye on this." He pointed at the dead bird. "Now, take care of this, will you? And clean up the floor a bit."

"Sí."

If only ritual sacrifice weren't so messy. But, all's well that ends well, he supposed. Martha was not a bad person. She cleaned, was great with the kids, and got along well with his wife. She could cook a mean chicken pasta, too. He watched her toss the perfectly severed chicken head into the trash and quickly sweep up the remains from the floor. Well, the woman *could* obviously butcher. Martha finished soon enough, and John continued from where he had left off before he'd spotted the creepy offering: cleaning the cabinet and all the silverware in it.

He let his hands roam all over the surface of the cabinet. The wood had worn out perfectly over the years, earning it the faded glow of a proper antique. Everything in this house looked authentic and beautiful. *Everything except for that painting above his head.* He didn't really want to, but he turned his gaze to the weary frame and all it encompassed. It was stained and old—really old—but there was no mistaking what it depicted. A prairie, or a field—some vast place where nothing seemed to grow above an inch.

In the middle of all the nothingness stood a statue, or a pile of some sort stretching way up into the air. Among the greenery, the amassment was all black, which in his opinion made the whole thing even more bizarre. He scrubbed the silver spoon in his hand again and again, completely unable to peel his eyes off the offending decoration. Maybe—just maybe—it wasn't so bad under all that crap. A thorough scrubbing would reveal the exact nature of the pileup. He dropped what had become the shiniest spoon in the whole world and let out a frustrated sigh. Oh, who was he kidding? No amount of cleaning could fix that mess of a painting. It simply didn't match the rest of the house's beautifully aged rusticity.

He was sure to find a lot of trash amidst the rubble—more crap than valuable stuff, which is what made him accept the deal in the first place. *The deal.* What a crock. As if anyone else, even any charity institution, would be interested in a run-down house in the middle of nowhere. It was either him or complete and utter oblivion for this house—of that he was sure. Still, there were rules in his uncle's will . . . rules he had to follow just to be allowed to step foot inside this dump. Rules . . . good rules, like to keep Martha on as a helper. Rules that seemed unimportant, like staying here at least once a year. But also silly, senseless rules, like to keep the painting right where it was. That horrid painting . . . that blackened, stupid thing in the middle of the hall. For all of time. Where everyone could see it.

He got up and closed the cabinet doors, emphatically refusing to throw another look at the half torn canvas above his head. The doorbell stopped him on his way to the kitchen.

"Coming!" He answered cheerfully, as if he was back in New York. But he didn't expect any real visitors. He'd only been here for a couple of weeks and aside from Amanda, his uncle's realtor, no one had stepped foot inside the house. Traveling the distance between the nearest places with any signs of life and here would have been quite the feat, apparently. That and the fact that active segregation was a practice here; a common thread among the native tribes of the wet and wild Scottish mire. They sure seemed to love their peace and quiet around these parts.

Sure enough, Amanda's face greeted him through the foggy stained glass of the door. She stepped inside, and pointed at the stack of paper peeking out of her bag.

"Can't sit for long . . . I just came by to drop off some papers for you to sign."

"More papers? What's it about?"

"Bunch of technical gibberish. You'll see."

He laughed as they both sat down on the couch near the entrance. "As long as it's not more rules and regulations, we're fine."

She threw a casual look at the picture on the wall. "You poor man. I would sympathize, but I've witnessed far worse deals than the one you got. You got a house. I mean, seriously—considering the kind of man your uncle was, I'd say you got off easy."

"Well, that's true. And you knew him better than I did. So still no idea what the painting is all about?"

"No. Your uncle was a very peculiar man, always searching for the most special things to collect. He was guided by the same rules you are. Trust him." She changed the subject swiftly. "The house seems to be getting better and better! You've put a lot of work into it."

They chatted while he signed the papers, and soon, true to her promise, Amanda rose to leave. Before leaving, she gently reminded him, "You got a good deal, John."

Her pristine demeanor softened, revealing a lot more than she had previously let on. "Just relax and enjoy it. This is going to be your home for a long time."

The door creaked shut behind her, and, just like that, he was all alone again.

Well, almost.

"Martha?"

Her pleasant face popped up from behind the kitchen door. "Sí?"

"When did they say they'd be back again?"

"They be back soon."

That was good enough.

He made himself a cup of coffee—coffee, not tea—and brought a lounge chair out to the patio. The view was less . . . *full* than he expected. When he'd first heard of this place, endless prairie to the foot of the forest to the west, he'd hoped all the mingling trees would be a relief from all the flatness. They weren't. It was the

middle of the day in spring and there was no sun, no real warmth
. . . nothing. He'd been having doubts; but on days like this one,
they were more than just doubts. They became huge, inescapable
questions which ate away at him. How would they ever get used to
this place? How would the kids adjust to their new schools? How
long before his wife was freaked out by the bad luck with *everything*? Before the emptiness would run her off?

But all this was too much to ponder now, so he zeroed in on the
easiest target—the one thing he could hold responsible for being
the bane of his existence. The one thing that, in fixing it, would
make everything else would run smoothly. Forever and ever, amen.

The painting.

Just as he shifted his attention, but before he got too wrapped
up in it—at precisely the right moment—he saw them pull up in the
car.

Together, they unloaded the groceries inside and talked for a
while before the kids ran off on a hiking adventure. He was left
alone with his wife, and they were enjoying the comfort of their
silent kitchen.

"Did you see how clean the cabinet is? It's perfect now."

"Yeah, but it's packed. We should secure it better."

"I can design some upholstery. Put a better key on the door. No
biggie."

"Fantastic."

"I'll clean up the painting, too."

Worriedly, she turned to face him. "Aren't we supposed to leave
it be?"

"I'll just clean it where it is. Nobody said anything about that.
Besides, who's gonna know?"

"Well, there's Martha . . ."

He shook his head dismissively. "I don't think the chicken-slayer will mind. Did I tell you I found another one of her macabre art pieces in the hall this morning?"

"Jesus. I'll have a talk with her."

Early the next morning he began creating a cover for the cabinet. He ground some planks together, sat them up, and joined them all at the base. It would need to be trimmed and painted, but it worked well enough around the cabinet for the time being. He put a new lock on the cabinet, and finally felt ready to proceed with the next project that had been bugging him for so long. Dozens of bottles, rags, and sponges surrounded him, and his ladder was propped against the wall. He debated whether or not he should take down the whole thing to clean it, but in the end, he chose to abide by the rules. At least until his hands got tired, and then all bets would be off. He meticulously watered down the painting; softly, so as not to soak it completely and ruin its texture. Little by little the darkness lifted, freeing the old color underneath. It was an arduous process, but he stubbornly got on with it because each tiny uncovered speck egged him on all the more. *More, more. You can do more.*

His hands were getting tired. With a swift move, he unhinged the canvas and began lifting it from the wall. He barely noticed the permanent shadow it cast on the wall as he carefully laid it on the floor. He worked and worked at cleaning the grime from the face of the painting; and finally, he saw what was hidden underneath for the first time. It didn't make any sense, though. The pile in the middle was an irregular totem of eyes looking back at him. *Eyes.* Realistic eyes of different shapes and colors; all of them fixed on the same spot somewhere outside their rectangular confines. Who would have thought the absurdist movement had predated Dali for so long? He was more confident than ever that the painting didn't fit with the rest of the house—but maybe there was some value to the piece anyway. Needing to share his excitement, John began calling for his family.

"Kids! Helen! Come check this out!"

"Kids are out. What's up?"

"Look! We got us some *art.*"

Horrified, Helen stared down at him on the floor with the painting in his hands.

"You took it down."

"Only for a moment. We're all alone, don't worry."

"Just put it back up, will you? Losing this house after all the effort we've put in to it . . . I don't even wanna think about it."

"Fine." He placed it back on the wall and turned to look at her again. "Isn't it bizarre?"

Freed from the anxiety of breaking the rules, she looked calmly at the painting as it sat in its proper place. Helen took her time checking it out, and answered him slowly.

"Very. What does it mean?"

"I have no idea. We should get an appraisal."

"Who'd come here to do that? We can't move it."

"I'll photograph it, and put it on the internet. I'll find someone who knows where it's from and what it is."

Helen left him be, and sure enough, he picked up the camera and began clicking away at the frame, ardently hoping that the painting's mystery would eventually be revealed. For a good long while, he had been unable to avert his eyes. He uploaded the pictures onto the internet—on all the relevant art websites anyway —and hoped to hear from someone soon. Throughout the rest of the day, he finished project after project, but made a number of stops in front of the painting until he had exhausted himself. He had gotten too tired, and the painting had drained him until he couldn't stop his eyes from closing and falling asleep.

He woke up before Helen and the kids, only to find himself standing before the painting again. There was something different in the air of the room now. He sniffed the air for a moment before crawling around to find it. And he did . . . right under the cabinet. It was fresh. *This is ridiculous,* he thought. *Most definitely not ok. Oh, no.* He picked up the second grotesque dead bird of the week and stormed into the kitchen.

"Martha! I don't care what reason you have for doing this, what bizarre belief system you subscribe to, whatever! This has to stop."

She just looked at him with blank eyes.

He waved the corpse in her face.

"Hey, you *comprende*? Don't do it again."

"Sí."

But he knew they were getting nowhere with this. Why did she continue this nonsense? Why in the house, always in his hallway? Why? He froze in place. Come to think of it, whenever he found a bizarre knick-knack, a dead bird just happened to appear flattened out underneath the cabinet. In fact, her ritualistic killings seemed to be placed directly below the giant, looming depiction of that old landscape on purpose. Lowering his voice, John gave Martha the most serious expression he could.

"You knew my uncle pretty well, right? Did he ever . . . did he ever tell you what this painting was all about? Is this some sort of idolatry?"

After his question to her, Martha shifted slightly. He knew that *she knew* exactly what he was talking about.

"No . . ."

He approached her easily, wanting to get to the bottom of the painting's mystery.

"Martha. The truth."

Her hands dropped to her side in exasperation.

"You don't understand. It is best left like this. Your uncle was a good man, he knew."

"Knew what?"

She fixed him with her sternest gaze. "He knew not to look."

What could that possibly mean? Wait a minute. Pointing into the hallway with urgency, he asked her. "So I cleaned it up. What about it?"

Eyes unwavering, her mouth no more than a tiny slit, she answered reluctantly.

"No wanna look. Never."

She turned to leave, but John quickly caught up with her. With the dead chicken still in his hand, he grabbed her face and forced her to face the wall. Wanting to prove a point, he made her look at the painting.

"Look! It's just a picture."

"No! Let me go!"

"What do you see? What?"

Her bulging, scared eyes ran all over the painting. "Guts, guts . . ." She turned to face him. "Why did you do that to me?"

She took off upstairs, and in the following moments he heard the sounds of closets opening and closing, and loud banging on the floor. Soon, Martha reemerged at the top of the stairs with her luggage in hand; and just like that, she was gone. She had packed her belongings into her car and left without so much as a word. As he was still trying to process this turn of events, Helen walked down the stairs and stood at his side.

"What was all the commotion about? What's that you're holding?"

He turned to the bird in his hand, then glanced back at Helen in a daze. "Martha. Another chicken."

"This is insane. She seems like such a nice person, too."

"Yeah . . ."

Helen was getting a little worked up; he could tell by the way she shot questions at him. "Is that why she left? You think she's coming back? We can't even fire her."

He dropped the chicken onto the table, grabbed her by the arms, and began dragging her to the hallway. Pointing at the painting on the wall, at the large pile of eyes staring at him, he asked her.

"Helen, what's up there? What is that pile made of? Tell me!"

She looked at him like he was nuts. "What do you mean?"

"Tell me. Please."

"I told you, it's bizarre. All these limbs . . ." Limbs. *Limbs.* She paused again, unsure how to answer. "They're so weird, so realistic. All different but all purposefully put in their right place. Where they should be. Take one out and the whole structure would collapse."

Not guts. Not eyes.

"Have the kids seen it?"

"I . . . I guess. How could they not?"

After talking to Helen, John couldn't shake off the way Martha was so scared of it—the way she had reacted to the painting. Dammit, *he* was scared of it.

"Helen, you should take the kids, and go. Go to town and stay there for a while."

"What has gotten into you?"

"Goddammit, just go!"

He must have gotten through to her, or at least seemed dangerously out of his mind—because that was all the coaxing she had needed. She hurried and packed the kids, leaving with some overnight bags in hand. At the doorway, she turned to look at him.

"Call us at the inn if you come back to your senses."

It wasn't going to be easy to do that. As soon as they were gone, he opened his laptop to find an explosion of comments about the painting, all equally exasperating:

```
Very interesting surrealist attempt. How old did
you say the piece was?
This structure of bony remains is extremely
intricate.
Um, I'm pretty sure it's made of lungs. It's what
human lungs look like.
What makes you say that? It's all random guts to
me. Long rows of pink, soft lining. Maybe pig?
Really unappetizing.
Just don't put it in the kitchen!
I SEE DEAD PEEEOPLE! LOL!
We probably need a pic with better resolution.
Very bizarre. Post a close-up.
```

He picked up the phone and called the only person he knew could explain this to him.

"Amanda? I cleaned up the painting. Whatever you have to tell me about it, now is the time. Martha's gone. So is my family."

He could hear her sigh from the other end of the line.

"Now, why did you have to go and do that? Your uncle resisted the urge for years. Couldn't you?"

"What is it? Nobody on the internet seems to know."

"How could they? It's so old. You could destroy it, but I have a feeling that won't be enough."

Another sigh. "If it was, it would have been long gone by now."

"What is it? Some sort of soul mirroring?" He couldn't believe he had even asked her that. "Everyone sees different things in it."

"God . . . your uncle told me too many stories. I wouldn't know which one to believe. All I know for sure is that he was scared of it. And if that burly, toughened-up asshole was scared of something, then I am too."

"This is not helping."

A moment of silence followed his statement, and then she answered.

"I'm sorry. Don't call me again. I'll be gone, somewhere far away from here."

And just like that—just like Martha—she hung up and was gone.

At this point, his head was throbbing, and there weren't many options left. He had to figure out what it was . . . or destroy it. He unhinged it from the frame and began checking it from top to bottom for any artist's signature or distinguishing marks. There was nothing. He grabbed it by the frame and began ripping it, trying to take all the pieces apart. He stopped when he spotted a little something drop near his feet. Enclosed in the lining of the frame was a folded piece of paper, looking as old as the painting itself, and he bent over to carefully pick it up. As he opened it, he noticed his hands were shaking. In stark contrast to the detailed depiction of the actual work, the paper was inscribed by a heavy hand and a rough prototype of the original. Standing in the middle of a field, where the undefined mass should have been, there was a giant human *body*. It was scribbled all over, with short strokes that either stood up straight, or bent over like wriggling worms. All entangled in perfect alignment, the scribbled strokes made up its whole structure.

Gaining awareness, he noticed that his headache was gone . . . vanished completely. He also realized that his own body was propped up against the wall. It was all starting to make sense.

With nothing left for him to do, he waited for the others.

He seemed to sleep for a couple of hours, until the sound of a car engine jolted him awake. He looked out the door, and noticed a heavy female form exiting the vehicle. *Martha's back.* She stepped inside and began making herself some tea as if nothing had happened, so he decided to join her. Soon, another car pulled up— his own this time. They were all here. Now that they had seen the painting, there was no escaping the truth. Something must happen. He hugged them all.

His youngest, his love, asked, "You wanna hear what I saw daddy?" He did.

More and more people arrived during the day. By noon, they all started moving toward the clearing, toward that green vastness of the painting. Critical mass reached. With enough of them, they would fill it up. Finally, they were going to breathe new life into it. One after the other, they gathered at the edges and melted into each other as they got closer and closer to the center mass. Once the first layer was done, they climbed on top of it, mixing more and more as each layer formed. All the bodies dissembled and re-formed, innards and appearances, all perfect in their hideousness. He said his goodbye to his family because he knew he would be the last to go.

When he finally made the climb himself, it was exhilarating. Like reaching for what he never knew he missed. At the top, his group clotted to form a layer over the bodies that preceded them. He didn't mind any of it, though—even having their rancid breath so close to his face. He didn't mind the bodies piled on top of him. From that point on, he was all eyes. He looked below, to the rest of them. The limbs, the heart.

"Glistening, daddy. It's so smooth."

Somewhere underneath the arch of carefully intertwined bodies, his family was scattered—scattered too far from where he was. That was the only thing he minded. Gazing at the world around him, he did not know what would happen next . . . because that wasn't his job.

He just watched as they started moving.

Door to Insanity

Mathias Jansson

He reached into the dark,
where insects crawled over his arms;
he felt the sticky switch of it
within his sweaty palms.

> *The deep sound from the thick wall*
> *slowly slid over the floor . . .*

A distant sound of fear,
a smell of hell so near;
and an abyss made up of stairs
leading down to *(where?)* nowhere.

> *He walked in silence,*
> *followed by demons*
> *whispering warnings in his ears;*
> *ancient spells of evil . . .*

When at last he reached the well,
an eternity of black,
he was trapped in his own hell;
the mirror showed him looking back.

> *Heavily he fell,*
> *sinking to the bottom*
> *as the watery darkness filled his lungs . . .*
> *and the demons sang a song*
> *that opened the door to insanity.*

BRANNIGAN'S
WINDOW

JOHN MC CAFFREY

Kelly?" Jim called, shutting the door behind him, "Hey, you home?"

He shook out of his jacket, hanging it on the coat tree by the front door as he listened for a response from his wife. Hearing none, he set his briefcase down on the floor and took off his tie and suit jacket, tossing them on the small table by the door. He looked at the dozen wilted flowers he'd bought off of a street vendor in hopes they might make up for last night's fight. He planned on taking her out for dinner; they needed to get away from the house for a while. He set the flowers down on top of his suit jacket and walked down the hall towards the kitchen rubbing his hands together, trying to rid his body of the cold November chill.

"Hey Kelly," he called louder. "You home?"

"Up here," came the muffled reply from upstairs.

He retraced his steps back towards the foyer, grabbing the flowers as he mounted the stairs two at a time. The smell of fresh paint and cut lumber permeated the upper hallway as he made the landing. The interior remodeling outfit they hired must have finally begun work on the upstairs, which placed them almost a week ahead of schedule. He'd be glad when they finished. It was becoming aggravating having the house in a constant state of disarray.

"You in the bedroom?" he called as he turned left on the landing, walking towards what would be their master bedroom.

"Yeah."

"Hey you," he said as he entered the room. "How was school?"

"Don't ask," she said without turning around. Jim noticed she'd already changed into sweats and sneakers and had pulled her blonde hair back into a ponytail, which he pushed aside to kiss her neck. He could feel the tension as he held her. They'd been arguing over the cost of remodeling their new house since they'd moved in. It'd been his idea to buy the place and renovate it. Kelly had been worried about the costs from the beginning, but he'd assured her it wouldn't be more than they could afford. If anything, it was far above what either of them thought possible and only seemed to be escalating. The money was quickly evaporating out of their bank account and it'd caused more than a few sleepless nights for them both. He was thankful Kelly had never once said I told you so, which was more than he felt he deserved. He pulled her close with his free hand as she leaned back into his embrace, her two hands gripping the arm that held her.

"The kids were monsters all day, and I have a ton of papers to grade this weekend," she said. "Judge agree to your motion?"

"Nope, hasn't ruled yet. He was more worried about getting off early for the weekend."

"Glad you're home early. These for me?" she asked, seeing the flowers in his hand.

"Yeah, cost me a fortune, too."

"I see that," she said. She took the wilted flowers and raised them to her nose to smell the fragrance. "I should put them in water."

"Later," he said, taking the flowers from her and tossing them to the floor. He turned her around, pulling her close. "Sorry about last night."

"Me too," she said.

"We'll be fine, Kel. I promise. I'll hold off on having the outside redone until next year, okay? That'll save us a lot. I know we've been spending more than we planned to, so the outside can wait."

She pulled back from him and looked up into his face. "You sure?"

"Positive."

"Okay, sounds good."

Jim smiled and glanced at the hole in the wall Kelly had been standing in front of when he entered. "Chris finally started in this room, I see," he said, releasing her. He looked around at the progress the workers had made. They were having the room they stood in extended halfway into the next by tearing the wall down, and the remainder of that room turned into a master bath with a whirlpool. The room they stood in now was bare except for the few items the carpenters left at the house. Ladders, a few tarps, large plastic pails of paint, as well as a few power tools were all placed in the far corner of the room.

"Yeah, you just missed them," she said. "Chris found something strange in there as they were taking the wall down. He showed me when I got home."

"In where?"

"In the hole." She motioned towards the four-foot wide gap in the wall, stepping closer to it. "Aren't you listening to anything I'm saying?"

He made a "hmph" sound deep in his throat and crossed the room to look.

"Chris said it shouldn't be a problem, but thought you should look at it first before they tore it out."

"Tore what out?"

"That," she replied, stepping out of his way so he could look past her.

He stepped closer to the hole and peered into the dark interior of the wall. It was obvious even in the gloom within that the space between the wall he stood at and the far wall was much wider than normal. It looked more like a hallway than an interior space for a wall. Jim squinted his eyes trying to see better but couldn't make out much more.

"Wow, that's a big space in there. But I don't see how that's a problem," he said as he pulled his head back from the opening.

"No, that's not it. Hold on a sec, let me grab a flashlight."

She walked over to the pile of tools in the corner and picked up the large flashlight the contractor had used earlier when he'd shown her the interior of the wall. She clicked it on as she walked back over to Jim.

He took the flashlight, turned, and placed it within the confines of the hole. He immediately saw he'd been right. The interior of the wall was much larger than the few inches in most houses between one wall and the next. This one spanned at least four feet from one wall to the next. He also saw what Kelly must have been referring to.

Within the confines of the wall was what resembled a large bay window. It stretched from floor to ceiling. There was rich burnished wood at the top and bottom, and looked seamless from his vantage point. Even from this distance he could make out markings in the wood. Letters and numbers as well as weird esoteric shapes. The only thing that seemed out of place, other than the fact that the whole structure was hidden within a wall, was there wasn't a proper window for the size of it. He moved the beam across it, trying to peer into the gloom. Where the glass should be was a four foot wide gray oval set in the middle.

"What the hell is it? Looks like a large window, or a mirror. It looks like glass in the middle, but whatever it may have been, it's been painted over." He pulled his head outside the hole.

Kelly shrugged her shoulders. "Beats me, and Chris had no clue. Whoever made it did so after the house was built he said."

"Weird."

"Yeah," Kelly agreed.

"Well, the realtor did tell us the Brannigans were weirdos when we bought the place." Jim said, referring to the previous owners of the house.

"She didn't say they were weirdos, Jim. *You* said they were weirdos. *She* said they were eccentric."

"Yeah, that's what I said. Weirdos."

"You're bad," she said, smiling at him.

He was glad to see her smile. The house had been a thorn in their sides these past few months and there had been little to laugh about. They'd purchased the large home from the son of one of the Brannigan's live-in domestic help after the old woman passed away. The son had let the house go for far below the value of the surrounding homes due to the state of disrepair, and Jim had wanted to live in this neighborhood badly. They'd signed the papers and moved out of their small apartment in the city and immediately started the renovations.

Jim stuck his head back in the hole and regarded the interior, lost in thought.

"What are you thinking about?" Kelly asked from behind him. He turned to look at her and smiled.

"Just thinking about what the realtor told us about the Brannigans. About how they were eccentric as well as wealthy." He accentuated the word wealthy, smiling at Kelly. "I was also thinking maybe we should take a closer look at the inside of that window in there."

"You think they stashed money inside of it?"

"I don't know, but it sure won't hurt to take a look."

He'd heard of stranger things happening . . . old flaky people stashing money in their mattresses and refrigerators. Why not inside a window? It would sure help the financial predicament he and Kelly were in if there was money there. He walked over to the assortment of tools in the corner and chose a sledgehammer as he eyed the wall.

Smiling at him, Kelly asked, "What are you going to do, tear the wall down?"

"Well, not like I'm going to ruin anything. They're going to take it down regardless, so we may as well have a look."

He handed her the flashlight and hefted the large mallet in his hands, trying to get a feel for the weight of it. He stuck his head inside the hole once more to gain a better location of where the window was, then walked over to the wall and swung the mallet, opening a large hole in the drywall. After a few minutes with the sledgehammer and with the help of Kelly, he had made a much larger hole than the workmen had made just to the left of the window.

They pulled back the last few large pieces of drywall. Jim took the flashlight from Kelly and flicked it on, pointing it into the gloom of the hole and the window structure within as he entered.

"It might be a mirror, but whatever it is they painted over the glass."

He moved the beam over the window. Someone had brush painted the entire piece of glass in dark gray paint. The light also showed the deep luster of the wood frame, and he could see the intricate carvings much better at this close range. There were indeed letters carved into the wood, but they were unlike anything he ever saw. They were large, and spaced symmetrically around the interior. There were mother-of-pearl inlays with etchings in gold underneath the middle in patterns that was beautifully rendered, but resembled nothing he was familiar with. The hardware used to house the glass was wrought of real silver, and he was surprised the previous owners wouldn't have taken it with them if for no other reason than the value of the materials. He moved the light around the interior, trying to gauge the reason behind the window.

"Okay, I'm going to open this wall up the rest of the way so we can go in." He grabbed the sledgehammer from the floor and handed the flashlight to Kelly.

"Maybe you're right, maybe it's hidden money," she said.

He smiled and started to bang away at the bottom of the wall. "Maybe I'm going to have a cardiac doing all Chris's work." Kelly grinned at him as she began to move away the pieces of drywall he tore off.

When they'd opened the wall up enough to enter, he walked back to the corner with Chris's tools. He found an extension cord with a light at the end and plugged it in, clicking it on. With the brighter light he stepped inside the opening and held it in front of him as Kelly followed. He stopped in front of the small structure and held the light up, peering at it closely. The whole thing was set in the adjacent wall.

"This is definitely a window. Kind of like a bay window, but not like one I've ever seen."

"What's that?" Kelly asked, pointing to his right.

He followed her gaze to the floor, seeing what she'd been referring to. It was a small cardboard box, like the ones used by clothing stores to put shirts and sweaters in. He handed the light to her and bent to pick it up. He felt something shift inside it as he stood back up.

"What'd I say? Stashing money in the walls. This has to be something. Let's look at this in the other room."

Kelly nodded as she hung the work light from one of the rafters over their head as they stepped back out into the room.

He grabbed one of the five gallon buckets to sit on, while Kelly chose one of the larger toolboxes. He opened the small box, revealing a red ledger and a white envelope within. Jim handed the ledger to Kelly as he ripped opened the envelope. He frowned in disappointment as he pulled out the envelope's only contents: two sheets of paper with handwriting on them. He unfolded the paper and began to read.

"What is it?"

Jim paused and looked up at his wife. "Well, it's not a treasure map," he said. "Listen to this."

I leave this letter in hopes that someone might one day be able to help the Brannigans, for my health has denied me the ability to watch vigil over what Mrs. Brannigan asked of me. She has followed Mr. Brannigan into the place he discovered many years ago even though he had made her swear she never would. She waited a year to the day and told me she would wait no longer. She has left me in charge of the house as well as the journal concerning the window, but I cannot understand what is written there. I fear Mrs. Brannigan has met with whatever fate the Master of the house did. I could no longer bear the things that I saw within the glass so I have had my son paint over the accursed thing. Now that my health has failed, I have also had him wall up the window, for it is unnatural and blasphemous and yet I cannot destroy it for it is the only way back for the Brannigans.

May God have mercy upon them both.

Jim looked up. "That's it, other than a small paragraph stating that she was the Brannigan's housekeeper with her signature and the date. I imagine right before they took her away to a nice rest home for the chronically delusional. No wonder her son sold it so cheap."

Kelly nodded and opened the red ledger and flipped through a few pages. "This is mostly in Latin if I recall it right from college. Take a look." She handed the book to Jim, who took it while handing her the letter to read. He glanced inside, flipping through pages. She was right; Latin filled the pages in neat, smooth characters. Some pages had small diagrams drawn on them, weird symbols and quotations. There were mathematical equations on others.

"Strange people for sure," Kelly said after reading the letter. "What do you think?"

"Well, I think we should take a closer look at that window. You never know, there still might be something valuable inside." He stood and motioned for Kelly to stand with him. "Look in that tool chest for a razor blade."

"Maybe we should leave it alone, Jim. You read what that woman wrote."

"You don't really believe that, do you?"

"No, but we should still leave it alone. It's spooky."

"It's kind of weird, but we got nothing to lose by checking it out."

"I suppose." She handed him back the letter, which he replaced in the envelope while she rooted around in the tool chest for a razor. She located a box opener knife and held it up for him to inspect.

"This?"

"That's perfect. Come on, let's go see this window of theirs."

When they were back within the wall, he unscrewed the box opener's handle and removed one of the extra blades from within, handing the rest back to Kelly, who placed it on the floor. Jim walked up to the window and began to scrape on the glass with the razor. When he'd removed a small space clean of paint roughly the size of a quarter, Kelly, who stood behind him, gasped in surprise and startled Jim.

"What?" he asked.

"Turn the light off."

"Huh?"

"The light above your head, turn it off. Hurry."

Jim groped above his head until he found the switch and clicked it off, darkening the interior of the wall.

He immediately saw what had excited her. Light was spilling out of the spot he had scraped free of paint.

"My God," Kelly whispered. "What the hell is it?"

The light shone pale blue in the gloom of the wall's interior. It fell on the floor in an oval shape between them both. The dust motes from their earlier work with the drywall danced slowly in the beam of light as they descended towards the floor.

"I don't know," Jim said as he bent to the window and began scraping off more paint. "But we're going to find out. Turn that light back on." When he'd widened the spot to roughly double its size, he reached up and clicked the light off again. This time there was little doubt; there was an ambient light shining through. Jim placed his face close to the glass and peered in. Grayish-blue mist swirled around on the other side of the glass. He tried to peer past the mist to distinguish any details, but it was far too thick. He stood up, peering at his wife in the gloom of the enclosed space.

"That's damn weird."

"Let me see," she said, squeezing into the space he'd vacated.

Jim stood up and turned the light back on as he inspected the frame of the window structure where it joined the far wall trying to figure out where the light came from. The wall, however, met the casement in a tight seal.

Kelly stood up. "What do you think?" she asked, but he barely heard her.

"Stay here," he said, stepping through the hole. He left the room heading down the hallway to the far room that the window was up against.

Kelly stared at the glass as if it might offer the answer to the puzzle it presented. The light still shone out, and the more she looked at it the more convinced she became that it was daylight and not some form of electrical bulb. Jim made a rapping sound on the other side of the wall suddenly, startling her.

"Hey," he said from the other side of the wall, his voice muffled. "You there?"

"Yes, you are to the left of it, or I should say it's to *your* left."

The hollow knocking sound he made as he rapped his knuckles on the drywall filled the small space Kelly stood in. She bent once again to peer into the small hole in the paint. He mumbled something, but Kelly wasn't paying attention. She was absorbed with the swirling mist through the glass. It was serene, almost hypnotic. She reached her hand out towards the glass, letting her fingertips lightly touch it.

It soothed.

She felt a humming coming from the cool glass beneath her fingers, as if some great and terrible machine pulsed deep in the earth beneath her. It was an almost audible throbbing. The mist danced just on the other side of the glass, beckoning to her. She felt the cool glass against the pads of her fingertips, but she also felt something more. Something that danced just beyond the sense of perception; not feeling nor sound. Something deeper within her being that spoke to her of shadow and despair. Something not quite right, something nameless and foul—and yet it still evoked in her a feeling of . . .

What?

She didn't know.

"Well, that's the damndest thing I ever saw," Jim said, startling her from behind. It seemed that no more than a moment had passed, and yet she hadn't heard Jim leave the other room nor enter this one.

"I can't find anything. Though I don't know what I'd be looking for anyway. I'm going to have another look in that journal."

Kelly nodded but barely heard him. The mist still whispered to her, the window still beckoned as if offering sanctuary. The light seemed to pulse and move as if a living thing, and she wondered what lay beyond the glass. She raised her hand to her forehead and rubbed at her temples. The light from the small hole Jim had scraped in the glass shone brighter in the gloom of the interior, seeming to overpower the bulb they'd hung above. It would be nice to enter the window and slip amongst the mist. All she'd have to do is open the window and climb inside, and she could . . .

Jim called to her louder, his voice breaking the feeling she had. She blinked her eyes rapidly and looked around in the gloom. She felt suddenly claustrophobic and left the darkness of the interior.

"Yeah?"

"I said, he seems to have written some in English. In the back of the book he has some notes. Listen to this."

I have obtained, through my contacts in the east, certain manuscripts that claim to hold the key to opening portals to other planes of existence. Whether or not they are physical worlds, or some form of alternate reality, I do not know. The manuscripts are ancient, and difficult to decipher due to the advanced state of decay of the pages, but I believe I can translate them. I have spent most of my inheritance in obtaining these books. I hope they are worth it.

I have always maintained that alternate, parallel worlds existed, and now I hope to prove it. We exist not in a universe, but within a multiverse

*and there must exist doorways between those worlds and ours. The fools
at the University who found it so easy to dismiss me from my position
might think differently with hard facts.*

Only time will tell.

Jim looked up at his wife and shrugged. "What do you make of
it?"

"I don't know. Strange for sure. Wasn't he a physicist at the
college?"

"Yeah," Jim replied as he continued looking through the ledger.
"Theoretical Physics and Cosmology, although this doesn't really
sound like science. Sounds more like supernatural crap to me."

He flipped a few pages and began reading from a different
section.

*I finally received the second manuscript last week, although it cost me
dearly. The book is written in a form of code which I have deciphered, and
translated. I have built the portal as a window, housing the opening in
wood and applying the wards around the center as instructed. There are
many destinations outlined in the book, yet I cannot tell by the names
given where they may lead. I will try each, exploring the realms beyond
the window in turn. With the application of the final ward, the glass in
the center filled with light. I believe I have been successful. If only my
colleagues could share in my discovery.*

Jim looked up from his reading. "Jesus, this guy was really into
this stuff. He mentions those books he bought. You didn't notice
them in the wall, did you?" Kelly shook her head. "We should look
around for them. He might've been nuts, but they sound valuable."
He started flipping through the pages again.

Kelly was troubled by what Jim was reading. The previous
owner might have been disturbed, but she couldn't deny the

feeling she had when she was in the room with the window, or the light and the mist beyond the glass. She was about to voice her concerns when Jim stopped flipping through pages.

"There's more."

Sounds come through the window when I open it. Wind, perhaps; but it reminds me of voices. Voices calling. I dare not leave the window open for too long, for I feel to do so might invite whatever is on that side to enter here. I cannot help but wonder what they are, or perhaps, who they are. It must certainly be only the wind, but it vexes me. The mist clears periodically but I cannot discern much through the opening. Only a journey through the gateway will yield the answers to the many questions the portal poses.

Jim stopped reading aloud and looked up at his wife. "This guy was really out in left field."

"Gives me the creeps," she said.

He continued thumbing through the pages. Now that they had found entries in English, he was eager to find out more. He began reading aloud again.

I have decided the only way to ascertain what lies on the other side is to journey within. The window calls to me in a way that I cannot describe. I sit for hours, listening to the voices, and while I am convinced no harm will come to me, I am still apprehensive.

Jim scanned over more of the text, then stopped on the following page and once again read aloud.

My wife fears the window. She too hears the strange voices when I have it open; and though I assure her not to worry, her dread grows. She has begged me to destroy the portal, but I do not think I can. I cannot locate the procedure in the book. To dismantle it in the wrong manner would be disastrous. The window acts as a conduit between this world and the other, and to destroy it would result in a catastrophe beyond what I can imagine.

The procedure to close it in the proper fashion was either on pages in the book that were obliterated, or in another book that I do not possess.

I cannot close this portal now. I must leave it as it is, because if I try and destroy it . . .

I don't even want to ponder what would happen.

I often sit now by the open window. The sounds I hear emanating from within have a soothing quality, and yet I am still afraid to enter. I wonder if the voices are those of sentient beings, or if it is in fact just my imagination. I would swear that I hear my name being called. I must make my journey soon, for only on the other side might I locate the way to close that which I have opened.

"Wow," Jim said, looking up.

Kelly said nothing as she looked towards the hole in the wall.

Jim stood up, closing the journal and setting it on top of the toolbox. He grabbed a crowbar from the pile of tools and headed towards the wall.

"What are you going to do?" Kelly asked.

"I'm going to take it apart and look inside."

"Weren't you paying attention to what you read? According to the book, that's the one thing that mustn't be done. He said quite specifically that destroying the window in any manner would be incredibly dangerous, Jim."

"Kel, come on. There's nothing to worry about. It's just a stupid book left behind by someone who was obviously not all there." He tapped the side of his head with his forefinger.

"Jim don't, leave it be. The thing gives me a weird feeling. I'm serious." She crossed her arms across her chest.

Jim stopped and looked at his wife, finally noticing how upset she was.

"Look," he said. "I think this whole thing is bullshit. But if it isn't, I want to take a look at it before the contractors come back on Monday. Like I said, there might be money hidden in there."

He reached his hand out towards her face and caressed her cheek. "Look . . . it'll be alright. I won't damage it—I'll just try to open it and see if there's anything inside, okay?"

"I don't know," she said, shaking her head. "Both Brannigan and his wife wound up missing. Hell, we both read about it in the paper long before we knew about this house. Remember? And while I'm not sure that they stepped off into . . ." her voice trailed off not knowing what to call it, finally waving her hand towards the hole in the wall. "They may not have stepped off into that thing in there, but hoax or not, I don't want to tempt fate."

"It'll be okay, you'll see."

He walked across the room, stooping to enter the hole. Doubt written on her face, Kelly hesitated a moment before she, too, crossed the room to join him.

When she entered the confined space she saw that Jim had placed the crowbar on the floor and was busy trying to find a way to open the window. He examined the frame that housed the glass and located a silver knob and accompanying latch to the left of it. He turned the latch and heard a click as the window popped open slightly. He grabbed the small knob, pulling the window open wide.

It was as if a pressure door had been opened. The air rushed forward and both Jim and Kelly's ears popped. The glass was thrown back forcibly and the open space where the window had been shimmered as if a fine silk veil hung from the frame. The ambient light now filled the space they shared, bathing both of them in a cool cerulean glow. Kelly stepped back from the window, placing her hands over her ears; but Jim leaned forward, trying to catch a glimpse of whatever might be below.

"Oh my God," he whispered as he placed his hands on either side of the frame and peered inside. The mist swirled and danced before the opening, caressing his thoughts and inviting him to enter. The feeling that came from the window was as familiar and alluring as a former lover. He smiled and looked back at Kelly. "This is no hoax," he said.

Kelly didn't hear him. Her own experience was completely different from her husband's. As soon as the portal had been opened she was assaulted by what sounded like thousands of voices calling out in anger and despair. They seemed faint, as if heard from a great distance; but to Kelly's ears, it sounded like a multitude beyond reckoning. She stepped back towards the wall, the sound filling her with fear and a sense of loss. They invaded her mind, overshadowing her thoughts as surely as nightfall eventually blankets the day. Her eyes rolled in her head and she blinked rapidly, feeling disoriented. She felt a pressure on her chest; an invisible and undeniable presence seemed to come from the opening, rush into the small dark room, and wrap its cold grip upon her mind and body. It was full of malevolence and desire, and on some primordial level, she was certain it meant them harm.

Jim noticed none of this as he continued to gaze in wonder out the window, trying to perceive what lay beyond the haze. He was trying to figure out what called to him. The light that spilled through the small opening they'd scratched in the paint earlier now bathed him in its soft eldritch glow.

Kelly found herself repulsed by the light, seeing it as cold and evil. She felt that what it touched, it soiled with its malignancy. She felt much the same about the voices and yet, deep in her mind, she was intrigued by the sound of them, for they were like nothing she'd ever heard. She lowered her hands from her ears and cocked her head to one side trying to concentrate on them. Though they were disturbing, she thought she could almost make out distinct words. The pressure on her chest lifted as the sound decreased in volume. She detected an urgency in the voices, a need. She squinted her eyes as if it might somehow grant her understanding, yet she couldn't make out anything distinct. Each of the voices overlapped the other. She was certain that these disembodied voices were aware that the portal had been opened and were looking for it.

Looking for them.

Now that she'd actually put her feelings into words, she knew she was right. Whatever beings she heard, she knew that they were aware of her and Jim and were searching for them. Searching for a way out. They'd alerted what was on the other side to their presence.

She looked at Jim as if seeing him for the first time and became aware of his fascination with the opening. She tried to find her voice to tell him to shut the window, to shut it now before it was too late—but she could do little more than move her lips. The presence she felt held her.

Jim, oblivious of his wife's predicament, gazed through the opening, the mist was calling to him. He too heard the voices, but to his ears they sung an invitation.

An invitation to descend and join with them.

He was bewildered and fascinated. The mist seemed to know his name. It spoke to him directly, whispering, sighing and captivating.

It called to him and he answered.

He turned and smiled at Kelly, who still stood in the same place, unable to move or speak. Kelly looked at her husband, but in his eyes she saw he was transfixed, as if in a trance. He moved slowly, exiting the hole to grab a ladder from the other room. He re-entered the hole and, lifting the ladder, he maneuvered it towards the window until he had it through the opening, lowering it to whatever was below.

Kelly wanted to warn him, to tell him to close the window while there was still time. There issued from the opening a great dread, but she could only gaze mutely as he grabbed hold of a rafter over-head, lifted his legs through the opening and disappeared through the window. The voices within the opening changed in pitch and seemed at once to grow closer. The sound now was one of wicked glee . . . it had found what it had been searching for.

Kelly found her voice the moment Jim disappeared through the opening. She felt that whatever had been holding her immobile wanted no interference with Jim entering the portal. She took a step forward as if to grab her husband . . . even though he was already gone.

"No!" she screamed as she grabbed the edges of the frame, peering within. The fear she felt at her husband's strange behavior and his sudden departure through the window left her the moment she looked through the opening. The mist swirled and glided around the edges of the frame and appeared inviting now that she could see them up close. The evil voices she'd thought she heard were also gone. She wasn't certain she'd ever heard them at all. The sound that now came from the opening seemed more peaceful, more comfortable and inviting, like a lazy brook on a summer day. No wonder Jim had gone through to the other side.

"Jim," she whispered as she gazed at the swirling blue mist. They beckoned and called to her. The mist knew her name and invited her to come and join her husband.

She hesitated, trying to recall the feeling she had a moment ago. Hadn't she been scared? She couldn't recall now. It was like the dull throb of an old wound, still present but barely remembered.

The mist swayed just beyond the jam, whispering and sighing. It echoed and breathed just beyond the oval in front of her, assuring and serene. She could enter and be with Jim; she could follow him and together they could . . .

The thought was left unanswered as she followed her husband into the swirling mist.

Within the confines of the room the light from the window pulsed and glowed. The mist caressed the jam and moved faster, swirling around the edges. The sound of voices—if they were in fact voices—rose in volume as they grew closer. But nothing was left to hear it except for dust and shadow.

The window began to swing inward, closing slowly until, with a click, the glass once again lay seated within its sturdy frame. The illumination from the work light hanging from the beam above was the only light now as the bluish hue from the scratch in the paint pulsed brightly, then winked out.

Chris sipped his coffee, warming up from the chill of the early morning rain as he looked at the large hole in the wall. He gazed about, trying to figure out the mess in the room. He shrugged and began to make mental notes of the supplies they would need to pick up later in the week. He listened as the rest of his crew began to arrive below.

"They home?" Mike called out as he entered the room. He was Chris's longest employee and one of his best friends.

"Nah," Chris said as he sipped his coffee. "They're gone. I let myself in with the key under the planter out back."

"Seen the cars in the driveway and figured they didn't go out 'cuz of the rain. How long you been here?"

"About twenty minutes." He pointed towards the hole in the wall with the hand that held the coffee cup. "Nice, huh?"

Mike looked at the hole. "They helping out with the remodeling now?"

"Beats me."

"What's the plan for today?"

"Well," Chris said, turning to look at Mike, "have Bob start cleaning up some of this mess while you and Pat take the remainder of this wall down."

He set his coffee down as he walked over to the tools and grabbed a large hammer.

"What'll you be doing, then?" Mike asked as he walked to the door to call to the others below.

"I," Chris answered as he walked back to grab his coffee, "will be inside here tearing down that God-awful window. I want to break early for lunch, so have the rest of the guys get a move on."

He stepped through the hole in the wall to begin dismantling the window within.

THE
SONG THAT CRAWLED

ADAM S. HOUSE

Requiem Æternam

In the summer of 1933, Adrian sat on his bed, humming a new melody in his head, trying to piece it together just right before he selected an instrument for its audible awakening into this world. It was a beautiful August day. A warm breeze blew through the curtains of his bedroom, tickling the bangs dangling in front of his eyes and causing him to push them back while trying not to lose focus of the song. The intensity with which he thought was awe inspiring. His eyes were closed but moved rapidly around the room, which caused his eyelids to flick back and forth as he thought. The pollen in the air blew past the curtain and brushed his arms in a soothing way, similar to walking through the fields of wheat surrounding the farm. For an instant, time stood still and he was at the centre of his own universe, completely engulfed by a sense of contentment. He could almost see himself sitting on the bed, pollen frozen all around him as though it had stopped with time, beads of sweat standing still on his brow, eyelids motionless. Suddenly, the notes required for this song fell into place and he opened his eyes. He picked up his viola and began to play.

It was a love song. One not meant for new lovers but a song for loved ones lost. He slid the horse-hair bow across the strings and released the mournful song into the summer breeze, which carried it past the shore and into the ocean where mythical mermaids cried. Upon hearing this song, their tears raised the tides on the shore. The birds stopped singing. The wind stopped blowing. The picturesque blue skies turned grey and the sounds of the ocean turned into nothingness, a void of complete silence.

As he played on he began to cry. He was so into the song that he was not aware if he was visibly crying or alone in his mind . . . but he was crying nonetheless. They were the tears of a very mournful goodbye. A goodbye he had never wanted to say. It was impossible for words to ever express the feelings behind this goodbye, as words powerful enough did not exist; only the song did. For Adrian, this was the only way he could possibly say goodbye to his mother and the only way she would have wanted it. She was on her way home from the market as Adrian played his song when her car blew a tire and veered into oncoming traffic.

Lacrimosa

Ever since Adrian was a young boy, it was quite obvious to those around him that he had a natural talent for music. More importantly, he was passionate about it. Every second of every day Adrian thought of magical melodies dancing around his head, reflecting happiness, sorrow, longing, love, and all the emotions he never knew how to express without the aid of an instrument. When he was happiest, he would play the piano with such exuberance it would make the elderly feel young and vibrant again. If he was sad, he would play the viola with such innocence a sinner would weep upon hearing it. To say he had a gift would be an understatement; he lived for his music and was able to write it in a way that would have made Mozart envious. He was able to bend notes in his mind and translate them onto an instrument with such perfection that it rivaled Giotto's perfect hand drawn circle for the pope.

His mother had always been the biggest influence on him and the only person he cared to please. He would play the piano every Sunday and she would dance in the light that shone through the windows and glistened off antique tea cups and gold-rimmed china plates. The smell of the warm ocean came in off the coast of Nova Scotia while the wheat in the fields swayed to each individual note. The music filled the air with purity.

Adrian's father James was not as interested in his son's musical talents. He was a farmer who woke up at sunrise, performed his duties on the farm, ate three meals a day and was asleep by nine o'clock in the evening. He lived a viciously monotonous life with which he was more than content, save one aspect that his wife had seemed to encourage—his son's love of music. For James, music was a waste of precious time needed for the farm. Crops needed to be harvested, soil needed to be tilled, and animals needed to be fed—all on a never ending daily basis—and God gave him a weak son who cared more about music then earning a living. As a result of this resentment toward his son, the relationship between James and his wife had always been visibly strained.

Adrian didn't understand how two people like his parents—two so completely different people—could have ever been together in the first place, let alone pretend to be happy with one another while both secretly wanting something more. James wanted a son who could handle and take over the family farm, and his wife wanted a husband who was a loving father and could appreciate the talents of his son.

Dies Irae

The two years since Adrian's mother had passed away were filled with sorrow and chaos. His father had been verbally abusive to him on a daily basis and berated him more every day. With his mother gone, his happiness turned to memories long forgotten. He stayed in his room and played his music only for himself, refusing to allow anyone to hear his songs for fear it would remind him of the happiness he could no longer have. His father routinely came up to the bedroom to belittle him for no reason other than personal enjoyment. A few months after his mother's death, the abusive tongue of his father turned into physical beatings on occasion, but Adrian never gave James the satisfaction of crying. He wasn't really sure that he could cry any more even if he wanted to. He had become emotionally numb to everything.

It was getting late and as Adrian sat on the foot of his bed, he was distracted from his musical thoughts by the familiar sound of his father's footsteps coming up the stairs. Adrian just sat there, staring at his instruments. The door opened and James walked in with his belt already in hand.

"Come here," James said with a raspy, drunken voice. "I've got something for you." Adrian didn't move, so James continued forward and proceeded to whip him repeatedly with his leather belt, causing numerous lashes and cuts up the back of his shoulders and forearms. After a few minutes James turned to walk away, but before pulling the door shut he looked back at his son and said, "You know, it's your fault she's dead, playing that sad music. It should have been you!"

Adrian lay in bed trying to think about anything other than the life he was living. He stayed there a long while, thinking and staring out his window as the constellations rolled by in the night sky. He kept his viola under the blankets with him and placed the scroll end on the pillow as if it were the head of a companion sleeping at his side. Since his mother's death he had personified his instruments in an unconscious attempt to deter his isolation.

Loneliness can drive anyone mad. As he watched the constellations disappear from sight he faded away into his thoughts . . . where he had the most fantastic dream.

Sanctus

He awakens on the sandy dune of a desert where the air is hot and dry. The sun is so bright it causes him to blink constantly and forces his hands to his face to try to block some of the unrelenting glare off the sand. He can see that the desert goes on for miles and miles; it looks like it goes on forever. In one direction he can see a structure, a massive obelisk of sorts, protruding out of the ground and jutting several hundred feet in the air. It is charcoal black, diamond in shape, and at the top it comes to a peak where a light emanates from it upward into the heavens. He starts to walk towards it for what seems like hours without gaining any distance.

Suddenly, the end of the light, which disappears into the heavens, descends rapidly and enters the top of the obelisk, and the peak glows brighter and brighter by the millisecond. With a thunderous bang, the structure explodes with magnificent force. A massive gust of wind passes from the direction of the structure and is instantly followed by a blaze that incinerates everything in its path except Adrian, who is merely a spectator in this fantasy. Within seconds, everything is flattened. There are no more dunes, there is no more obelisk standing. There is nothing. The sand of the desert is vitrified and smooth as glass. Adrian looks up and the sky turns to night right before his eyes. The constellations look nothing like those he had viewed through his bedroom window. The sky is filled with a yellow-green tint that ripples in waves like the Atlantic off Nova Scotia during the changing of tides.

He feels a cold wind tear through him and lowers his view. No longer in the devastated desert, he sees he is in a frozen wasteland filled with mountains of ice and caverns littered with bones that appear intentionally thrown about. It is snowing consistently and blowing hard, but he does not care about the cold. He doesn't feel anything, but is simply *aware* of it. Through the darkness of night and the whiteout haze of the snow, Adrian can faintly see a figure in the distance walking towards him. It is tall—at least seven feet. Its features are hard to distinguish, as it was wearing a heavy black robe. The small, visible bit of jaw bone reveals it is scaly in appearance, as do its exposed hands. It is almost skeletal—or possibly reptilian looking. As the figure comes closer, its eyes shine bright red for a split second, alarming Adrian to the reality of this fantastic, unimaginable dream.

The figure stops in front of Adrian, looks down at him, and speaks. "You have suffered a loss . . . a death sensation has brought you to me." Its voice is rough and haggard, sounding like a deep-toned man speaking as he gargled corrosive cleaner. "In the Sea of Sorrow, you will find the song that crawls. Play it for the one." The figure turns and walks back into the snow covered darkness, and disappears into the haze of the snow just as mysteriously as he had appeared. Adrian turns around and sees a path where no snow is falling or blowing, as if it were laid out especially for him.

He walks along the path for a few minutes and reaches a small dock with a small rowboat secured to the end. He sits in the rowboat, and the moment he touches the oars he is in the middle of a sea with massive waves crashing down on him from every direction. He finds himself thrown into a storm of epic proportions, and is virtually helpless against its ravaging force. Through the sinister crashing waves he occasionally sees glimpses of massive, scaly, aquatic life that resemble nothing he can fathom. He closes his eyes, thinks of his music, and drifts away in his head. Soon the harsh sounds of thunder clapping and waves crashing turn into

more peaceful ones of a full orchestra within him. He is the maestro, and his mind is the baton. He can feel the movement of the sea wither away beneath him to the calmness of his thoughts. He opens his eyes to see the water level depleting as if it were a massive bath and someone had removed the plug. It lowers at a moderate but steady pace, and eventually lays him upon the muddy bottom of the sea. He steps out of the boat and sees a rock mound ahead. There is a faint sound of music coming from the direction of the rocks.

Upon investigating the rock mound, Adrian discovers, to his absolute astonishment, a doorway embedded in the stone. He opens the door and descends a long spiraling stairwell that feels like it goes on for hours. Eventually it comes to an end and opens into a large room that is dome shaped. Six different indents along the wall are each lit by a torch. The indents all contain statues, each one as smooth as the vitrified desert floor after the explosion . . . and they resemble beasts that can't possibly be real. They are not statues of humans or animals, but almost a bizarre hybrid of the two. In the middle of the room is an altar that holds a manuscript of some sort. Adrian can no longer hear the faint music that led him to the doorway and down the stairwell, but his eyes light up with pure excitement when he looks upon the manuscript. It contains the musical notes for a song that he himself could never conjure up on his own. The formation of these notes and the unique time signatures of the piece defy everything he ever thought about the way music could be written. It is more like a mathematical formula than a simple melody.

From the corner of his eye Adrian notices a faint yellow-green glow coming from the darkness of the room. He walks over to where he thought the light source was coming from and notices a hieroglyph-type painting on the wall. It depicts a creature hideous in nature coming up from the depths of the earth and devouring all that is presented to it. It appears to sustain itself this way. Adrian takes another look at the manuscript, closes his eyes, and sings the song in his head, trying it with various mental instruments in order to determine which would be best suited for this master-piece. He hears a glass-shattering shriek, and is slowly pulled back to reality.

Agnus Dei

Adrian sat up in bed, closed his eyes again, and started to play the song over and over in his head. He felt the notes crawl from one to another and ease their way into a cosmic bliss known only to a select few musicians throughout history. If the world were flat, this song would force it round, bringing everything together in a way so connected that all would be known, shared, and loved. Time and space would intertwine so flawlessly that anything and everything could be permitted. Memories would be the future and a place would just be a thought. He wondered if man was ready to hear such a piece of music. Would man even be able to comprehend it enough to appreciate its true potential?

A few hours went by while Adrian dwelt on the melody in his head, reminiscing over the strange, archaic world he visited within his dreams. The experience felt so real and alive that he questioned its authenticity. Regardless, the song that crawled out of the dream world when he awoke was very much a real, living piece of music. He was not yet sure of the reason for the song, but knew it had a very significant importance to him and his well-being. He felt the song could take his whole life and make it complete; a life he longed for where he could be alone and lavish in the joys of his songs.

Hours passed as he was left in solitude with his thoughts, and it was nearing dinner time. He could hear his father in the kitchen, throwing things around as if he was engaged in a battle. He headed down the stairs and sat at one end of the table. A small bowl of soup had been placed on the placemat in front of him. His father sat at the opposite end, eating a large piece of roast beef, mashed potatoes, and assorted vegetables. There was also a large bowl of soup with several packets of sodium crackers piled next to it, and a large pint of Indian Pale Ale. Adrian looked to the left at the empty place where his mother once sat, looking radiant and pleased as she discussed the joys of music with her beloved son. There was no more conversation of such things; just an empty seat at a cold table. He ate his soup slowly but steadily, every once in a while giving a quick glance around the room. He noticed his father's eyes were always maliciously fixated on him.

James stared at his son with a look of pure hatred and disappointment—almost as if he blamed the entire world's problems on his son—but Adrian was more than used to this, as it happened every time he ate a meal at this lonely, long dead table. Once he finished his soup, Adrian slowly picked up his empty bowl and made his way to the sink where he rinsed it. As he let the cold water from the well splash back and forth on the bowl, it slipped out of his hands and shattered throughout the big farmhouse sink. Before the sound of the breaking bowl faded, he heard the sound of his father's fork and knife slam into his plate, causing Adrian to turn around just in time to receive a thudding backhand to the left temple. He dropped to the floor from the near-knockout blow. As his vision started to return, he felt an unrelenting pain in his chest. It was the impact of his father's work boots making an imprint with each stomp he took, forcing the boy to the hardwood floor and into unconsciousness.

Lux Æternum

Adrian awoke on the kitchen floor. The night sky was already dark through the picture window. He found it difficult to breathe, and his chest was severely bruised from the assault he endured. There was a midnight-black welt on the left side of his temple and trails of dried blood from both nostrils. He picked himself up slowly and limped to the washroom to clean up. Through the doorway, he could see his father passed out in his chair in the living room, empty bottles scattered all around him. The door made a slight creaking sound every time it moved, so he tried his best to quiet it as he carefully closed it behind him. Like a cat in the night, he made his way up the stairs of the old farmhouse and into his room. He climbed into bed and stared out his window while watching as again the constellations slowly drifted by over time. He closed his eyes and thought of all the things he missed. He thought of that far-off world in his dream and wondered if he would ever see that place again. He felt a glare through his eyelids as he lay in bed, as if someone suddenly turned on a light in a darkened room. His eyes opened, and to his astonishment, he was back at the doorway at the bottom of the drained sea.

Libera Me

The door is already open, and he hears the beautiful song coming from the depths of the long spiraling stairwell. No time is wasted as he immediately heads through the door and begins his descent down the stairs into the unknown dream that awaits. Once he reaches the bottom, he is again in the dome shaped room—but he isn't alone this time. Off to the side, he sees the outline of the figure that met him in the frozen wasteland. The figure makes his way towards him, and with a slow methodical gesture lowers the hood of his darkened robe to expose his face. It is large and scaly, yellow-green in complexion with ridges and tiny skeletal horns protruding from it in symmetrical sequences all over. Its mouth is not the same shape as a man's, as it appears to open in two separate directions: top to bottom like a man's, but also left to right. When opened, it looks like a perfect circle. Most of its teeth are small and sharp little nails, except for four, which are large fangs, and located on each side of the mouth. They almost appear to be too big as they extend past the opposing sides of the mouth. Next to its ears are extensions of webbed-reptilian skin which jut out a few inches and descend downward, ending as they join the collar bone.

For a second, the creature's eyes shine a glowing red color, and as they dissipate it speaks. "Play the song . . . see the one . . . crawl." The creature's eyes begin to glow red again but they do not fade away this time. They grow brighter and brighter, then quickly become so bright that Adrian can see nothing but red and is forced to shut his eyes and cover them with the palms of his hands. A moment passes and Adrian lowers his hands. He is in his room, sitting up in bed and sweating profusely. He takes a moment to gather his composure, but he knows exactly what he has to do. He has to play the song.

Without hesitation he reaches for his finest viola and makes his way down the stairs. His father lay sleeping in his chair, still passed out from the consumption of too much pale ale. With his instrument ready, Adrian sits in the love seat on the opposite side of the room, the place he used to sit to entertain his mother on those longed for Sunday afternoons. He raises the viola to his shoulder and places his chin on the guard while extending the wooden bow until it hovers over the strings. He begins to play. A song is heard throughout the farmhouse that can't be described in words. It echoes a history of untold musicians and defies everything of which a song is capable.

His father's eyes open immediately, but he cannot move. He is paralyzed in the chair and completely entranced by the song being played. Adrian sees a black mist forming at his father's feet, spiraling faster and faster as it grows in size, like a tornado preparing to release itself on an unsuspecting landscape. Within the growing vortex that is forming, he sees flashes of electricity and what appear to be stars; complete constellations. These are not the usual constellations he is accustomed to, but the unrecognizable ones he had dreamt about in that fantastic land of mystery. He plays on, harder and with more emotion than ever before. He feels alive again for the first time since the loss of the only person he ever loved, and when he realizes the joy he is feeling, he begins to cry. The moment he sheds his first tear, two hands are thrown out of the vortex and rest on either side of it. Using the hardwood floor as leverage, something forces its way out. A creature begins to crawl its way into this world. It is the massive reptilian from the dream. Its yellow-green eyes begin to glow red as it crawls slowly out of the vortex and clenches his father. Adrian smiles and vigorously plays the impossible song with more emotion than ever imaginable. His father's eyes are wide open and his skin is a pale shade of white, but he is unable to move in any way. The creature creeps complacently back into the vortex as the song crawls along . . . and James is no more.

In Paradisum

After James missed several appointments to deliver livestock, the market began to call his house on a regular basis to inquire about the deliveries. They tried for two days before sending a representative to check the old homestead for fear James may have fallen ill, or possibly been injured while tending to the farm. When the representative arrived, James was nowhere to be seen; but

Adrian was in the front room playing the piano peacefully and beautifully. At this point, the representative decided to contact the local authorities to report a missing person.

After two days of searching the area, Adrian sat alone in the back of the sheriff's patrol car smiling uncontrollably at the happiness he had felt since his father's disappearance. He spent the time reminiscing about his mother and played music for her memory on the piano she used to adore hearing. Over the seat and through the front windshield of the Ford Model cruiser, he could see Sheriff Mackay and Deputy Grant walking out of the farmhouse. They looked distraught and confused. As they approached the cruiser, Adrian could hear them as they tried to figure out what exactly happened to his father. They leaned on the hood of the cruiser and began to talk about the matter as if he wasn't even there.

"I don't get it, Sheriff. We've checked this entire homestead for two solid days now, and we haven't found a thing," The deputy sounded frustrated. "There isn't one single piece of evidence here to help us out."

"Well, who says he wants to be found or helped?" Adrian's smiling face fixated on the Sheriff though the car's windshield, curious about their theories as he knew no one would ever be able to comprehend the true horror which had taken place in the farmhouse. "Truth is he probably hitched a ride down to the harbor and jumped a merchant ship out to sea for a new life. Just had enough of being alone on this farm here."

"Sheriff, what kind of grown man abandons his young son and takes off for a new life?" Adrian could see the Deputy looked even more confused at this point. "That makes no sense to me at all!" the deputy said disgustedly.

"Come on, Deputy, you know it was no secret what James thought of the young lad here. I'm surprised he didn't do something cowardly like this shortly after his wife died, or even worse, cause some harm to the boy." Adrian could see from the sheriff's eyes that he truly did not like James, and would not likely be too upset to find out that James had expired. "What we have to do now is get this boy where he needs to be. I'll have the dispatcher at headquarters notify personnel at the Waterville asylum of Adrian's arrival and arrange to have him transported there first thing in the morning."

"You're going to send him to the Waterville asylum, Sheriff?"

The sheriff gave a stern look and took his hat off so the deputy could see the seriousness of his face.

"Deputy, do you really think any families in these parts are going to want to take in a mute, mongoloid boy who has lost both his parents? I hate to say it, but the asylum is really the only option."

Adrian turned his attention from the police officers and looked over the landscape. He looked past the fields of wheat and out into the open Atlantic. He watched the mist from the waves breaking on the shore as it spread through the sky, causing small rainbows to appear and disappear in seconds. He smelled the pollen as it floated in the breeze and penetrated the senses like no other form in nature. He smiled continuously and joyously as the song crawled around his mental orchestra as if guiding him to a world of bliss that he had longed to feel for so long. For Adrian, everything was perfect.

HUNGRY
AS THE WIND

JONATHAN MOON

Detached. Cold. Distant.

Check, check, and check.

What else had she said? Oh, yeah—"Goodbye."

Why am I thinking about this now? Is this my life flashing slowly before my eyes? Rendered into a series of depressing snap-shot memories to distract my mind from the goddamned howling of the wind? My regrets will make my fear seem hollow, and I've seen the wind chew them up—all of them. I know the wind is still hungry. Always hungry.

The tent flaps at me from every angle, as cyclonic winds batter my feeble shelter.

Detached. Cold. Distant.

There it is again. I don't think this is some instinctive coping method. This is something more than that. The wind beckoned me away from her, right down into this graveyard canyon. And soon, soon it will snatch me up with its terrible claws and tear me into pieces.

Detached. Cold. Distant.

I'm not enough weight to keep the tent on the ground. It's going to wrap me up, my own nylon burial shroud. I'm going to go outside. And when the wind grows tired of toying with me and finally comes for the kill, I'll let it take me . . .

Because I'll be taking it to Hell with me.

Two Weeks Earlier

Matt stands in front of the window overlooking the back yard, his cell phone held up to his ear. The look on his face may be slack and blank, but the gears in his mind are grinding along steadily enough. His eyes are bloodshot and cheeks bearded with three-day stubble, pale under the dark fuzz. In a single glance he notices the ancient swing-set in the backyard with the crabgrass clustered around its metal support legs like the fur on Clydesdales, the billowing cotton-like seed from the popular trees coating everything in a layer of slick tree-born white . . . and Lisa, standing behind him with her arms folded across her chest and her scowl telling him everything she wants to but won't because he's on the phone with his boss.

He processes a mental mosh pit of thoughts for each visual observation: *I promised Lisa five damn years ago we'd be married and have a child in six months. I'd pointed at the swing-set and told her I would fix it up as soon as we knew the sex so I could paint it pink or blue. I need to mow the damn lawn—looks like fucking meth-heads live here. If the cotton is falling from the trees then it must be full-on summer, the sappy pods of spring having left their stink and stain for another season, God bless ya, nature.* He recalls the recent souvenirs taken from Vegas: beet-red skin and tender bags under the eyes . . . three bruised ribs. *I look like shit and we both know it. But that's what work gives us besides gobs of money. Affliction. Some skill set there, pal. You've become pretty adept at trading the freedom of others and your own for cash, all in the name of financial security.*

These observations tie directly to the next blurry rail. *Look at her. She is going to leave you this time. No excuses, no promises, no nothing. She is done. We are done.* Those words she had screamed in his face, a vain and childish attempt to draw any form of emotion from him, still hum and burn like freshly swallowed whiskey.

Detached. Cold. Distant.

And all this while his boss William Baird rambles on about how Matt is going to be spending his weekend. He tells him to pack his sleeping bag and shotgun and he'll be picking him up in half an hour, be outside and ready.

Matt ends the call and turns to face Lisa. He can't read her expression beyond the obvious anger. He doesn't know what she wants to hear or what he should say. So he is honest.

"I have to go camping this weekend."

Lisa scoffs, "Oh, is that right? You got home less than forty-eight hours ago and already can't wait to get the hell away from me?"

"I'm doing all this for *us.* You know it's not personal, and I really don't want to fight about it. Just one—"

"Oh, there's no fight *here,* Matt. It's not personal—*right?*" Her tone echoes Matt's and with brutish certainty he knows what she is going to say. *Here it comes. Don't act surprised, stupid—you knew this was going to happen. You knew and you did nothing.* "I'm leaving now, Matt. I can't fucking do this anymore."

He says nothing. Not even when she begins crying. Not even when she leaves the front door open and storms out. Not even while she sits in the driveway with tears streaking down her face, letting the car run for five minutes before finally pulling away.

Matt grabs a beer and sits on his front porch. He's on his third with no sign of stopping when his aptly named boss pulls up in a forest green Escalade.

William's thick dark beard presses back the collar of his army fatigue jacket. He sees Matt waiting and taps his faded blue fishing cap at him. The thick, elaborately twisting mustache twitches, signaling a smile as he hangs out the window and shouts, "This is going to be a *fun* job. I love chasing these survival nuts down. I'm hoping we can bag these shitheels quick enough so I can get some fishing in, ya dig?"

"I hear you." Matt crumples the can and chucks it over his fence. He stacks his sleeping bag, backpack, tent, and duffel bag in the cargo space next to William's tightly packed supplies. Under a flap of canvas Matt sees the corner of a charcoal crate with the unmistakable "HK" painted in red. He takes a quick mental measurement and the sober words form in his mind, killing his buzz: *Grenades. What the hell are we doing with grenades?*

Deciding not to say anything about them yet, Matt closes the back and moves to the passenger side. "Survival jobs, huh. So—what's the take?"

William Baird laughs and his mountain man beard quivers. "Juicy, friend. *Real* juicy."

Matt doesn't smile—in part because he didn't receive a real answer. But he nods it off for now, knowing he'll circle back and squeeze it from the tight lipped William Baird soon enough. He settles into the passenger side, using the first several moments of the drive to adjust his seat with the assortment of knobs and switches he finds at the base.

While he is maximizing his comfort, wishing he'd had the foresight to grab his flask, William makes an announcement. "Gotta pick up Rocco and Lance and then we'll be headed up into the hills."

"Both of them? I thought they hated each other."

"They do." The twitching mustache signals another smile hidden somewhere under the caveman face-do.

Matt can't shake the image of the red letters and the slim case in the back. Throwing the other two savages into the mix makes him uneasy. "And how many people are we chasing down if there are four of us?"

William waves the question away, knowing Matt can get on a roll with his questions and can work that roll right back around to the subject of payment. He's known Matt longer than the others in his employ, and still has the hardest time reading him and not being walked in whatever circles Matt calmly chooses to manipulate him into. It's one of the reasons he likes Matt so much more than the others: his tact. The brutes Rocco and Lance, the *Brothers Trouble,* tended to fall short in that category.

William loves his job. There's no reason to hide one's motives in the human tracking business; you can really see what makes a man tick when you hunt other human beings for a living. Matt works for William The Beard because he can utilize his cold determination, tracking skills, and calmness under pressure. Rocco works for The Beard so he can beat people up and flex his tattooed arms while doing so; a rabid animal whose savageness can be reasonably focused for whatever brutal tasks are set upon him. Lance works for The Beard to supplement the meager disability the military pays him for taking a few chunks of shrapnel the size of a soda bottles to his neck and leg just south of Bagdad. That, and the rigid, socially-awkward, six-foot-six ex-soldier has himself a few vices which require him to assume the mercenary role from time to time (like a monthly need for a good rail or two of Dirt to keep the night terrors away), of which William has no problem taking advantage.

This is the first time he has had to call in his three best for a job. William wanted the score to be a surprise, especially for Matt—but he knows Matt isn't going to let it go. He can already tell that the wife thing has gone downhill, and he doesn't feel like getting the blunt end of Matt's mind-shovel today.

William The Beard pulls down the floppy bill of his fishing cap and hunches his shoulders with a sigh. "Two of them. So—" he holds up his fingers, "that's four of us, two of them. Fair odds, right?"

Matt nods at this logic, but it's plain to see his gears are still turning. "Okay, normal enough. It's always at least the two of us. And then the other two psychos as backup . . ."

Used to Matt's little mind traps (like assuming the last was spoken as a question), William elects to play dumb and remain silently hidden under his scowl and beard.

"But what I'm wondering *now*," Matt continues, "is what kind of badasses would require all three of your most adept players, when we all know you have those who are cheaper. *Much* cheaper."

An uncomfortable silence. Then déjà vu all over again, and William wonders: *Haven't we been here before? Right. Fucking. Here? No wonder Lisa's gone, buddy. Your relentless mistrust probably picked every bit of meat off her soul, too.*

Through with games, Matt springs the trap. "What's my take, Will?"

William licks his lips. His pink tongue darts from his mass of beard and he clears his throat. "If we get both of 'em—and there's no *if* there, my friend . . ." William lets it hang in the air to build suspense. Then, without fanfare: "Two hundred K."

William is pleased to watch this bit of info act like a wrench thrown into Matt's mental gears. For a full minute there is a no sound but the road under the wheels and wind pushing through the cracked windows.

"So," Matt begins, "we are chasing down a million dollar bounty this weekend." He nods his understanding without needing his boss's confirmation.

William's arched eyebrows tell him he is on the right track. "Yeah, yeah." Another wave in the air swiping away the conversation, and now the beard can't hide William's defeated irritation. "You figured it out, smart guy. We are following a couple of big bounties into the wild frontier this weekend. If you can wait until we meet up with the rest of the crew, I'll go over everything in a nice little package. That okay with you?"

"Two hundred K?" Matt squints one eye at his agitated boss.

"Okay, if you can keep it to yourself, I'll throw in a fifty K bonus, 'cuz I know you just got back from that Vegas job and didn't get your R and R yet."

Matt opens his mouth to thank him, but William chuckles and quickly adds, "Shit, I bet Lisa is pissed."

Matt says nothing.

"So? Is she pissed or what, asshole?" William slaps the steering wheel in frustration.

Matt tilts his head to the window as he considers the question. "Yeah. I guess you could say she's pretty pissed."

William is floored by actually reading an emotion from Matt—it's happened maybe twice since they first met. There's a glimmer of something which could be sadness or longing in those clear, blue eyes—and it worries him. He decides not to pick at the obvious wound. Instead he points at the trailer becoming visible up the gravel road and the two huge men standing chest to chest and nose to nose in front of it.

"Guess Rocco decided to meet us here. Must be *real* excited for this hoorah." William chuckles deviously under his beard and pulls up behind Lance's jacked-up F250.

Matt curls the corners of his mouth in an effort to fulfill the acknowledgment of humor, but the action is shallow and awkward. William honks and the two giants turn their angry stares on the Escalade instead of each other.

"William, goddamn it!" Lance shouts before William can even come to a complete stop. "Why are you sending this crazy scumbag to my home?"

"Your home has never been so classy as when I stood on your rickety-ass porch and knocked on your fiberglass door." Rocco backs up his taunt with an arrogant grin that crosses his smooth, handsome face. It's no secret that he considers himself the Casanova of the human recovery biz.

The smell of charged sweat in the air could rival a pit-fight arena. Stepping toe-to-toe with the other brute, Lance's neck muscles twitch and William shouts over them both in an attempt to defuse the dangerous situation. He jabs at his watch. "Hey! We're on the clock, fellas—clamp the shit and climb in. We've got a bitch of a drive ahead and then one hell of a hike waiting at the end of it."

Lance thumbs in Rocco's direction. "I am not riding in the same vehicle as this asshole. I'll follow in my own rig."

William smiles at Matt as the burly bounty hunter stomps off to his old beaten Ford. William leans across Matt's lap and shouts out the window at Lance while Rocco slams his backpack into the remaining cargo space. "Hey, don't you wanna hear about the job? About your take?"

Lance doesn't even turn around. He answers as he opens the mismatched red door on his otherwise blue pickup with a hateful squeal of metal on metal.

"Later."

William nods and shifts the Escalade into gear. They roll away from the trailer park.

"Rocco wants to know about the job and the take, don't you, Rocco-ol' pal?" Matt says while looking out the window at the stop-motion scenery.

Rocco is kicked back against the leather, sunglasses hiding his eyes, thick head resting back against his palms to give him maximum flexing potential. He smirks at Matt, but it fades as he considers it.

"Yeah, I guess I do."

William flips Matt off. "Fine. Rocco, we are chasing down two high dollar bounties this weekend, and they are supposedly survival nuts—more paranoid than Lance's meth-head neighbors. We are following them into a thick forest up on that Hoo-Doo mountain. Nasty terrain, and spooky as hell anyways. Everybody else is looking in the wrong spot . . . but I got the golden tip others just don't have a clue about."

"*So . . .*" Matt verbalizes for a speechless and confused looking Rocco.

William huffs, "So? So big pay day, Rocco. We nab them both and you're pocketing fifty K."

The resounding celebratory sound Rocco makes is reminiscent of drunken frat boys and dying elephants. Matt winces at the sound while The Beard laughs out loud and turns up the classic rock radio.

There is very little conversation for the remainder of the ride.

Matt, always more content being observant to those around him rather than left alone to his own thoughts, keeps an eye on Lance in the pickup behind them. The old truck belches black puffs of exhaust smoke as it drifts across the double yellow line and back. Matt shakes his head when he notices Lance alone in his pickup talking to himself in a rather animated and irritated fashion. Somewhat content, Matt sighs. He'd easily take Blue Oyster Cult over Lance's—or anyone else's, really—ranting and raving any day of the week.

Time passes quickly enough, and before nightfall the men are pulling up to a motel in the town of Dry Hill at the base of the mountain. William springs for two rooms, but Lance refuses to sleep indoors with any of them; his expletive-ridden objections are barked across the parking lot and punctuated with a hoarse "Nothing personal" before he slams the truck door behind him. The others shrug it off, and William takes the second room for himself without bothering to ask. Matt and Rocco each crash on a twin bed in the first.

Matt tosses and turns, the sleep of the heavy-headed. In his dreams her words echo endlessly in a wind that roars around him, though the tall pine trees surrounding him remain anciently still.

Detached. Cold. Distant.

He finally feels the wind, her words slicing at his flesh like verbal razorblades within the howling gale as it engulfs him. The pain is terrible, and as it reaches a crescendo he awakens to Rocco's Budweiser-reeking snores and early morning sunlight spilling in through the cracks of the heavy brown drapes.

Matt wipes the sleep from his eyes, and within minutes The Beard is knocking at the door. Matt looks at Rocco, chainsaw snoring nearly as loud as the pounds on the door, then gets up to let his boss in. He opens the door, blocking the morning glare with his forearm. William and Lance stand there, shadowy hulks, ready to go.

William looks like a cat digesting a canary ever-so-slowly while the big man over his shoulder is looking twice as bad as he did on the drive up yesterday. Matt leaves the door open for them while he takes a leak and grabs his jacket. Lance refuses and returns to his pickup to let it run. William walks around the bed and the snoring Rocco. He pinches the giant's nose closed and with a few muffled snorts Rocco is coerced into reality. They grab a dozen doughnuts and coffees—which Lance rudely refuses, "Fucking sulfates!"—and are on the road within fifteen minutes.

William leads them with a map he doesn't let Matt or Rocco see, and within an hour they are deep the bowls of the gnarly Hoo-Doo forest at a point too tangled and wild for the vehicles to maneuver any further. They strap into their packs and, after William consults his mysterious map, head deeper into the shadows of the trees. Within ten minutes they find a highly-enhanced Jeep wedged between a boulder and the trunk of an ancient evergreen. A fierce looking rock outcropping has buried itself in the Jeep's under-carriage like a knife in the belly.

Smugly, William fluffs his dark beard and twists on his mustache. "You three may be damn good at what you do, but I assure you, gentlemen—I am also *damn* good at what I do."

He looks at his crew and smiles with a mix of pride and un-spoken worry. Matt is climbing and crawling around the Jeep, searching intently for any clue of the direction the men went on foot. Rocco kneels down and pulls out his twin shock batons: two inch-thick alloy rods with electrified tips. Lance digs into a duffle bag and retrieves an assortment of tranq-guns, which he loads and distributes to Matt and William. Then he digs out a pair of AK-47s and four magazines.

Matt eyes the rifles with mild suspicion. "That's some heavy hardware, Lance."

He says nothing of Lance's trembling pale hands that engage the mags.

"You ain't got a fancy shotgun in your duffle bag there, cutie-pie?" Lance snarls back.

"I do," Matt admits. "A damn *fancy* shotgun. But it shoots special beanbags meant to subdue—not buckshot meant to slaughter."

"You ain't gotta shoot 'em. I brought 'em for the boss and me anyhow." Lance nods at William, who solemnly accepts the gun offered to him. He avoids eye contact with Rocco and Matt as he leads them past the Jeep.

"Where you going, Will?" Matt asks.

"You find anything to tell me where they went, Matt?" he snaps back.

"Nope. Not a damn thing."

"Yeah, I didn't think you would. So, I'm going to follow my gut feeling," he gives his modest beer belly a loving jiggle, "and it says *this* way."

Matt has a number of questions, and he knows asking them and receiving their answers will only lead to more. He chokes it down and falls in line. Just beyond the totaled crawler the air takes on a thick, almost metallic taste. Lance begins talking with himself under his breath, rotating between whimpering, laughing, and crying. He begins staring up into the trees with wide eyes and gaping jaw. Matt opens his mouth to say something when the big man moans something about the wind, but William grabs his arm to silence him in advance.

Matt looks at the hand gripping his bicep as if it is a riddle just beyond his wit. William explains quickly and quietly. "You might give Lance some space today. He was curled up in a ball and crying his eyes out this morning when I tapped on the window to his truck. He started ranting about the wind and how it blew so hard it was rocking his pickup all night."

"I didn't hear any wind last night," Matt notes.

"Yeah," William acknowledges, "but don't try telling him that. He said he heard it sharpening its claws across the hood and roof of his truck."

"What?"

William chuckles nervously. "Yeah, and when he told me he heard it whispering his name, I asked him if he wanted to sit this one out."

Matt watches Lance from behind. The big man is a mess today and would have a hard time sneaking up on a dead beaver, much less a couple of men skilled in wilderness survival.

"And he didn't."

"Nope," William answers, shaking his head, "but that fella walks a fine line between psychotic and out and out crazy. So let's just play it cool around him, huh?"

Matt wants very badly to ask William why the hell he would encourage someone so obviously unbalanced to tote around a fully automatic weapon. But before he has a chance to question his boss, Rocco and Lance find something, signaling back with a well-rehearsed whistle. Matt finds himself hurling calmly towards a chaos he can feel like static on his skin.

The others end up waiting on Matt, who has more difficultly navigating the dense woodlands with his full pack. It's as if the signals supposed to be going to his limbs are getting caught in the tangled mess of his mind. He finds them standing around a small handmade log cabin. A cow skull hangs on the weathered front door, and two small windows with colorful yet dusty blanket drapes are on either side. Two pipes protrude from the sharp A-frame roof and smoke drifts out lazily. William and Lance have their AKs aimed at the front door. Having taken the time to roll up the sleeves of his tee shirt, Rocco holds a shock baton in each meaty fist. Matt shakes his head at the lot of them.

"Don't worry guys, I'll knock." Matt lets his pack crash to the ground alongside his beanbag gun. He swaggers past the others to the front door, ignoring their protests and curses. As he steps on the rickety porch a round tanned face pops up behind the window left of the door. The dark eyebrows raise, the wide forehead taking on an excess of surprised wrinkles. A face very similar pops into the opposite window and mimics that of the first man. The two men stare past Matt to the armed hulks: Rocco flexing and swiping shock batons as if striking at the ghosts of his past captures, Lance twitching and growling with the AK butted up to his muscular shoulder, and William The Beard cradling his AK comfortably, long thick beard hanging to the middle of his chest and mustache twisted like a flamboyant western gun fighter, shadowed by the floppy circular bill of his blue fishing cap.

Matt realizes how crazy they must look, and the overwhelmed terror etched on the worried faces of the two Native American men confirms this. He raises his hands and does a slow turn to show nothing hidden in his pants. He snaps at the others to lower their weapons. Rocco and Lance both look to William, who finally nods and lowers the Russian death machine to point at the ground instead of the cabin.

By the time Matt is facing the cabin again, his hands held open at shoulder-height, the two native men are standing outside their respective windows. Each has an ancient rifle trained on him; one aimed high, and one aimed low.

The same expression can be seen in each bounty hunter's face: *Jesus they're quick!* The situation teetering towards volatile, Matt throws a look at Lance, whose trigger finger has crept back onto the AK's sweet spot. Matt makes sure that the brute's eyes meet his own and hopes his point makes it across: *Stand down, dammit!*

"Sorry if we spooked you, sirs," William offers as he slips comfortably into business mode. "We're bail bond collectors, with strong evidence that a couple of skips are hiding somewhere nearby."

"Well, ain't nobody been around in a long, long time," the taller native expresses.

His counterpart adds, "We're the only ones living out here, and we'd know if people came sneaking through."

"I understand that, sirs," William retorts, "but maybe you could just hear us out a minute." He commences explaining the soft version of their mission and the terrible men they are chasing. Busy eyeing the damp ground around the cabin, Matt hears the spill on a subconscious level. He hears his name spoken as William makes quick introductions of them all, and he gives a wave without looking at the men. Luckily, the situation grows calmer and the talk more friendly. Matt catches their names as Gil and Fred, but doesn't look up to see which is which. He's more interested in the shallow boot print stamped into the pine needle-littered mud twenty feet north of the cabin.

The natives are bragging about their claimed status as sentries to the gorge-carved mountain side beyond their cabin, which is considered sacred land to their tribe and their holy duty to protect.

Matt interrupts them. "I found a boot print, Will."

The natives scoff at the deadpan tracker. William's mustache curls up with his smile, and he tips his cap at the two men before turning to see Matt's find. Gil and Fred share a look of doubt, but Matt sees a more intense emotion growing just under the surface. Something darker. Like dread, perhaps. The bountymen give in to their curiosity and hustle over to see the reported print.

"I'll be damned!" William hoots.

"It could just be one of theirs," Rocco complains, pointing a shock baton at Gil and Fred.

"Different tread," Matt explains. Everyone leans in to take note of the firmly cut print left from a nice new pair of tactical boots. All together they turn and look at the knee-high moccasins Gil and Fred are wearing. As if to show the boot print is no fluke, Matt crouches next to the print and points in a path running past the cabin at an angle. While everyone else leans forward to see what Matt is showing them, the natives both go pale. Gil and Fred gawk at the three bloody limbs, fractured and hanging in the unnatural brown smear across the nearby rock formation. The natives both sit down on the same downed log, their souls paler than the white men surrounding them.

William's ear to ear grin shines through his facial hair. He turns to the natives. "We gotta chase 'em down, boys. We'll be able to compensate y'all for passing through once we have 'em in custody."

Galvanized by the prospect of chase, Matt, Rocco, and Lance all start down the path before them slowly and cautiously. William looks to both Gil and Fred for acknowledgment, but they only sigh and stare at each other, as if neither wants to give it. Before his men can move more than ten feet, both shout at the same time.

"Stop! Hold it right there! You don't want to go any farther . . ."

Only Matt obeys. The sudden shift of the natives' composure has him spooked. Rocco only scoffs at their words and horrified tones, and Lance rambles forward, looking like the only voices reaching him are in his own head. Gil and Fred jump up and wave their arms at Rocco and Lance as they disappear into the thick dimness of the forest.

"You'll never come back—you'll only find death in the gorges! Your death with come with the wind!" Their panic is primal and electric and has William visibly shaken. He gets the feeling the men would raise their rifles and stop them with flesh-wound warnings if he didn't still have his sweaty hands on his AK47.

"They aren't going to stop," Matt tells the natives, in hopes they will at least stop screaming.

From the copse beyond the cabin, Lance lets go a wild scream; then comes his ragged guffaws, like an enraged idiot child.

"Will, we have to go after them. If there is something you fellas know that could give us an edge against the scumbags we are chasing down, that'd be mighty keen."

Gil speaks through numb lips. "Ain't nobody going past here will be coming back. The *Wendigo* dwells on the mountainside, hunting through the many small gorges. We were supposed to keep people away . . . to keep them safe."

A cavalcade of shouts erupts down the path. Neither Matt nor William wait to see if the men have anything else to say, or if they follow. After sharing a long worried look, Gil and Fred do.

As the others reach the sound of conflict, the rattle of rifle fire cracks through the air with electrical force. William, Gil and Fred all duck and cover, while Matt remains standing, wincing as he stares at the result of the clatter.

Lance is standing over a man wearing camouflage fatigue pants, a sweat and blood stained t-shirt, and boots looking like they'd match the track at the head of the path. The bullets tore through the corpse's chest, leaving several fist sized craters dotting its torso. Blood is splattered all over the small clearing. Standing behind a green tarp hanging between two trees is a blood soaked Rocco.

William slowly stands back to his feet and approaches the chaotic scene. He sees the bullet-riddled corpse. He sees his payday splattered all over the clearing.

Having already seen the corpse, Matt instead focuses on the murderous glow in Lance's eyes. He senses the big man has gone around a bend from which he won't be coming back . . . and wonders if he might just take as many people with him as he can.

William's fury is evident; the little flesh uncovered with fur on his face turns a scarlet red. However, once he is close enough to feel the madness coming off of Lance in waves he turns his attention to a slack-jawed Rocco.

"What the *fucking hell* happened?"

Rocco opens and closes his mouth a few times before any words come tumbling out. "The guy was just sitting here, crying and . . . and cutting away at himself. He was so excited to see us—he jumped up and started waving his bloody arms around." The tough guy lowers his voice, careful to turn away from Lance's ear. Lance is staring at tree tops again. Rocco nods at the corpse. "Then the asshole started talking crazy, saying the wind was going to eat him up. Said it already ate his buddy. Said . . . said it was gonna eat us up, too."

Having weaved through the carnage, Gil nods solemnly at the man's final words. Fred can't take his eyes off of a drooling and chuckling Lance. Rocco's eyes dart from his crazed partner to the men around him. His knuckles are white from clenching his batons.

"That's about when Lance smashed his face in with the butt of the AK. Dude hit the ground and Lance lit 'em up. Bang bang, game over, muthafucka."

"So the other guy ain't here?" William huffs.

Rocco waves his shock baton around the small clearing. "What you see is what I see, boss."

"He was telling you the truth," Gil states sadly. "Your bounty was right. None of us will leave here alive."

William's sudden shout clatters around the rocky canyon. "Oh, well, with this asshole *dead* and his asshole partner missing, I'm sure's shit not sticking around! Many a hope and dream has just been smashed for me, thank you fellas. I'm leaving—and if anyone gets in my way they'll end up looking like GI Jack over there. C'mon, boys. We're going fishing."

Nobody moves to follow William, and he stomps past them all before Rocco finally stumbles after—slowly, as if trudging through muck and mire. Gil and Fred exchange doubtful looks, but shoulder their rifles and follow. Matt watches Lance, snapping his head back and forth and growling in a strange echoing way through the rivers of drool drizzling off his chin.

"Will—what about Lance?"

"He is no longer under my employ." Gil steals a frightened look back, but William shouts without turning. "And he has his own

truck, so he's on his own. I'm not sticking around anymore. This forest creeps me out."

"Yeah," Matt manages, hoping the word sums up the building nervousness he feels.

"No one is leaving." The words crawl from Lance's throat, though it sounds as if they pass through Hell first. *"I'm still hungry."*

Gil and Fred scream "Wendigo!" in frightened unison, then shoulder their ancient rifles.

Rocco spins around with his batons at the ready. William doesn't even flinch; he raises his middle finger over his shoulder and continues walking. Then, smiling so wide the tips of his mustache nearly tickle his ears, he feels wind on his face; a hot, fetid wind reeking of carrion and filth coming out of nowhere.

William wrinkles his nose in disgust—"What the fuck?"—then screams when something in the foul wind slices at his face, tearing away a strip of beard-covered cheek flesh. William's hand flies to the gash and blood instantly oozes between the fingers.

The strip of furry flesh is carried on the reeking wind as it blows past Gil and Fred, then past Rocco and Matt to land at Lance's feet. They all look from the gruesome fold of William-flesh to Lance. His eyes are now glowing with an unholy orange sheen, and his teeth have grown so long and sharp his facial structure has undergone significant stretching to allow room for them. The what-was-once-Lance kneels to pick up the skin and tosses it into his mouth. He chews happily at it and raises his AK, firing randomly at the group. His head snaps in unnatural, choppy jerks. Most of the bullets end up buried in tree trunks or dirt.

Gil and Fred stand their ground and return fire. Their aim proves much better as homemade bullets sizzle into Lance's meaty muscles. The big man staggers back when hit, but does not fall down. He turns the AK, still jerking, and almost as if by accident manages to cut down Fred with a lucky shot to the side of the head.

Gil does not see the spectacular gush from Fred's skull and drops down on top of his dead friend, not yet knowing that Fred's soul had been instantaneously freed from the body.

Matt hands Rocco his tranq-pistol and pumps two bag rounds into the chamber of his "Riot Ender" shotgun. William, still refusing to look back, keeps his hands tightly clamped to his disfigured cheek and trudges forward. Rocco tilts the tranq-pistol sideways and stomps towards Lance, plucking at the trigger with every step. Six long strides, six high-powered tranq-darts in a perfect line from Lance's inner thigh to his cheek. By then Rocco is close enough to use his batons and Matt is close enough to use his shotgun.

Assuming the most drastic course of action is required, Matt lets the first barrel go two feet away from Lance's crotch, and the second six inches closer and ten inches higher. At the same time, Rocco swipes one baton downward with all his strength, shattering Lance's shin bone, then brings the other baton up, burying the electrified tip under the fiend's chin. Lance finally crumbles under their attack.

William stops walking against the terrible wind when it begins slicing away at him more and more with every step. He feels blood trickling off of him in streams running far too fast to be just cosmetic. Then his flesh is torn away in strips. He opens his mouth to scream, but the wind silences him and lifts him off his feet, tearing him into such small chunks that only a few spatters of blood are wasted, splashed like rain across the shocked faces of his companions.

Matt and Rocco grab Gil and stagger away from the carnage. They stumble over the small ridge line, and down into the next tree-choked gorge. Gil orders them deeper into the mountain, believing the Wendigo will find them wherever they go, but silently promising to at least make the bastard work for it.

"We knocked it out," Rocco pants. "We can cut back the way we came . . ."

"Rocco, the wind just ate Will right before our eyes." Matt's voice is chilly with a finality that Rocco's thick head won't absorb.

Gil just laughs madly over his shoulder as he leaps over logs. Every twenty paces or so he spins around with tears in his eyes . . . but he doesn't stop. None of them do. "It's not *knocked out.* It was skin walking. You might have just killed its host, but it is all around us . . . you dead men just don't get it."

The three scamper to hide in the folds of the mountain. They finally stop in a small ravine within a slender gorge, in between two other larger ones. Night falls and the wind screeches restlessly through the crevices of the Hoo-Doo, hungry and smelling of rot.

Despite the roaring wind that searches for them, the men slip into exhausted sleep and wake up two days later.

Gil gives Matt and Rocco the skinny on the demonic, cannibalistic Wendigos. He explains William's death and Lance's transformation; how the demon can take many forms at once. It can take the form of a wind which can literally chew the flesh from bone. It can also take the form of some hideous demon made of dead forest animals, with monstrous antlers designed in Hell. The Wendigo can be both of these while possessing humans; it completely hollows out everything human about its prey, leaving only a decrepit shell that's rotted from the inside out.

Gil tells them that they were on the Wendigo's part of the mountain, its territory, essentially. The first fools stumbled into its home trying to run from the law, running stupidly into the gorge that grandfathers had warned of entering since their people had come to the mountain. And now there was no escaping it. Now it would feast on them all.

Unwilling to accept their ends so quickly, Matt and Rocco group their meager supplies and make a half comfortable camp in their small ravine. Come afternoon they sneak gingerly back the way they'd come and find the site of the attack largely unchanged . . .

Except that the three bodies, counting Lance's, are all missing.

After collecting William's AK, now speckled with dried flecks of his blood—*Bad fucking job, amigo,* thinks Matt. *Sorry it was our last*—the two men rummage through the camp. Within minutes they find a duffel bag with a dozen MREs, a cooler stuffed with water bottles, an FN Ballista sniper rifle with scope and a quarter box of ammo . . . and two old school hand grenades. Matt thinks about the crate of HKs still sitting in William's Escalade. He grins darkly, similar to what William may have done.

Oldies but goldies. These will do.

William's Escalade and Lance's beat up Ford sit less than a mile away, each having at least a quarter tank of gas. But Matt and Rocco won't have any of that backing away from a fight shit. Hell no, not William The Beard's Red Cap Clan. *Death afore Submission,* thank you kindly.

They return to camp with their goodies, but Gil is only excited for the water and MREs. He tells them weapons are useless against the demon Wendigo, and that their death is at hand. Then he stuffs his face full of freeze-dried chili and climbs into William's tent to perform an orchestra of snoring and intestinal distress.

With nightfall comes the full force of the wind.

It rips at the trees of the mountainside, an unseen demon prying them apart to look for its hidden prey. It howls and screeches all around them, carrying voices of the damned which plead for their surrender in soft sultry tones one moment and then scream for their warm souls the next. Matt hears Lisa's voice on the wind, begging him to join her in the sharp hellborn currents. Wrapping his pillow around his head does little to muffle the sound of the voices on the wind, but enough so that he doesn't hear Rocco storm out of his tent and run to the crest of the next gorge.

Matt and Gil both hear the rattle and clatter of the AK as Rocco fires it into the hideous wind. They peek at him from the screened window flaps of their tents. A maelstrom surrounds the giant tattooed man, flinging sticks and debris across the cluttered forest floor. Rocco stands in the moonlight, pale and crazy and firing his gun in random directions as the wind whips around him. He screams, and Matt watches vicious wounds open all over Rocco's flesh. The thug lets the AK slip from his blood-slick hands as he droops to his knees.

With one triumphant gust, the wind picks Rocco's crumbling form up and takes it into the night sky. Matt and Gil listen to Rocco's screams in the wind for the next few hours, making sleep nearly impossible.

The days and nights blur together in a wind-driven nightmare. Finally they run out of food; a day or two later they run out of water. The day after that, Matt watches Gil climb out of his tent at dusk, naked as the day he was born, with his black hair braided tightly behind his head. Matt says nothing as Gil looks at him, tears streaming down his filthy cheeks, and nods. He doesn't say anything when the weakened man trips and falls and has to struggle to get back to his feet. He watches raptly, and silently, as Gil struggles up to the top of the hillside, only to be plucked upwards by a wind which singes the branches of the trees around him. Gil's screams last a day and a half.

Matt sinks into his mind.

Detached. Cold. Distant. Over and over and over and over.

One day Matt emerges from his tent, naked from the waist up and oozing from deep, self-inflicted gashes. He holds his hands at his sides, a trembling grenade clenched in each bloody fist. A gentle breeze tickles at his fresh wounds as he chooses the ridge to sacrifice himself from. The horrible wind welcomes him, clearing his path of obstacles as it licks the blood from his wounds with burning tongues and assaults his senses with the reek of carrion and decay.

Matt's mind is calm and blank, blissfully so as the Wendigo digs its unseen talons in and tears away its first bites with the breeze.

Detached. Cold. Distant.

Matt struggles on, the wind encouraging him and debasing him in turns. It cuts with teeth and words.

Detached. Cold. Distant. *Just can't wait to get the hell away from me, can you, Matt?*

Matt reaches the peak and the wind engulfs him in a razor blade embrace as it pulls him into the air. It fills his ears with the screams of the damned and his sinuses with the rot of death.

Detached. Cold. Distant. *I'm leaving now . . . I can't fucking do this anymore.*

Matt feels it feasting on him. His head flops to the side and he absentmindedly notices the scenery whipping by below.

Detached. Cold. Distant.

Matt's body twitches as the Wendigo feasts, but he doesn't scream. In fact, he smiles as he uses the last of his strength to demand his thumbs pluck the pins from the grenades.

Her words never cease as he rides the flaming winds all the way to Hell.

The
GOOD MAN

DAVID DUNWOODY

Rogers let his head fall back. Broken glass scraped his neck and pate as if he were in the maw of some beast—but instead of hot, damp breath, there were tongues of cool air that moved ever so gently across his skin. It almost took his mind off the pain—which reminded him about the pain—and he balled a wet fist against the hole in his side.

Hammond lay in the aisle directly in front of him, surrounded by torn Frito-Lay bags. Blood had pooled around his entire body, and Rogers imagined the corpse would be epoxied to the floor by the time the meat wagon rolled in. Rogers didn't want to know how badly he himself was bleeding. He was still lucid, and the throbbing wound was still white-hot—so that had to count for something. Maybe he'd still have a pint in him when somebody showed up. Maybe he'd make it.

He was seated against a half-shattered cooler door at the back of the store. He could smell beer and figured one or more of the bullets—perhaps the one that had punched through his mid-section—had killed a 12-pack. Whoever owned this dump was going to hit the roof. Unless the cashier was the owner, in which case he wasn't hitting anything ever again.

God, I'm gonna have to write all this up. The pettiness of the thought gave Rogers a bitter smile. *Yep, I'll make it. Because that's how the luck of the Rogers clan works. I'll drown in paperwork before blood.*

Hammond, being between Rogers and the register, had gotten the worst of it. That went without saying, given his present condition. He'd probably saved Rogers' life just by pausing to move a pack of Zingers someone had misplaced. Hammond always did shit like that. It was annoying. Hell, one time Rogers invited him over for dinner with Ellie, and he and the girls had alphabetized their bookshelf while the table was being set. Hammond would have made a good detective.

I hope Bollywood up there triggered the silent alarm while he still had a face.

It was dead quiet. Rogers realized his ears had been ringing all this time and had only now stopped. The pain was everywhere. Fuck. Things wouldn't have gone down like this if the cashier hadn't brandished that sawed-off. Why in the Christ had he done that with two beat cops standing right there to take care of it? The perp hadn't even noticed them when he came barreling in; their cruiser was parked on the side street, and they could have married him to the floor before he even smelled bacon. But Bollywood wanted to be the hero. He had probably been the owner.

Rogers sucked air through gritted teeth. With his free hand—the one that wasn't pressed against the hole—he made another try at grabbing the radio mic off his shoulder lapel, but the pain corkscrewed through his torso and his hand fell limp. His eyelids fluttered and he saw colors exploding as agony flowered; then it retreated into the wound. A dull throb now. Maybe better to slip his phone from his pocket and call the wife. Maybe it was that time.

He fished the phone out, noticing as he did that his pistol was lying on the floor in a pile of glass. He returned his attention to the phone. He had Ellie and the Belly set as his wallpaper. She was seven months along. They hadn't settled on a name yet. Typical cop story; wouldn't be a box-office hit if he didn't kick the bucket. As his trembling fingers brushed the keypad, he tried to think of a good name. He wanted that to be the last thing he said.

Out of his line of sight, the front door opened.

Ding.

The phone fell into Rogers' lap. He tried to straighten up and felt glass teeth nip the back of his neck. He tried to call out, but only a soft sigh emerged from his lips.

A boy who looked to be maybe twelve stepped into the aisle where Hammond lay. The boy was dressed in blue jeans and a striped shirt. Tiny horizontal strips of white, orange and red. Rogers' vision began to swim, and the stripes scrolled up and down over the boy's chest. Kid had a weathered red ball cap. His eyes were dark and they studied Hammond's body with curiosity.

Rogers tried to speak again. The boy looked up at him, and, stepping over Hammond, approached.

The kid had a denim knapsack slung over one shoulder. One hand gripped the strap, and the other swung lazily at his side. Tufts of brown hair stuck out from under the red ball cap. He was looking at Rogers like the cop really *was* something out of a movie, or a video game. Goddamn kid's face was blank as a . . . something or other. Rogers was running out of similes faster than blood (although that line wasn't half-bad, he'd save that for the boys if he made it).

He set his jaw and tried to work his voice box. A wheeze, then a croak, passed his parted lips. Then he said, as steadily and clearly as he could manage, "Call 911." After that, the air went out of him.

He pointed to the phone in his lap. The kid knelt, studying Ellie and the Belly. *Pick it up,* Rogers' mind screamed. His eyes drilled a telepathic beam through the boy's forehead.

The boy picked it up.

He put the phone in his pocket.

As he knelt to unclip Rogers' mic from his shoulder and unplug it from the radio, the cop watched in a wondrous daze. He wanted to laugh, he really did. Little shit was robbing him. The last thing Rogers would see was this tiny smug-faced prick shoveling armfuls of chips into his backpack. This badge, so heavy on his chest now, was the cosmic goof he'd always suspected it to be. KICK ME, it may as well have said. They'd bury him in white gloves and black shoes shined for the first time in a decade.

The kid took the radio, too, dropping it next to Hammond before he knelt over the body. The kid rolled back his striped sleeve. Then something emerged.

Rogers didn't want to believe it—but he had no choice, because it was happening. From a razor-thin slit in the boy's forearm—from beneath pale flesh which now resembled tissue paper, like a sleeve itself—emerged a long, wet, gray mass of what looked like coiled spaghetti. The foul wormy thing slid out of the boy's arm and touched down lightly on Hammond's chest. The individual noodles, trembling gray appendages, separated from one another and drifted in the air over Hammond like . . . like tentacles, or maybe antennae . . . like they were sniffing around. And the boy's face was calm and still.

He's no boy, Jesus, you gotta know that. Rogers' head bowed slightly as he nodded to himself. He pulled bloody knuckles across the tile, toward the holster on his hip.

No, no, the gun was over there! In the glass! *Snap out of it, asshole. Somehow you know this is your only chance, your one shot. As long as he's doing whatever he's doing with Hammond—and let's face it, you know what he's doing. He's doing what monsters do with corpses.*

Rogers did know, but it still caused his murmuring heart to jump a little when the noodly things began sucking at Hammond's wounds. The gray tendrils grew fat and pink and the boy's face flushed.

Sweet Jesus. The gun, the gun!

There was a sound coming from the boy as he—it—fed. It did not sound like liquid being gulped into an empty bladder, as Rogers might have expected; it sounded like rain on dead leaves. The cop sensed that there was something in the boy that could never be nourished and that he just fed for feeding's sake. Idle and bored, like any kid . . . in that sense, at least.

The boy detached from Hammond and looked back at Rogers. His eyes were wide now, and so dark. God, they were all-black.

Rogers managed, again, to speak.

"No."

The boy came up so that he was standing at Rogers' feet, and he knelt between them. The pink tentacles wavered over Rogers' wound. The cop pressed his fist into that bullet hole until fireworks went off in his brain. *Not my blood. Not getting mine.*

The boy spoke. He spoke in a weird, terrible falsetto, as if his voice were being dubbed by an adult in a piss-poor imitation of a little boy.

"You're an ugly treat," the boy said, and frowned.

He knocked Rogers' fist aside like a wet sock and the noodles lunged at the wound.

Rogers screamed as they struck home. The tentacles convulsed and went from pink to black in an instant. They convulsed again. What was this fucking thing doing to him? He could see now that the tendrils were quite translucent, and that the fluid rushing through them was going *in, oh Christ Jesus,* going *into* his wound.

Ellie.

His hand grabbed the boy's shirt and the fabric snarled around his trembling fingers. With the last of his strength, he shook the dully-staring thing. "Fuck you. Stop. Stop."

The kid smiled and withdrew.

And Rogers, who expected at that moment to die, did not.

As a matter of fact, he got up.

Life surged through his limbs and the pain faded from his wound, and he pushed himself to his feet with his eyes locked onto the boy he was about to kill. He bent quickly to snatch up his gun, and his finger was already pulling back on the trigger as he thrust the weapon forward.

Had the smiling thing in his sights. Right there. *Right there!*

His finger went numb. He couldn't pull the trigger.

Rogers beat on his arm as the numbness spread, then took the gun in his other hand. It immediately lost all sensation, and the gun clattered on the floor.

He staggered towards the boy, who danced backwards to the register.

"Hobbled hobbling hob," sang the kid in that hideous falsetto.

Movement made Rogers glance to his left. There was a big, round mirror affixed to the ceiling at the top of the last aisle to offer the cashier a bird's-eye view of whichever minorities he stalked through his little piece of America. Rogers saw himself lurching over Hammond's body, but no kid. Not exactly surprising. What surprised him was when he looked back down and the kid was actually gone.

"Shit. Shit!"

His first thought was that he had to get to the car and call it in. His second was that the kid's black blood was in him now, and had healed him. The third was that it had also prevented him from firing the gun.

He retrieved his piece and went outside. The street was empty, the night sky a blank chalkboard. There must have been black clouds obscuring every star . . . or maybe the planet had just fallen into another dimension. Each seemed equally plausible at this point. Rogers rounded the corner onto the side street, and before he could say "no more surprises," he saw the mangled wreck of the cruiser and howled.

Goddammit! Little fuck had thought of everything, hadn't he? The radio in there was probably ripped apart. Rogers had to check, so he crept forward. He wondered how long the kid had been out here, slowly and silently warping the car into an optical illusion. Maybe he had some telekinetic powers or magic or something. Rogers thought about the boy's lack of a reflection and wondered if the boy would photograph. Needed his phone with its camera—

The kid had his phone. He had Ellie and the Belly. They weren't *ugly treats.* Ellie was worn in places, sure—but Rogers knew and loved every one of them: her popping right elbow, the creases of her always-laughing eyes. Somehow he knew that the kid could see all these things now, too. Was that why he'd done what he did? Forget the phone . . . was that why he'd put himself into the cop? To get into Rogers' head? To get his *address?*

He broke into a run. He didn't know where he was going, he just ran.

Phone, asshole. Pay phone, bar, whatever, just call this in and get a black-and-white to the house!

"Officer?"

Rogers turned, his gun snapping up at the sound of the man. He fell into a firing stance, then ice flooded his veins as that familiar tingling crept into his fingers and they went dead.

The man stood at the mouth of the side street, observing the heap that had been the cruiser. His face was white and his eyes were black like the boy's. They glittered as he looked from the car to Rogers.

"Did he touch you?" the man called.

Rogers let his arms drop. The man nodded at the unspoken answer.

"You'll die soon if we don't find him," the man said. He was calm—way too calm—and it was no put-on. This character was all business.

"They'll die, too," he went on. "Whoever they are, they'll die first. And once he doesn't need you anymore he'll take back what he's given."

"Given?"

"An extension, so to speak, on your life. Enough time for you to reach a hospital if we're quick about this."

Rogers kept his gun at his side; feeling was returning to his hands, but he knew it would be gone in a second if he drew down on this thing again.

"They're my kids," he said. "My baby. He's going after my family."

"And he is my son," the man said.

"What are you?"

"Pick a name that suits you."

Rogers didn't bother. He holstered the gun and fingered the hole in his uniform. The wound was gone, replaced with smooth pink skin. An extension.

"I suppose I'll die if I kill him," he muttered.

"One way or another." The man pulled his dark winter coat tight around his torso. "As I said, he's my child. We each understand the other's predicament, yes?"

"Okay," Rogers said. His head was swimming and he placed his hand against the side of the store.

"Are you lightheaded?" asked the man.

Rogers nodded, knees buckling.

"It'll pass," he heard the man say, and Rogers felt hands gripping him under his arms, and then he was somewhere else.

Dad likes to take apart old TVs and put them back together. Mom has a big map with quarters glued on it. Boy is far away. You see one time he went to the woods to find a hobby and there was a torn dog there. Its belly was open down to its privates and it lay in a way that stirred the boy, inviting him to come closer and see. "You see with your eyes, not your hands," Mom would say. But Boy felt bold all of a sudden and he put his fingers inside to explore the cooling guts. He breathed their scent and laid flat on his stomach and entered the dog up to his elbows. Something violent moved inside of him and he knew he had found a hobby.

Mom and Dad and Boy have been alive for a very long time and there is a room where Mom keeps all her old maps with all different types of coins and a room where Dad keeps all his TVs plugged in and sputtering. Boy does not ask for a room, instead he does his new hobby far away. You see one day he dashed a bird's head with a rock and he saw its little brain and with the legs still kicking too. He got real close and squinted into the brain but he didn't see a soul. All things have souls, even people like him. He knows that but he can't ever see it, can't see himself at all, and it bothers him. He can't ask Dad or Mom about it so he keeps his questions to himself.

One time Mom asked him where he goes far away. She saw the blood under his nails. He lied and said he ate the birds but really he keeps them out there and watches them soften and squints in search of a little pearl or string or something that might be a soul.

Dad has talked to him before about how they can't eat people and lately Dad has been bringing it up a lot. It gets the boy thinking. Maybe people have souls big enough to be seen by the naked eye.

One day not long after that he walks into Dad's room where Dad is hunched over a Fifties TV set and muttering while he picks through it. He stares at the back of Dad's head for a long time and then he goes away again.

Rogers came back screaming. He had seen it all, in moldy sepia tones; but it wasn't what he'd seen that had rocked him. It had all seemed pretty goddamned boring, matter of fact—couple of uninvolved hoarder parents and their coming-of-age psychopath —coming of age at one hundred fifty years, sure. But kids were kids. No, it was what the kid had been thinking, and how the thoughts had seemed like Rogers' own, and how he'd grown erect at the last one.

And good ol' Dad was cradling Rogers now and telling him to breathe. Rogers jerked away, going for his gun again. He felt his hand go numb and threw it against the side of the building so hard his shoulder almost came apart.

"Kid's a monster," he snarled. "You're just gonna take him home, is that it? Send him to his room?"

"What I do with him once I have him is no concern of yours." Dad offered a hand to help Rogers up.

Rogers thought back to poor Hammond and the boy feeding on him. He remembered sensing that the feeding was unimportant to the boy, perhaps even unnecessary. No, the kid needed his breakfast; but it didn't satisfy him the way it did to see an animal lying prone with its skull split like a walnut. He would forgo a century of nourishment for the freedom to explore the human mind.

Rogers rose on shaking legs. "We've gotta get home. My home. You have a car?"

Dad gestured in the direction from which he'd come. "You're handling this better than most," he said as Rogers fell into step beside him.

"Just get me there."

His head still felt a little foggy. He wondered if the boy had been in his head as he had been in the boy's. What would he have seen? Rogers didn't remember much about being little, and certainly not his sexual awakening. He remembered fumbling around with Jake Savage's mom at eighteen, but that had been late in the game for his generation. He remembered Larry Thomas telling him that getting a hummer from Mrs. Savage was about as smart as banging a petri dish. He'd shaved his entire lower body and spent the rest of that summer looking for warts and crabs. Goddamn dork. Worse in college, courting dollar-store cashiers in that dumpy closet of an apartment. He was pretty sure the space heater he'd bought off some classmate had been a Lite Brite. Never warmed the apartment. Two hundo a month for that pile. Oh yeah, he used to say "hundo." Goddamn dork.

He had always been into older women, though. He thought maybe that preceded Mrs. Savage, who'd kept drunk-dialing him at his parents' house and who he'd finally told to go nest in the roof of a cave somewhere (the monster might have appreciated that line). Ellie was his age, but she was definitely more grown-up than he was. And she was a mom, a damn good one, and there was nothing sexier than that in his book. Younger men like Hammond didn't get that.

The kid wanted Ellie too, for different reasons. The horror of it sang in Rogers' bones.

Dad led him to the passenger door of a startlingly inconspicuous blue Ford hatchback. It looked like a Nineties model and Rogers almost walked past it before the man caught his arm.

"No kidding," Rogers muttered as he settled on a beaded seat cover. Stale cigarette smoke and smudged fingerprints on the dash. He eyed the change in the ashtray, counting up eighty cents, and as Dad started the car and Rogers pulled his seat belt over his chest he had to remind himself he was sitting next to something inhuman.

As if reading his mind (and maybe he goddamn was) Dad said, "It's good I don't frighten you."

"Not any more than the man who shot my partner," Rogers said. Then, thinking of the boy, "But he does."

"That's good too," the man said. Was that resentment in his voice? Probably ate at him that he'd had to lay low for ten lifetimes, that he could only take apart TV sets and had to leave dismemberment to the Dahmers of the world. *But there's still a ghoul in there. You should be scared of dear ol' Dad. Don't get too comfortable. You don't know Count Dracula and you don't know him.* Hell, even the Muppet Count could have spent his off-hours eating rats and prostitutes for all anyone knew.

"One generation's monster is often a jester to the next," Dad said. *Was* he reading Rogers' thoughts? The man slowed to make a right on a red.

"Just go. There's no one coming." Rogers fingered his holster. "How am I supposed to help you once we find him? I can't make a move against him."

"You'll help your family," Dad replied.

The words didn't make sense. Rogers' brain was doing the backstroke again. He pressed his fingers into his eyes and tried to will the boy away, but memory overcame him like an icy wind. This time it was his own.

Fresh out of college and already lost. Drunk, again, in his apartment. He considers wandering the halls for a bit, maybe finding some of his three-AM-friends whose names he doesn't know and whose loping stoner walks are more recognizable than their flushed faces. Gets off the couch, spins in search of his shoes and decides against it. When a man can assess the whole of his existence in a 360-degree turn, something's wrong.

He's thought about suicide before but never seriously. Zip-tying down the trigger of an Uzi and eating a couple dozen rounds. Let the papers figure that one out. But as he sits back down on the couch young Rogers has a serious thought.

Why not?

He's not in pain. He hasn't been robbed of anyone or anything. It's just this ennui that doesn't feel any different from what he imagines death to be like. It's his whole life and the long, boring trip it's been, no highs, no lows.

He has a gun, the one his dad carried on the job. He's thought about taking after the old man but he doesn't want the numbing comfort of following some well-worn path. Are there any surprises left after your tenth Christmas, or is it all just this?

He pulls the pistol out from the bottom of the sock drawer and steps over to the mirror. Was he really almost about to go out of the apartment? He's dressed only in his briefs, shrunken in the wash, one ball hanging out. It looks like a hydrocephalic wearing a bandana. They'll find him like this.

Rogers howls with laughter until he's on the floor crying. Still holding the gun, he wipes the tears from his view and, standing back up, fixing his junk, he admires the way that the firearm wears him. Most men can't even pull that off in pants.

"Are you back, Officer?"

"Get him out. Outta my head."

"That's where he likes to be. Sometimes quite literally. Please understand that despite what you may now know of us, what my son is doing has nothing to do with sustenance. He kills for his pleasure."

Rogers shook his head back and forth. It felt like a sack of potatoes. "What time is it?" He rubbed his eyes and yawned. He felt like he was losing chunks of nighttime. How long had they been driving? He didn't recognize the back streets outside.

"Where are we going?"

"Your home. This way is quickest."

"Did I tell you the address?"

"I know it."

"Will the kid have to fall back when the sun comes up?"

"The sun doesn't affect us," Dad said.

Rogers should have suspected as much; the memories of the boy that he'd experienced had seemed oddly bright, but he'd thought it was the light of recall rather than Sol adrift in the sky.

"Are you in my head too? How do you know the address?"

"I retrieved it from your wallet."

"Oh."

"There—*damn!*" Dad slammed on the brakes, the car fishtailing. Rogers gripped the door handle and fought against inertia and his own sluggishness to stay upright and see outside. The car lurched and came to a stop sideways in the road. The street was empty.

"What!" Rogers exclaimed, but Dad was already out of the car.

"I saw his eyes!" the man cried, running down the street.

As Rogers began to climb out, he felt the fog growing thicker in his head. God *damn!* He tried to call to the kid's father, to let him know he was going the wrong way, but the thoughts came back— the boy's thoughts, memories, and a rush of raw sensation that was so abrupt and so real that Rogers felt as if his soul had been forcibly penetrated. He saw and knew it all and he could not make words from the screams that came.

Vaguely, he detected footsteps approaching, Dad coming back. He felt hands shaking him. Finally he could speak, and Rogers slurred, "He killed his mom."

"What?" Dad knelt and held Rogers' head in his hands. With his thumbs he pried the cop's eyelids open. *"What did you say?"*

"He thought about it for months before he did it. He split her head. She was dead before she fell down the stairs." Rogers stared blankly into the eyes of a fiend who was suddenly very human. He didn't want to tell the rest, but it left his mouth anyway, what the boy had done with his mother's remains before Dad had returned home and found—

"He was crying," the man stammered. "Don't you see? *Didn't* you see? He was *crying* when I found her. He was hysterical. She fell. He would never—never."

"He did." Rogers blinked wetly. "You can't see in his heart. I can."

Dad sat in the street beside Rogers, leaning back against the car. Rogers was reading him clearly now. The reality Dad had been trying to chase away had turned on him like a feral beast. It had been inevitable, Rogers realized, that in his efforts to contain the boy and the boy's urges, Dad would be forced to accept the truth. Maybe tonight's melee was the only way Dad could bring himself to do what needed doing. Seemed that way. Dad went to the back of the car and returned with a small black box which he set in Rogers' lap.

"I can't open it. There's silver inside." Dad held out his hands. "Before you do this, know that the silver will affect you too. It's going to open that wound of yours. Just touching it."

Rogers lifted the box's lid—heavy for its size, like it was solid lead—and saw bullets of varying calibers in foam bedding. The ache in his side came on immediately.

"He won't be able to stop you this time," said Dad. "Not with silver in hand. But you have to go now—Officer, you're already bleeding again. Please."

Rogers emptied the magazine of his gun and replaced the rounds with silver, silent all the while. He chambered the first bullet and looked up at Dad.

"He's going to kill my family."

"Not if you get after him. Now."

"Wouldn't have to if you'd done it back then. Wouldn't be bleeding. Wouldn't be fuzzy. Wouldn't have to bury Hammond. Wouldn't be here."

Rogers shot Dad through the neck—he'd been aiming for the head, but had stumbled while getting to his feet. Still, it was good enough, and Rogers took the car keys from the man's coat, not bothering to take in the spectacle of bubbling and melting flesh, instead making his way to the nearest intersection so he could get his bearings and get home.

His awareness of time and distance came and went with the pain, the silver affecting him even with the gun resting in the passenger seat. But at least he was free of the other fog, the boy's intruding presence. He found familiar streets, empty and dark. He rolled up onto the curb in front of his house and steeled himself against the dull but insistent pull of his ebbing life. Crossed the yard, threw open the front door. No time for strategy. No bullshit. Storm the castle.

Boy.

Boy.

Been there and gone already, the monster.

Rogers spent some time among the remains before his friends arrived, having been called by some passerby who'd glanced through the open door. He tried to stop them from photographing and cataloguing the scene, from collecting and labeling his family, because he knew that when this was done Ellie and the girls were going to be taken away from him, and, after all, he still hadn't found the baby who wouldn't even have a name for his grave marker.

Boy.

Baby.

Boy.

Some years later, Rogers handed a fat wad of bills to a stone-faced Mexican and said, "Hang around and there'll be extra in it for you."

"I won't go in," the man said firmly.

"I know. Just stay out here. If something—if it goes bad, just make sure you burn everything."

Rogers turned to the shack. In the blazing sun, heat rippled off the corrugated metal in waves. It almost looked like a mirage in the middle of the desert, and Rogers felt a pang of fear—what if it was?—but told himself to go in and make it real.

Wearing heavy gloves that still didn't quite protect from the heat of the metal, he pried open the door and entered the shack. Darkness, wet and thick and boiling, enveloped him. He closed the door behind him, reached down, and felt for the electric lantern.

It snapped on and the pale blue light played eerily over the boy's blistered flesh. He'd been cooking in here for a while now. The silver chains wrapped around his bare skin now touched only corroded tissue and bone. He was half gone already, the thing, but still smiling.

Rogers felt he had to ask. He didn't want to, because he didn't want the illusion of hope to return, nor did he want to allow the boy to play with him, but he had to ask. He had never stopped being a dad. That wasn't something that was ever undone, not even when a man was left all alone. It defined a life that otherwise would have been cashed out long ago.

"Where is my baby?" Rogers said quietly.

The boy's grin spread wider, blisters peeling at the corners. "Not a baby anymore," he sang in a hoarse voice. He stuck out his swollen tongue.

"Where?" Rogers repeated. He took pliers he'd fashioned himself from his jeans pocket, slippery in his sweaty hands. The heat was making his head swim. It felt just like the good old days.

The boy wagged his tongue at Rogers.

Rogers fingered the scar in his side and said, "You know the silver doesn't bother me anymore. But I remember what it felt like. And I know you won't let me see it, the way it feels when I'm taking you apart, but I'll still know."

He crouched and took hold of the boy's tongue with the pliers. "That your life never had meaning—that you never had love, not even from your parents—that you never gained anything you could lose, maybe you think that makes you strong. But the truth is you're empty. On the other hand, this will haunt me for the rest of my life. As much as I hate you, what I'm about to do will ensure I never sleep another night without dreaming of it. That's because I have loved, and was loved. And because I'm going to do it anyway, that makes me stronger than you."

The boy made a noise in his throat like he was going to say something. Rogers didn't wait.

He walked to the edge of the Rio Grande and stood there for a long time with his father's gun in his hand. As the sun went below the earth, he threw it into the water.

Thirty years on. Another night in the trenches.

Rogers' figure was slight and unimposing, and no one questioned him as he took the elevator up to the NICU. He looked like
someone's granddad, and the bag he carried probably had some
overnight stuff for a new mom or even a handycam, although the
hospital's infant charges were all asleep at this hour unless something was wrong.

He stood at the viewing window and looked over the tiny bodies
in their clear bassinets. Twelve in all, all nearly identical—but with
names and mommies and futures.

"Sir?"

He turned to see a young nurse. She eyed him with concern.
"Are you looking for somebody?"

"I am," Rogers replied. "Maurie. She works on this unit."

"Oh. Well, that's me." She frowned. "What's this about?"

Rogers nodded toward the window. "Could they be any more
helpless?"

"Sir, I think you'd better tell me who you are."

With one of the fingers that gripped the bag's straps, Rogers
tugged stealthily on the zipper. "How much blood could they give
you? Surely it's not enough to live on."

His eyes met the nurse's. "You must just get off on it."

She grabbed at him but he hit her with the bag, and as she
recoiled in shock, he pulled a silver spike from it. It cleaved
through her sternum like a pin popping a balloon.

The nurse sagged and Rogers let the spike go down with her.
Her face began to run and she gasped, "Don't hurt him. I was only
trying to take care of him."

Rogers had no idea what she meant, but her brain was turning
to soft-serve so she probably didn't either. When she was good and
gone he retrieved the spike and wiped it clean with a towel.

Daddy?

Rogers stiffened.

I knew you'd come, Daddy.

He looked through the window and knew which one it was, the one whose thoughts called to him. Rogers walked into the room. Past the other infants, the innocents, was a fat pink cherub with blue eyes and a smile that was oddly warm and so terribly familiar.

Daddy.

Rogers pressed his fist against his teeth. "No."

I knew you'd come. Can we go home?

Rogers' eyes drifted to the tag on the bassinet—*Baby Doe,* it said, and at first he thought the moniker was meant to describe the child's perfect eyes until he realized it was because they didn't have a name. He must have been "found" and brought here by Nurse Maurie. Maybe they'd even done this routine before. How many hospitals, then, had the pair worked together? How many babies had they bled? In his pursuit of the nurse, how long had he also been on the trail of his own . . .

"Thirty years," he whispered. "You're more than thirty years old."

Daddy. The infant's tiny arms strained.

"You're not a child."

I need you, Daddy.

"I can't help you now." Rogers' voice broke. He reached into the bag.

I need you, Daddy. Gray tendrils, thin and weak, squirmed beneath the infant's skin. *Don't lose me again.*

"I can only do what needs doing," Rogers said, "but I'm doing it myself because I still love you." Because he was still a dad—that could never be undone, not even now, nor when he left the hospital and returned to the night alone.

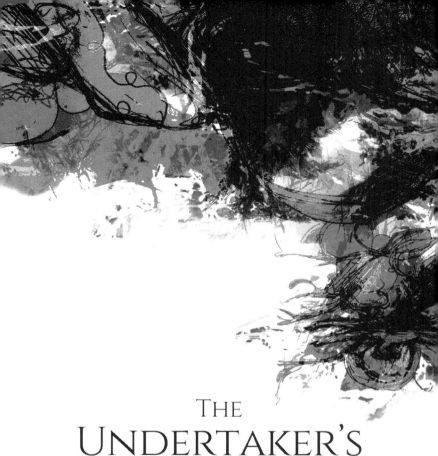

The
Undertaker's
Melancholy

Sydney Leigh

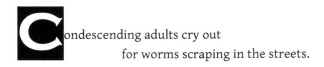ondescending adults cry out
for worms scraping in the streets.

A slap in the face is a passive yellow warning symbol. The
path of least resistance leads to
red spongy moss
growing on slimy tree frogs

Consistence and endurance can be held only until
the sun fades to
gray and purple polka dots

Eating books in abhorrence is flattering to the orange sewer rats
shrieking their hideous laughter *Stop it Stop it Stop that laughing*

Reaching to mules with leeches sucking blood Sucking blood
Sucking *green* blood Sucking *blue* blood Sucking *my* blood
Sucking *your* blood as

you watch revolving globes sinking into
the shattered ribcage
of an indian summer

Skeletonsburiedinyourgarbagedisposal

Desperation
is a bottomless pit (filled with emptiness)

Nomadic attics
defining an oasis in the sulky desert where the TraNsfoRMatiOn
of
a scaly snake to a furry moth can be
        succulous solubility

until. the. day. comes. when. hell.
thaws from its frozen state and turns homosapien camels
            into the hearts of   bayed satisfaction
                    how do you do how do you do how do you do

    A chanced lethe, an unsaturated exigent Homogenous matter
                    conforms to poisonous mushrooms and Leaps,
unheeded,
into the darkness of the calendar,

                            Causing
                        a moldy, bloody, mucous,
discharge Flowing, Flowing, Flowing, seeping into your
ears, My
ears, Dripping out of

            The Undertaker's Melancholy,

m I s c o n s t r u e d enough to sleep in order to adventure
tree root and scary slug nightmares *Don't look Don't look at Don't
look at me I don't want you to Look at me*

while I sweep away the avenging fantasies
> up

>> into the glistening, sparkling water

>>>>>>>> fall

of hollow memories of hairless, limbless canines
> like stony, distorted faces,

mothers' fluttering wings with mace and s|t|r|a|i|n|i|n|g smiles,
> waiting
to conceit and deliver the danger; the incrafted sarcasm

>> *leave me alone leave me alone leave me alone*

The ancient witchcraft legacy is rid of bequeathing bloody spurs;
the crazed shutters

>>> trailing Traitors trailing Villains trailing Murderers
with honorable patience

Naked reverence compels the sacred inflammation of

>>>>> *BENDING HEIRS,*

>>> wounds descending the issue to resolve an
unknown testament . . .

Daggers
piercing skin piercing skull piercing heart,
> leaving tearing flesh wounds Begging to default the
promissory corpse,

>>>>>> compounding

>> total madness.

THE
TUNNEL RECORD

J. DANIEL STONE

Night.

Dark green night beneath the velvet shower of city stars, and Delilah was the only girl left on the rooftop; ghost-girl spilling liquid shadow as a cold slice of moon ravaged her swaying body. The clove cigarette was down to the filter but she took the last pull anyway, tasting vanilla, spice, and everything not-so-nice as the smoke twined tendrils around her calm drunk-face and through the tangle of her blue-black dreadlocks.

There were cans beneath her ragged Grinders, PBRs, BOMB craft beer, and she kicked them over the side of the tenement, peering down to look upon Avenue A, Oval Park, and the crazed night-drivers along the FDR Drive. The cans clattered to the concrete, but she wished for the crash of glass. It would liven the night so.

"You'll fall if you look any farther," a voice said.

Rez stood firm and handsome, choppy black hair pushed to one side, the usual William S. Burroughs book clenched like a pistol, a quill pen wagging free like a bird in flight. Sapphire eyes marked the night, the most beautiful color Delilah had ever seen. Then again, those were her eyes too because Rez was her twin brother.

"They're down there," Delilah said, pointing to the black below her. "I heard them in the pipes."

Rez nodded, lit a cigarette, and peered over the edge. He looked much younger than his twenty-two years tonight. It seemed the stressors of life did not scar time across his soft face, they simply reflected upon his attire. If one looked hard enough they'd see a glimmer of pinstriped sock through the left sole of his Converse sneakers—reflected upon his fingernails too, bitten down to bleeding nubs. He wiped his nails across Delilah's King Crimson t-shirt, the psychedelic print resembling a silk Chinese fan.

"I heard them too," Rez said. "And not the *voices* you think."

A story begins and ends. A story is formed. But no story, big or small, could encompass the adventure of two siblings looking to catch up on a lifetime.

A tricky side of the borough. Yawning streets and people hovering like will o' the wisps. Nervous fingers balance cigarettes and bottles of rotgut. You can meet your best friend here or encounter a stolid rock star as your mind is ciphered out of reality and pulled into another dimension. Rez and Delilah found themselves traversing these streets looking for something to do.

Take into account a girl who just moved to New York in search of a dream long forgotten: a promised career in music. Take into account her twin brother who could hear things that others could not; consider the two of them put together after being separated at birth the first two decades of their life. There was much adventure to catch up on.

The Bowery at midnight glimmered with an air of gentrification and gloaming. New money brought in posh retail, sandblasted brick and the sweet smell of expensive perfume, but old traditions still said that struggle was the norm. Beat poets polluted every corner complaining about the best minds of their generation destroyed by madness and thrown into poverty looking for an angry fix.

"They're everywhere," Delilah said.

Squatters, bums, transients and stragglers. The streets were teeming with signs that said they they'd do anything to make a quick buck. *For my family,* one smelly man whispered, *WILL TELL JOKES FOR A DOLLAR!* written in scrappy magic marker across his cardboard box. Delilah bypassed a line of them digging into sloppy plates of street-meat, had to pull Rez forward so he would stop staring.

"I wanna party," she said.

A sickly blue-veined hand reached out and gripped Delilah's leg with a strange force. She looked down to see eyes white and glazed as lychee fruit.

Help me. Haven't eaten in two weeks, its mouth croaked. *Need to survive. HUNGRY!*

She remembered that Rez had once given a street dweller a falafel sandwich only to have it thrown in his face, insulted that neither Rez nor Delilah, young like him, did not offer not play into the loneliness attained after the last sip of the bottle.

"Off me!" Delilah said.

". . . hungry . . ."

The bum's mouth was opening wide, showing off a row of brown teeth rotted to fine apex points. *They're underground too,* it whispered, and then those teeth were coming for Delilah's flesh; fingers were breaking the skin of her ankles. Delilah kicked the spidery hand away and kneed the bitch in her piranha mouth. Snot and blood smeared across her knee, her black jeans ripped. But those long thin fingers were back again, so her boot came down like she was squashing an insect. The sound of crackling bones left horrible music in her ears.

SO WRONG! the bum screamed. *YOU'D HURT A HUNGRY OLD WOMAN!*

Hungry for flesh? Delilah thought.

"Fuck was that?" Rez asked.

"Squatters," Delilah said.

The block they turned onto was narrow and dark, lit only by the passing of the occasional car and the red-webbed glimmer that spoke of a stumbling drunk's eyes. There came the cool sizzle of neon lights and girls ready to play for pay. Kids huddled in front of tenements that seemed to be built from charcoal; carnal desires glimmered from the windows; lace and leather, glass dildos, whips and butt plugs. Tendrils of smoke smudged like streaks in a window you just can't clean as Delilah pointed to the club called *CHUDS.*

"This is it?" Rez asked.

"Music. All night."

As they slipped through the door, the ground seemed to shiver and beat along with the heavy metal music thumping inside. The smell of whiskey and wine crept into Delilah's nose. They moved so deep and so fast that Delilah was certain she'd run out of oxygen. *Down into the basement of the city.*

"How deep we going?"

"As far as it takes," Delilah said.

The glow of spiral light bulbs reflected Delilah's hair spidery white; made her skin so translucent one could see the row of teeth beneath her lips as if it were some kind of X-ray. On the ground floor ears popped to the sound of glass breaking and virulent laughter. Drugs were passed around like candy, blotter acid stamped with languid skulls, GHB in tiny vials and a new drug called Bath Salts. *The Zombie Effect.*

"That's the one I like."

Rez made the exchange with the random pale hand, didn't bother to look at the face and swallowed the pill as Delilah took hers in a shot of Jäger. The drug hit Delilah in an instant. At first the club lilted in a shattering juxtaposition; there was a separation of reality like tearing paper in half, then a wave of colors mixed before her eyes and burst like a supernova as the music came to life.

The bar area was in full swing. Kids hounded for alcohol, their dyed hair stiff and filled with static electricity; faces marked by steel piercings, skin scrawled with flamboyant tattoos. The artistically inclined, the hipsters and the metal heads. They sat around in packs or cliques ordering beer and paid attention to nothing but the band on stage, knuckle-deep in the brain of the most irrelevant gossip Delilah ever had the curse of hearing.

Like life matters anymore? she heard. *Can we still smoke cigarettes down here?*

"So thirsty," Rez said.

His eyes fixed upon the vast selection of craft beer on tap. Weyerbacher, Dog Fish Head, Dragon Slayer, Ommegang, and Brooklyn. Delilah ordered a Dragon Slayer IPA and Rez a Weyerbacher Sour Black. Beer in hand, Rez ventured away and touched everything he could: the obscene grime built upon dust, the insignias of magick, delirium, and the swirly band patches stapled to the lone billboard. It was then that Delilah saw the screaming graffiti: *LiVe FoReVeR!* and *THE TUNNELS TaKe YOUR LiFe!*

The tunnels, Delilah thought.

Living in the big city, rumors were bound to make waves. She'd already heard the stories encircling the Cannibalistic Human Underground Dwellers; how they lived below the streets, how they made the train tunnels their home of party and decadence. New York City is a puzzle on the outside as much it is on the inside. To imagine the life that thrived beneath her feet enthralled Delilah. To experience that life with Rez was all she could ask for.

"Party time," Rez said, beer in hand and smiling.

They were on the dance floor now, sycophants twisting in sweaty unison, the strobe lights blending them into one knot of flesh. Mosh pits and violent dancing. The music jangled and raged, filling the room with a fear and loathing that rose above the horrible laughter of the crowd. And then Delilah saw why.

"No fucking way."

They shuffled in packs, albino forms that looked as if they'd grown up in basements. Bodies were plucked off the dance floor like flower petals and pulled into dark spaces between the walls until Delilah saw black puddles of blood. Fish gill eyes shimmered, webbed hands outstretched and grins of sharp decayed teeth brought the smell of rot to the dance floor. But it seemed nobody paid any attention, too preoccupied with music and drugs.

"Get behind me."

Delilah grabbed Rez, but soon they were upon them—ravenous forms in black and silver. Something tugged her dreads, and a hand came up between them like a tongue from hell and separated Delilah from Rez. Delilah let out a heartbreaking cry. With her mouth open and voice wailing, a wobbling assailant affixed rubbery lips to Delilah like suction cups; a slug-tongue dug so deep into her throat she felt her gag reflex take charge.

Another one came upon her left and assaulted the maddened patterns of her tattoos, the fine points of her bones with blood-slimed lips. Delilah pushed it down, but its sharp fingernails dug into Delilah's arm and chest, bringing bright beads of blood to the surface. Its nose crinkled in delight at the smell of her blood and it came back for more, smearing red down her belly into the hairless cleft between her legs. Time slowed to a crawl; the neon became as bright as the sun as the Bath Salts took charge. It made her feel strangely hungry; that is until she saw her brother scared out of his wits.

They formed a circle around him, writhing to the crunch of the metal band like a ritualistic dance that sent shockwaves of bodies to the floor. Hands groped Rez's beautiful black hair, sweet face, and exposed chest, sliming his xylophone ribs. They were drawing blood;

a bite mark resembling tattoo of a hemp leaf was carved into his sharp shoulder. *Cannibals.* Delilah immediately elbowed one of the mole people in the face, its soft gummy features spattering green goo onto her arm. That's when they began to scamper away, dragging Rez in the direction of a hole in the wall she hadn't noticed before.

"Let him go!"

She lifted a bottle of Old Number 7 from the bar and swung without looking, connecting it to the head of a bum—but the bottle didn't break—rather, it sunk into its skull like Jell-O and formed a crater that quickly filled with swampy blood. Somehow they received her angry message and let Rez go. Off they went, slithering into the hole behind the poster board of cryptic advertisements, gone as quick as they came.

"You okay?"

"Only in fucking New York," Rez said, dizzy.

"I'm going after them."

Rez reached for his sister, but before he could stop her she was already diving into the deep dark chasm, holding her breath, ready to swim the murky waters of the city beneath the city and kick some mutant ass.

It all started when Delilah saw the news report: thriving homeless communities discovered *beneath* the streets of New York City. Pulled out of their dank caves by angry police, lugubrious forms with talons for fingers and rat teeth, others strung out and blinded by the sun. Their lizard eyes were glossed over and they did not speak like that of the world above them. Sadly, this was a glimpse of how a city could degrade an entire population so badly that they were forced to seek life in the tunnels below the black top. It was a sight straight out of a Rob Zombie film.

Some of them lived so deep they became blinded by sunlight, an officer said.

Some live only in the train tracks . . . others live deep as deep can get. We needed gas masks so we could stand the stench.

Delilah was still living in Pennsylvania and hoping that Electric Orchid would be her one way ticket out of the boondocks. After the band had traveled to New York City and won a battle of the bands contest for the contract of a lifetime, the thought of the mole people came right back into Delilah's head.

She came, she conquered, and she thought she saw it all in New York. But there were still the mole people. Alphabet City is where Rez resided, where the beatniks partied around huge garbage can fires, drinking and pissing in the same clothes day in and day out. Alphabet City is where she first heard the sounds from the bathroom pipes. So many fucking sounds, yet not ones like you'd think.

Deeper than the clatter of resting drainage, not the flush of a toilet two floors above you; it wasn't the dark glittery tap-tap-tap of insects invading various apartments, or the sound of a leaking drain patting against rusted metal. She heard voices that belonged at the bottom of the sea. It was the secret tongue of muck and grime. Fish gossip, zombie-stomp, *mole people.*

"I hear them down there," Delilah said as she took her head away from the shower drain.

That night she found Rez resting upon the couch, jotting things down in his moleskin notebook, trailing the pen along his one arm with the raven quill tattoo, swirling the black ink in the same pattern that twilight was descending upon his window. Blood orange light crept over everything; it illuminated the array of posters tacked to the ceiling, magazine cut-outs he'd saved since he was a teenager. He wore glasses now that he could afford a pair, tortoise print Converse frames, and they sat upon his aquiline nose like a maddened librarian as he flipped through a book called *The Mole People*, which was written by a famous journalist accused of fabricating the entire manuscript.

Life in the Tunnels beneath New York City.

But with every story, falsified or not, comes a history. Delilah thought about Manhattan in the days when it was a growing baby, its shape still being kneaded out around the edges. She thought about the story of the pirate ship buried beneath Front Street; she thought about how Wall Street got its name, a literal wall that was used to block the Indians from the Quakers over three hundred years ago. She thought about the families who escaped to the underground to get away from the poison of modern society. There was so much to discover.

A city beneath the city.

The tunnel was a whorled oblivion that branched off into endless directions. You couldn't tell time here, couldn't tell which way was north, south, east or west. Could you even go more south once you'd landed yourself skyscraper-deep into the city's underground?

"Anything?"

Rez waited for something to mark his sensitive brain, but nothing came to him. There was only the snap of electric lines, the humdrum rush of water in pipes, the hissing of toxic chemicals eating away the asphalt. He looked up and saw a dazzle of darkness, and to the left of that a pile of what seemed to be the skulls of rats.

"Smells like shit down here," Delilah said.

Each step they took brought out a new stench, a spiral of sounds. To Rez, this echoing catacomb was like living in-real-time—that pivotal moment he'd read about a hundred times in *House of Leaves*— Navidson uncovering the secret to his dreamy Virginia home, that the internal measurements were slightly bigger than the external ones . . . and then all hell breaks loose. Random doors appear across blank walls, the house growls, and the honeycombed darkness begins its ascent until Navidson becomes controlled by it, led willingly into the never ending world of nothingness.

This is what happens when you hurry through a maze: the faster you go, the worse you are entangled.

"Might we go forward?"

Rez's mind rode the tunnels. It was a jungle of darkness; within lay cadaverous hands and thorny teeth. Down here the ghost of trains still slithered, BMT and the Lexington line that formed the veins and arteries of the boroughs. The sporadic light bulb lured them in no straight direction, but now that there was some light Rez could see the source of the sweet smell of garbage and the angry state of mind in the tunnel art.

MoDeRn SoCiEtY Is GUILTY of INTELLECTUAL TerRoRiSm.

ThE FaBuLoUs FiVe FoReVeR!!!

"They seem angry," Rez said. "I can feel it."

"Bitter is a better word," Delilah said, lighting a cigarette.

Get out! said a snake voice. *WE DON'T NEED ANY HELP!*

Rez saw reptile eyes; Delilah tensed in a protective stance and then charged ahead. She swung her fists, hitting nothing but the thick darkness, the reluctant ghost. But what followed were the noises. Weird whistling like a phantom train, like a rat's throat being ripped out. Rez thought about the rats, how big they were above ground, and could not imagine the size they would grow to down here. If the squatters had webbed feet and bathed in the sewer water, then the rats would be big as dogs and hungry as lions.

"It's a labyrinth," Rez said.

"But a labyrinth *leads* to something," Delilah's eyes flushed the color of inquisition.

"To the mole people."

A homeless man reached a leathery hand out, snatched Delilah's cigarette out from her mouth and showed off his meaty smile. His clothes were shredded and Rez could see his penis, the color of overripe fruit; his arms were marked up like mad from the needle still plunged into a bleeding vein. Rez and Delilah stepped over him and held their nose to his carrion comforts. But their cautions superseded them. Another whistle-like sound panged into their ears and the man's eyes shot open; his bony hand reached up like the arcade claw and latched onto Rez's pant leg.

"Haven't eaten in weeks," he said.

"Eat this!"

Delilah's boot found the man's nose with a wet crunch. A freshet of blood sprayed, slicking Rez's hand coolly as he bent to supply the man with a warm touch. They ran, but in what direction they didn't know. Rez imagined the streets above him, the smell of roasting Halal meat, dirty water dogs, charred pretzels and the indie book, forging a map in his mind. He thought about Tompkins Square Park and the families of lost youth in full regalia, the beatniks leading the pack, the bums who beat tin garbage cans for change, the leftover Occupy Wall Street kids with instruments on their backs putting on a show for free; the skaters scratching off the paint on the hand rails with their boards, the punks in leather who still rocked out with boom boxes on their shoulders. But it was of no use trying to think about all of this. The avenues and walkways were clouded; the numbers and figures were incalculable. The streets of Delancey, Bowery, Orchard, and Hester were all useless down here. The tunnels didn't abide by traffic laws or governmentally placed pathways.

No single blueprint of New York City exists! Every day you wake up to a big change, something vastly skewed. One who spent his days dreaming of a concrete map would only find himself lost in his own heady version of the city, the old Dutch colony that never truly was.

"Down here man becomes an animal. Evolves," Rez said.

"Yeah . . . well animals work in teams and have means of communication."

Like families of maggots vomiting their brethren . . .

Like peace in the dark?

A string of rats scampered over their feet. Rez saw huge black eyes, mutated legs, and razor teeth; he heard the hissing of steam pipes, smelled their fetid drool. *Track rabbits,* he thought. *They're prey as much as they're predators.* But the rats did not look for the attention of the two pale shadows in the tunnels; rather, they began nibbling the corpse of a woman still clutching her malnourished child. Her breasts were leathery, her nipples dried and dead as the stems of funeral flowers. One of the rats had already dug its way into the eye socket of the infant until a jellied mass of flesh rolled free like a squashed grape.

"This is just sick," Delilah said.

Rez nearly cried. There would be no funeral for this woman, no one to mourn her existence like so many people above ground took for granted. Not even her child had survived. *The tunnels take your life,* he thought. Rez could tell this woman would not even be useful to medical science if she was excavated and studied for her abilities to live so long down here. Her body was too decomposed to determine the cause of death; too much of her meat had been stolen by the rats. But one could say her death had to do with the array of broken whiskey bottles and hypodermics lying by her side.

"The Dark Angel must be down here," Delilah said. "Like we read in the book."

"Matted feet, long hair . . . the ruler of the drippy underworld. Delilah—"

"Truth is stranger than fiction, is it not?" Delilah's eyes were wide sparkling sapphires.

"Yes, it is. But once you get your mind wrapped around something you don't stop even if it will kill you!"

It will kill you.

The sound of another whistle commenced and Rez instinctively ran toward it. If the people turn to animals down here, then these sounds warranted a warning, a signal . . . something. They stumbled over more drunken bodies with flippers for hands and gills for lips. One could hear the slither of worms returning to their chemical holes it was so quiet, and the slush of water mixed with exhaust dripping upon their heads.

No strangers in here, a voice said. *No one from above!*

"We mean no harm," Rez said.

I can't hurt you, but I can hurt the ones you care about.

"No."

You've a fascination with the darkness of my tunnels. The evil within. And it is evil!

The voice skidded into Rez's head. A schism ripped through his brain and poured out his ears hot and thick as plasma. He fell to his knees and listened to where the voice was taking him. To a nightmare of loneliness, a fountain of pain. There were the sights of desperate clawing youth running from the society that deemed them wastes of life and useless to their cause; the homeless that were asked to leave the shelters that clothed and fed. Down into the burrows to create families bred by darkness, riots and blood. People who avoided daylight for the comfort of the bottle and the sweet alien warmth of it.

But they were like anyone else: people with opinions and feelings. But down here they were free from the strict perversions of the world upstairs, from the sickness that wept stale tears through the streets of Manhattan. Rez saw all of them huddling away from sunlight, from wind, from warmth. He saw them cutting up junk, melting it in spoons, saw the needles filling with diaphanous swirls of blood. He saw mothers eating their children out of desperation, felt the angel-headed hipsters cling to the starry dynamo of dream and false hope. He breathed their sadness, tasted their shame.

He felt their anger.

OUT!

The hands were many. The faces were peaked like bird beaks and their tongues were sluggish; their fingers kissed Rez's face like octopus tentacles, tugging his hair and biting his neck. Delilah tackled a whole pack of them into the near wall and she became lost within a sea of gummy appendages. Rez ran to her aid and pulled four gooey bodies off of Delilah. As she rose from the frenzy, Rez heard another one of them whistle.

"We're outnumbered."

They came from all directions now. Though he had never felt more peace than when he was in his sister's presence, and wasn't a violent person to begin with, he couldn't bear the thought of anymore of *them* getting in the way—especially if they were going to hurt Delilah. So with all his might, Rez completed a roundhouse kick and knocked the whistling sewage squatter to the ground. He felt the snap of its brittle bones and the wail of its pain radiate up his leg.

"Out now!" Rez yelled.

"Fuck the Dark Angel and fuck this place!"

But the walls were caving in somehow; the air was rising in temperature, choking them. Behind them were the hungry mole people; in front, a wall of blackness. *Could this be the end?* thought Rez. *All my life I've fought to get out of danger, and this is how I'm repaid?* Just like in that tormented Virginia home, there was no certain way to piece their way back up into the city. They hadn't left a trail of breadcrumbs, and so they might be trapped here and become one of them. But it was a destiny Rez refused to accept.

Their eyes . . . their eyes can't take the light! Rez remembered.

He lit his green butane lighter, found a dry walking stick a brown paper bag and crumbled cigarettes. He crushed everything together and lit it like a torch. The squatters squealed.

NOOOOO LIGHTS! NO LIGHTSSSSS!

When he found his sense of direction, Rez noticed that they had not moved five feet from where they initially dropped through the hole in the club. The burrows had played a trick on them. But Delilah backed into the wall, looked up into Rez's eyes, and nodded. He read them clearly: *step on my shoulders and get up there.* Rez reached for the small door, swinging his homemade torch like a crazy person, and pushed it open. The sound of music and the saccharine smell of craft beer teased him as he used all the energy left in his body and climbed through, throwing the stick at the hobbling squatters, grey hair shielding their eyes, hands clawing for Delilah's knees as he pulled her up.

"I'm never trusting you again," Rez said.

Two days later, they had a few bruises and a new nightmare to worry about—but everything was fine. Electric Orchid was due to play a show; club was bloated with gossip. Their fans were growing in numbers—it was only a matter of time before Electric Orchid was going to make it even further than New York. But she didn't want to think about that tonight; how the band's music promised disaster and hope, how her sibilant melodies sounded like demons pissing on Heaven's gates.

Tonight she wanted to spread a message.

Delilah had written a few new songs and wanted to try them out. Songs about the Dark Angel, the squatters, and the infamous underground. Her first solo set, opening for her own band, a new rock 'n' roll riot within this new day of rage.

"It was a nice change of scenery."

"Yeah, a nice way to rot in hell . . ."

Delilah hit the stage. The kids didn't make any noise for her at first, not like she cared anyway. Delilah didn't need anyone's confirmation to judge the quality of her songs. The music cued and Delilah began to hum behind the keyboard's spiking rhythm that bordered on the insane, the drums that beat in time with her, slow and mischievous. The guitarist crept up to the chorus pressing various pedals, mixing wah-wah, distortion and overdrive like some crunchy rhythmic beat. When Delilah opened her mouth, the crowd seemed to sober up and stood attentive; their graceless hands moved into the air and began to clap. Her voice was ripping but soft, like that of a goddess, and she told her story through the lyrics, wondering if they were listening.

There is a city beneath the streets, and with it comes peace in the dark.

SERVA ANIMUM · CASTELLUM CUSTODITUM · HORTUM BENE CURATUM · FLUMEN NON OBSTRUCTUM ·

Did you enjoy the book?

We welcome all feedback and queries.
Villipede.com

Kallirroe Agelopoulou is a med intern with a severe case of sci-fi and horror addiction. Writing helps. Some of her work appears in *Dark Bits, Sanitarium, Dark Edifice, Bewildering Stories, Gone Lawn, Fiction Vortex, Thick Jam, and MicroHorror*. She keeps trying to hit her daily writing quota in Athens, Greece, but it's been a while since she's updated her blog: **kallirroe.blogspot.com.**

Pete Clark has a number of stories published on webzines, and in the anthologies *Detritus* (Omnium Gatherum), *Short Sips* and *Here There Be Dragons* (Wicked East Press), *Fresh Blood* (MayDecember Publications), *Thirteen Volume 3* (13 Horror) and *Time of Death* (Living Dead Press). He was awarded an Honorable Mention in the L. Ron Hubbard Writers of the Future contest (2nd Quarter 2011). He includes Stephen King, Clive Barker and China Miéville among his many influences. Writing numerous short stories and his first novel, he lives in North West England with his wife, two children and a growing collection of guitars.

Stephen Cooney has been a fan of art for as long as he can remember. Watching fantasy and horror in his youth served as a model of inspiration for his art, as did his dreams of designing heavy metal band album covers. He attended Exeter Art School, but felt it was not a good fit as his teachers didn't fully "get" the dark nature of his artistic inclinations. After years of painting, a tattoo artist fell in love with Stephen's work and hired him to design tattoo flash, which in turn led to him taking up the art of inking clients himself. Since returning to his first love of painting, he has involved himself largely with horror and fantasy projects but welcomes opportunities to move outside of those genres. His influences include Derek Riggs, Ken Kelly, and Edward J. Repka, all artists who design album covers.

Stephen and his wife Amanda live in the UK and have two children, Hayley and Steven Junior. Look for his website soon.

Dennis A! is an artist, sculptor, and illustrator from SW Lower Michigan producing the second generation of Zombie Toes, one-of-a-kind "dismembered" toes of the undead—each sculpted and hand-painted to be both gruesomely realistic and charmingly hilarious. Dennis also creates original Rock and Metal posters for bands such as Steel Panther, OTEP, GWAR, Mastodon, and the legendary Alice Cooper. He is currently working on The Rise of Cthulhu series, a fan art "mash-up" homage to some of his favorite pop culture characters taking on the tentacled creatures of Lovecraft lore, and original skateboard designs for an ArtDeck Co. skateboard art show this fall. **parabolastar.com**

Adam Domville is the writer and illustrator of *Atheniens*, a four issue limited series that was published in Athens, Greece. Adam is a versatile artist whose credits include: book illustrations, tattoo art and design, poster art for rock bands, corporate and promotional art, logo design, and commissioned original paintings. Most recently his work is featured in *Panels for Primates*, published by Monkeybrain and available at comixology.com. Born in Montreal, raised in Greece, Adam has traveled the world and currently lives in Victoria, BC. His work can be seen at **adamdomville.com**, and he can be contacted at **adamdomville@hotmail.com**.

Born in Texas and currently living in Utah, **David Dunwoody** writes subversive horror fiction, including the *Empire* zombie series and the collections *Dark Entities* and *Uunbound & Other Tales*. Most recent is his post-apocalyptic novel *The Harvest Cycle*. His short stories have been published by outfits such as Permuted, Chaosium, Shroud and

Dark Regions. Favorite authors include Lovecraft, King and Barker. More info and free fiction at **daviddunwoody.com**.

Matt Edginton's art has always leaned to the darker side. Because of this, in his youth he was once subjected to an impromptu exorcism, which worked . . . for a few months. Matt's father has served as a constant artistic influence throughout his life, as well as the work of Brom, Jae Lee, Giger, and many more. Battle Beasts were and are his favorite toys, and if he could meet any two people of historical significance, they would be Bruce Lee and Rick Moranis. Matt makes metal do his bidding, coordinates Villipede Publications, and lives in Idaho Falls, Idaho, with his beautiful wife and three wonderful daughters.

A filmmaker and writer of short stories, poetry and screenplays, **Tony Flynn** is fantastically afraid of most everything, and therefore has a particular interest in the horror genre. Previously, his work has been published by Mocha Memoirs Press, Daverana Enterprises and Sirens Call Publications. Other works in writing and film can be found via **tonywritesstuff.tumblr.com** and **vimeo.com/tonyflynn**.

For handcrafted home decor, art inquiries, and tegu breeding techniques, contact **Eric Ford** at **aveolive@live.com**.

Geoffrey H. Goodwin does not know.

Adam S. House is a Canadian writer living in Beijing, China, where he is a contributing editor for a Canadian-based video game website as well as a podcast personality. He is a lifelong fan of horror, science fiction and fantasy stories in which the reader is allowed, and encouraged, to dream the impossible. Since 2005, he has divided his time between China and his home in Nova Scotia, Canada. Find him at **adamscotthouse.com, thesurrealhouse.com**, and Twitter: **@HaggardMess**.

Mathias Jansson is a Swedish art critic and poet. He has been previously published in *The Horror Zine Magazine*, *SNM Horror Magazine*, and *The Poetry Box*. He has also contributed to several anthologies: Horrified Press' *Just One More Step*, *Suffer Eternal* volumes 1-3, and *Hell Whore Anthology* volumes 1-3. His homepage is **mathiasjansson72.blogspot.se**.

Lisamarie Lamb started writing in her late teens but it was only with the birth of her daughter that she decided to write more seriously, with the aim of publication. Since that decision in 2010, she has had over 30 short stories published in anthologies and magazines. In November 2012, Dark Hall Press published a collection of her short stories with a twist, entitled *Over The Bridge*. In November 2013, J. Ellington Ashton Press released a second short story collection entitled *Fairy Lights*. She has collaborated on—and edited—a project entitled *A Roof Over Their Heads*, written by six authors from the Isle of Sheppey about the island where she lives with her husband, daughter, and two cats.
themoonlitdoor.blogspot.co.uk
facebook.com/lisamarielambwriter

Sydney Leigh is the evil literary double of a mostly sane writer, editor, photographer, artist, English teacher, and native of the North Shore. Inspired by a one-eyed muse, her poetry, drabble, and short fiction has appeared in numerous anthologies and on the skin of willing victims. Forthcoming publications include Firbolg Publishing's *Enter at Your Own Risk: The End is the Beginning*, which will launch at this year's World Horror Convention in Portland, Oregon. Look for her on Goodreads, Facebook, and at Villipede Publications, where she spends her days charming letters and constructing nightmares—or drop into her website: **thespiderbox.shawnaleighbernard.com**.

John Mc Caffrey writes tales of horror, the supernatural, science fiction, and fantasy. He was born in Illinois and grew up on the south side of Chicago. While still in grade school, he developed a passion for reading through the works of Tolkien, Poe, and Lovecraft, as well as being addicted to watching Hammer Film's at the local Saturday matinee. Today he lives in northern Indiana with his wife and two dogs where he writes in his spare time. His works can be found at Amazon, Barnes & Noble and Smashwords as well as various anthologies. **jmccaffrey.com**
facebook.com/pages/John-Mc-Caffrey-Author/503178623071533

Adam Millard is the author of sixteen novels, seven novellas, and more than a hundred short stories, which can be found in various collections and anthologies. Probably best known for his post-apocalyptic fiction, Adam also writes fantasy/horror for children, as well as bizarro fiction for several publishers. His "Dead" series has been the filling in a Stephen King/Bram Stoker sandwich on Amazon's bestsellers chart, and the translation rights have recently sold to German publisher, Voodoo Press. Adam dwells online at **adammillard.co.uk** and **@adammillard** on Twitter.

Jonathan MoOn is the strange bastard behind *Worms in the Needle*, *Heinous,* and *Stories To Poke Your Eyes Out To*, among several other terrible things. He eats souls, drinks whiskey, carries knives, and wears masks. **mrmoonblogs.blogspot.com**

CONTRIBUTORS

Monstark (Mark Thompson) loves to make monstrous things. He resides reclusively in the San Francisco Bay Area, where he is slowly procuring the means to trans-shape from human form into beast. He will continue to make art, zines, comics and music until he finds his hands too large, his claws too unwieldy, to use tools. **monstark.com**

Patrick O'Neill is a rising new talent in the world of horror fiction and resides in Dorset, UK, with wife, Nikki, and son, Benedict. His dark and unsettling tales have been featured in numerous anthologies and he is currently working on his single author collection, *The Darkest Eyes*, and on his debut novel, *No Contrition*. Patrick can be contacted at **padzoneill@hotmail.com**.

Becky Regalado lives in north Texas with her husband and son. When she's not writing, she enjoys reading and jewelry-making. She is working on her degree in Library Science in between working full-time at a university library and querying her first fantasy novel. She was a semi-finalist in the *2005 L. Ron Hubbard's Writers of the Future Contest*, and one of her satirical works was the Editor's Choice piece in the May 2011 edition of *Writer's Beat Quarterly*. Her short horror piece "Awfully Disappointing Either Way" was also published in *The Fringe* online magazine in June 2011. You can view her blog at **beckah-rah.blogspot.com** and follow her on Twitter **@Beckahrah**.

C. Deskin Rink is a human organism. His work has appeared in the anthologies *Dark Tales of Lost Civilizations*, *Torn Realities* and at Pseudopod.org. Follow him at **ankorsabat.blogspot.com**.

Lawrence Salani lives on the coast in Australia, near Sydney. Always having lived by the sea, it is sometimes reflected in his writing. As well as writing horror he enjoys fine arts painting and drawing. He feels that painting and writing are analogous and that inspiration and ideas from one can be used in the other. Favorite authors are H.P. Lovecraft, Austin Spare, William Blake, and too many more to mention. His published works include "A Fragment of Yesterday" in Eclecticism E-Zine, issue 5; "Summer Heat" in the *Night Terrors* anthology (Blood Bound); and "The Angel of Death" in the *Danse Macabre* anthology (Edge).

David Shearer is a Fraser Valley based freelance Master Graphic Designer and Illustrator. Since his childhood he's been blessed with talents in both fine and technical art and has focused a great deal of time in honing the creativity and problem-solving skills that come naturally to him. Compromises or half-way solutions are not in his vocabulary as he constantly pushes the envelope, thinks out-of-the-box, and drives towards clean and uncluttered design—while at the same time providing a tangible representation of his clients' vision. His decade-long track record proves that he consistently delivers excellent customer satisfaction.
Please visit his site: **theartofoneness.com**.

Luke Spooner a.k.a. "Carrion House" and "Hoodwink House" currently lives and works in the South of England. Having recently graduated from the University of Portsmouth with a first class degree, he is now a full time illustrator for just about any project that peaks his interest. Despite regular forays into children's books and fairy tales, for which he has won awards for literary and artistic merit, his true love lies in anything macabre, melancholy or dark in nature and essence. He believes that the job of putting someone else's words into a visual form, to accompany and support their text, is a massive responsibility as well as being something he truly treasures. Visit Luke's site at **carrionhouse.com**.

J. Daniel Stone was germinated in New York City and is still thriving there to this day. He's only been on earth for 27 years but has already been published by Grey Matter Press, Prime Books, *Icarus: The Magazine of Gay Speculative Fiction*, *The Dreadful Cafe* (Fall 2014), and more. His first novel, *The Absence of Light*, was published by Villipede Publications. Currently, his second novel is looking for a publishing house; simultaneously, he is hard at work putting together his first short story collection. Come find him on Twitter **@solitaryspiral**.

Jonathan Templar lives in Cheshire, UK. He copes with the constant, constant rainfall by writing in a variety of genres, from horror and fantasy to children's bedtime tales. Jonathan's recent acclaimed work includes the story "The Meat Man" in the charity collection *Horror for Good* and "Basher" for the shared world anthology *World's Collider*. His novella *The Angel of Shadwell*, the first in a series of stories for steam-punk detective Inspector Noridel, is available from Nightscape Press, and Jonathan recently published his first collection of short stories, *The Geometry of Hell*. He has an author site with a full bibliography at **jonathantemplar.com**.

Justin Wheeler is a very passionate and driven individual with an extremely diligent work ethic.
justinsanedesign.com and **justinwheelerportfolio.com**

Dot Wickliff is a hopeless necromantic v.3 ultra grey-human hybrid with cerebral Jujutsu add-ons and reinforced sham-animisti Apache genetic matrix. While you ponder that, go see more of Dot's thoughts at **epochellipses.blogspot.com**.

Wednesday Wolf wants to make the world a little stranger. He is a member of the human species, a variant of ape originating on the third rock from Sol. His homeland is Hong Kong, though he currently reside in New York (completely legally—there is no need to check the paperwork on the matter). He paints with watercolour, ink, spit and blood. Everything on his paintings, dear reader, is a slice of his mind. If you find anything offensive or profane, he recommends googling small animals. If you find anything arousing, titilating or intriguing, inform him. If you are alone, lonely and isolated in the dark of the night, know that he is sitting up with you.

wednesdaywolf.com

Printed in Great Britain
by Amazon